倍斯特出版事業有限公司
g Ltd.

U0066423

一次就考到

雅思
聽力 6.5+

MP3

倍斯特編輯部◎ 著

運用影子跟讀法 同步強化「聽力專注力」、「準確定位關鍵考點」和「應試時答題穩定性」

4大學習法

❶ 「短對話」影子跟讀：穩拿section 1和 2中20題得分
▶ 強化聽「短對話」訊息，前20題較簡易的題目都答對，輕易獲取聽力6.5+。

❷ 「短段落」影子跟讀：強化聽section 3和4中的學術段落題型
▶ 提升聽「段落」訊息的專注力，準確定位在關鍵訊息上，減低干擾訊息影響答題的能力。

❸ 「長段落」影子跟讀：大幅提升section 3和4答題應對能力和穩定性
▶ 試場答題穩定性飆升，完成聽力考試能信心滿滿地接續寫閱讀試題，不影響後續閱讀和寫作答題成效。

❹ 關鍵必考聽力字彙：記憶考場必考的字就夠了
▶ 背誦關鍵字彙並強化拼寫這些字彙的能力，不因「拼字錯誤」或「聽得懂卻不會拼字」所造成的聽力失分。

Editor's 編者序 Preface

　　雅思聽力與考生所熟悉的傳統聽力考試不太同的地方是，它包含了填空題，而填空題無法像選擇題聽力那樣大致聽懂主旨等，選出對的答案或是儘管在聽不懂或來不及答完試題時用猜的。雅思聽力一共有 4 個 section，總共 40 題試題，有時候整場考試下來，於填完答案卡後一數，涉及拼字的填空或摘要題多達 30 題，這部分也顯示出除了要聽懂外，更要能拚出該單字。很多時候單字是你我都熟悉不過的單字，例如**冰箱**等生活場景的字彙，但有時候考生太久沒用卻忘了怎麼拚了，而造成失分。有時候卻是因為答案不只一個單字，可能是

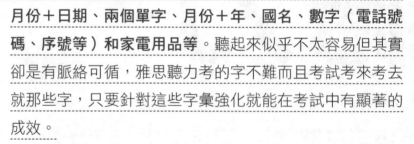

月份＋日期、兩個單字、月份＋年、國名、數字（電話號碼、序號等）和家電用品等。聽起來似乎不太容易但其實卻是有脈絡可循，雅思聽力考的字不難而且考試考來考去就那些字，只要針對這些字彙強化就能在考試中有顯著的成效。

　　書籍中一共規劃了四個部分，影子跟讀「短對話」、影子跟讀「短段落」、影子跟讀「實戰練習」和雅思必考字彙。規劃影子跟讀的用意是強化考生聽力專注力，考生可以藉由每個單元練習數十次的影子跟讀，並於熟悉語速後逐步拉長影子跟讀的句子，在能聽到更多訊息後再跟著讀，能大幅強化應考實力。**影子跟讀「短對話」**可以強化 section 1 和 2 聽短訊息時的能力，要注意的是別因為這兩個部分較簡單，而因為分心造成分數失分。**影子跟讀**

「**短段落**」的部分則包含試題練習，先由短段落練習影子跟讀並用後面規劃的試題演練大幅強化聽**月份、數字、年、日期和家電用品等雅思必考字彙**。影子跟讀「**實戰練習**」也包含了長段落影子跟讀和試題，試題能有效強化聽 section 3 和 4 的應考實力，考生常會在聽較長訊息時會因許多因素，如較不專注或看題本某題空格遲遲未聽到該題相關聽力訊息、誤判定位等使自己在 section 3 和 4 的答對題數不理想。建議可以多練習這部分影子跟讀的次數並確實完成試題，直到每個填空題都能答對為止。

　　最後的部分是**雅思必考字彙**，必考字彙更便於考生在考前觀看和熟悉生活場景字彙（其實程度很好的考生，可能僅看下必考字彙單元就能於考試中拿到聽力 7-7.5+左右的成績。）。此外，聽力前三部份的設計和量，其實非常紮實，做數十次後其實遠比數學期聽力課效用更高，也很適合欲累積**逐步口譯能力**的考生不斷作練習並增進自己的能力。最後祝所有考生都能考取理想成績。

倍斯特編輯部 敬上

機場接機

▶ 影子跟讀「短對話」練習 🎧 MP3 001

此篇為「影子跟讀短對話練習」，此章節規劃了由聽「短對話」的 shadowing 練習，能從最基礎、最易上手的部分切入雅思聽力備考並提升考生的專注力。雅思聽力中尤其 section 1 跟 2 雖然對話不難但很容易因為分心而錯失聽力訊息，而 section 1 和 2 是最好拿分且最好都要拿到全對的部分，整體分數才容易接近獲取聽力 7-7+，現在就一起動身，開始聽「短對話」！

Customer service: I am afraid all our drivers are flat out at the moment. I would suggest you take a taxi from the airport to the campus, but it would cost you an arm and a leg.

客服：很抱歉我們司機現在都很忙。我建議您自己搭計程車到學校，可是車費會很貴。

Mark: Would you refund the cost of the pickup service since I was not picked up?

馬克：那你會退我接機的費用嗎？畢竟沒有人來接我啊。

Customer service: Unfortunately, it has all been prepaid, and it is customer's responsibility to provide us the correct flight details.

客服：恐怕不行，因為接機服務都是預付的，而且提供正確的行程表是客人的責任。

Mark: That is totally unfair! I did provide the correct itinerary to my agent. It is not my fault if the information somehow got lost in the system. I can't get hold of my agent due to the time difference. If I would be charged anyway, I would rather stick around here for your next available driver.

馬克：這真是太不公平了，我有通知代辦中心我更改了機位，你們沒有收到正確的訂位紀錄不是我的錯。因為時差的關係我聯絡不上代辦中心。如果你們堅持要收費的話，那我情願等你們的司機有空。

影子跟讀：「短對話」

影子跟讀：「短段落」

影子跟讀：「實戰練習」

雅思聽力必考字彙

70個單元的影子跟讀「短對話」練習，section 1和2答題正確率提升至**100%**！

✦ 務必實際照著音檔語速跟讀，逐步漸進拉長句數，確實做數次至數十次練習，大幅強化聽力專注力和答題正確性，修正至前兩個section答題正確性能到100%

✦ 此外，聽力訊息稍縱即逝，要特別注意別因為這兩個部分較簡易，因為分心而造成失分。

超海量練習，完全切中考生弱點，自己狂練後即可應考！ 應考填空、摘要題答題正確率100%

✦ 規劃24個聽「短段落」單元，聽力練習練到飽，狂強化「數字」、「日期」、「日期＋年」、「日期＋月份」、「家庭用品」等各式搭配的挖空考題，練習至每個空格都聽出答案和拼對答案，應考填空題100%答對率。

✦ 每題填空題均挖空必考雅思字彙，寫完練習後可以將參考答案字彙列入自己的筆記本中，時間花在刀口上，聽力字彙背這些就夠了。

▶ 影子跟讀「短段落」練習　 🎧 MP3 077

此部分為「影子跟讀短段落練習❷」，請重新播放音檔並完成試題，除了能提升並修正拼寫能力外，也可以藉由音檔注意自己專注力和定位聽力訊息部份，短段落聽力的提升能強化 section1 和 2 答題的正確性，現在就一起動身，開始完成「短段落練習❷」吧！

　　The 1._____ of Facebook started to grow in 2007. Most of the 2._____ back then joined Facebook in 2007. Late in 2007, Facebook had 3._____ which allowed 4._____ to attract 5._____ and introduce themselves. The 6._____ of this 7._____ just kept blooming, and on 8._____, Facebook set up its international 9._____ in Dublin, 10._____. Statistics from 11._____ showed that over 12._____ are shared on Facebook, and over 13._____ accessed Facebook through their 14._____ which is only about 33% of all 15._____.

　　Born in 1984, Mark Zuckerberg was born in White Plains, 16._____. Zuckerberg began using computers and writing software in middle school. His father taught him Atari BASIC Programming in the 1990s, and later hired 17._____ David Newman to tutor him privately. Zuckerberg took a 18._____ in the subject at Mercy College near his home while still in high school. He enjoyed developing 19._____, especially 20._____ tools and games.

▶ 參考答案

1. popularity	2. youngsters
3. 100,000 business pages	4. companies
5. potential customers	6. business potential
7. social network	8. October 2008
9. headquarters	10. Ireland
11. October 2011	12. 100 billion photos
13. 350 million users	14. mobile phones
15. Facebook traffic	16. New York
17. software developer	18. graduate course
19. computer programs	20. communication

影子跟讀：「短對話」

影子跟讀：「短段落」

影子跟讀：「實戰練習」

雅思聽力必考字彙

Instructions
使用說明

24個單元的影子跟讀「短段落」練習，section 3 和 4 訊息「定位」能力和「專注力」強化，聽力分數卡在7.5分學習者更要練習！

✦ 除了影子跟讀練習外，務必要完成每篇短段落練習後的試題，並聽至每個答案都答對為止，若難度太高，寫試題時請播放音檔兩次再寫，漸進強化至播放一次，就答對試題為止。

✦ 這部分的練習跟試題的撰寫能無形中強化學習中忽略的訊息「定位」問題，其實聽力練習到夠專注時，聽力定位問題所造成的失分就會消失，能更精確達到更高的分數段，例如7.5分或8.0分以上成績。

短段落 | UNIT 10

塑膠工業之父

▶ 影子跟讀「短段落」練習 🎧 MP3 080

　　此篇為「影子跟讀短段落練習」，此章節規劃了由聽「短段落」的 shadowing 練習，從最基礎、最易上手的部分切入雅思聽力備考並提升考生的專注力，雅思聽力中尤其 section 3 跟 4 雖然話題不難，且很多時候不是考生程度沒到某個分數段，但確實很容易因為定位錯誤而錯失聽力訊息或誤判題本的上該題訊息已經唸過了，強化這部分能提升 section 3 和 4 的得分，整體分數要 7+或 7.5+其實這部分要很費心的喔！現在就一起動身，開始聽「短段落」！

　　What are plastics exactly? The majority of the polymers are based on chains of carbon atoms along with oxygen, sulfur, or nitrogen. Most plastics contain other organic or inorganic compounds blended in.

　　塑膠到底是什麼？大多數聚合物都基於碳原子和氧、硫、或氮的鍵。大多數塑膠混有其他有機或無機化合物。

　　The amount of additives ranges from zero percentage to more than 50% for certain electronic applications. The invention of plastic was a great success but also brought us a

---

serious environmental concerns regarding its slow decomposition rate after being discarded. One way to help with the environment is to practice recycling or use other environmental friendly materials instead. Another approach is to speed up the development of biodegradable plastic.

　　在一些電子應用上，添加劑的量從零至 50%以上。塑膠的發明獲得了巨大的成功，但也給我們帶來了關於其被丟棄後緩慢分解所造成嚴重的環境問題。練習回收或改用其他對環境友好的材料是幫助環境的一種方法。另一種方法是，加快生物分解性塑料的開發。

　　The father of the Plastics Industry, Leo Baekeland, was born in Belgium on November 14th, 1863. He was best known for his invention of Bakelite which is an inexpensive, nonflammable and versatile plastic. Because of his invention, the plastic industry started to bloom and became a popular material in many different industries.

　　塑膠工業之父，利奧‧貝克蘭，於 1863 年 11 月 14 日出生於比利時。他最為人知的是酚醛塑的發明，這是一種廉價，不可燃和通用的塑膠。由於他的發明，塑料行業開始盛行，在許多不同的行業成為一個受歡迎的材料。

實戰練習 | UNIT ❻
無尾熊

▶ 影子跟讀「實戰練習」　🎧 MP3 100

此篇為「影子跟讀實戰練習」，此章節規劃了由聽「實際考試長度的英文內容」的 shadowing 練習，經由先前的兩個部分的練習，已經能逐步掌握跟聽一定句數的英文內容，現在經由實際考試長度的聽力內容來練習，讓耳朵適應聽這樣長度的英文內容，提升考場時的答題穩定度和適應性，進而獲致理想成績，現在就一起動身，開始由聽「實戰練習」！（如果聽這部份且跟讀練習的難度還是太高，請重複前兩個部份的練習數次後再來做這部分的練習喔！）

Koalas are recognised as a symbol of Australia, but the species face many threats in this modernised world. Land exploitation in areas where koalas used to live has posed various risks to this cute creature. Urbanization is depriving and fragmenting koala habitat; human-induced threats such as vehicle strikes or domestic dog attacks are also threatening koala's life. It is also believed the increasing prevalence of koala's diseases are to some extent due to the stress caused by human activities.

無尾熊是澳洲的象徵，但是此物種在現代化世界中面臨許多威

脅。無尾熊過去棲息的地方遭受的土地過度利用，這對這個可愛的生物造成不同的風險威脅。都市化正剝奪或肢解著無尾熊的棲息地。人類引起的威脅像是汽車攻擊或家庭飼養的狗攻擊正威脅著無尾熊的生命。據說，無尾熊疾病的逐漸盛行某些程度上是由於人類活動所引起的壓力。

Some koalas live in the sanctuary where they are cared for by experienced staff. While most koalas live in the wild, they are easily recognized by their appearance and the habitat they are from. Koalas may be given a nickname by local residents if they show up frequently in the neighborhood, so they are more like human's pets rather than wild animals. People enjoy seeing koalas and they make a lot of effort to protect them, such as planting trees and controlling their dogs.

有些無尾熊生活在保護區，在那裡受到具經驗的員工照顧著。雖然大多數的無尾熊生活在野外，能由外表輕易地辨識出它們和它們所處的棲息所在地。如果它們頻繁地出現在社區的話，當地居民可能給予無尾熊暱稱。所以，它們更像是人類的寵物而非野生動物。人們喜愛看到無尾熊而且他們為了保護無尾熊做了許多努力，例如植樹和控制他們的狗狗。

The biggest threat to the koala's existence is habitat destruction, and following this, the most serious threat is death from car hits. I'm going to talk about the koala and the car accident. A koala hit by a vehicle could be killed

8個單元的影子跟讀「實戰練習」，除了section 3 和 4 訊息「定位」能力和「專注力」強化外，大幅強化答題穩定度和適應性，答題正確率能提升至100%！

✦ 能專注聽長段落訊息是 section 3 和 4 拿分關鍵，除了練習數次影子跟讀練習外，也務必完成每單元後的試題。

✦ 跟著音檔覆誦除了提升聽力專注力外，同步利用「聽」與「說」的關聯性

強化「聽」和「說」的能力，每個句子都能無形成為口說中寶貴的語庫，無形增進口說時的表達能力，口說無形中強化數個分數級距，大幅降低雅思四個單項的準備時間。

✦ 除了雅思考試外，長段落的部分更能增進短逐步和長逐步口譯實力，在實力遠勝於學歷和證照的時代中，畢業後即刻與職場接軌。

Instructions

also threatened by pollution and 11._____ from climate change. It is also the largest animals ever to have lived, since they are much larger than 12._____. Their heart has the same size as a small car, which bumps tons of blood through the 13._____ of the blue whale. The largest blue whale that was ever found was 33.58 meters long and weighed 14._____ tons. The blue whale has a very small 15._____ and relatively small 16._____. In terms of feeding and distribution, the blue whale feeds almost exclusively on 17._____ and you can find the blue whales worldwide.

Hence, it is now listed as 18._____. The fin whale prefers to stay in deep water and it is also distributed all over the world's ocean. Unlike the blue whale, the fin whale is more 19._____, which means they live in flocks and are more sociable. Fin whales are generally seen in groups of 10 or more. They mainly feed on 20._____, such as crabs, lobsters and shrimps. The next one is the grey whale, which appears only in the North Pacific Ocean. The grey whale is baleen whale as well. In summer the grey whales move to the 21._____ to feed and in winter they travel along the US coast down to the Mexican coast. They are 15 meters long on average and weigh about 20 tons. The skin of the back of the grey whale has yellow and white 22._____ caused by parasites.

Only the male sings. On the way up, fishes are encircled in a 23._____ and swallowed by the humpback whale. This type of whale also travels long distances; they spend the winter near Hawaii and move to the polar regions in summer. The humpback whale is up to 19 meters long and 48 tons in weight. It feeds on krill, sardines, and small fishes. The humpback whale is considered a vulnerable species and 24._____ is prohibited as well.

參考答案

1. baleen whales	2. fish-rich water
3. viviparous	4. lungs
5. blowholes	6. maintain breath
7. pattern	8. low frequency sound
9. illegal whaling	10. fishing nets
11. habitat loss	12. dinosaurs
13. circulatory system	14. 190
15. dorsal fin	16. tail flukes
17. krill	18. an endangered species
19. gregarious	20. small crustaceans
21. Bering Sea	22. coloured patches
23. bubble net	24. whaling

✦ 參考答案的答案是不適挺熟悉，常見的雅思聽力和閱讀中挖空會出現的字，例如habitat, dorsal fin, gregarious, dinosaurs等字，快來練習吧！，高分正等著你。

✦ 快跟坊間數萬單和單字書說再見吧，聽力考來考去就這幾百字，背這些就夠了！

✦ 把雅思官方聽力試題每篇挖空部分和音檔出現的字，抄在筆記本上，大概就是這些單字，家庭用品等生活主題字彙，過難的真的不會出現！快將時間花在刀口上吧！

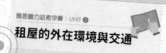

雅思聽力必考字彙｜UNIT ❷

租屋的外在環境與交通

找房子時，房客聯繫房東詢問是否還有空房（vacancy）並預約（make appointment），看房（house inspection）。房子的地點（location）是重要的考量因素，因為關係到就學和打工的方便度。一般來說住在市中心（downtown）相對比較貴，而住在郊區（suburbs）較為便宜。要考慮住家附近是否有方便的大眾交通工具（public transport），到距離最近的公車站（bus station）或地鐵站（subway／metro station）要步行幾分鐘。如果自己駕車，則要詢問是否有停車位（parking lot）。另外也要確認住家與醫院（hospital）、學校（university）、超市（super-market）的距離。簽約時要註明租住時長（duration），多久續租一次（renew the lease），何時可以入住（move in），以及開始付房租的時間。

重要字彙	
vacancy	空房
make appointment	預約
house inspection	看房
location	地點
downtown	市中心
suburb	郊區

Instructions

CONTENTS 目次

Part 1 影子跟讀「短對話」

Part 2 影子跟讀「短段落」

機場接機

▶ 影子跟讀「短對話」練習 🎧 MP3 001

此篇為**「影子跟讀短對話練習」**，此章節規劃了由聽**「短對話」**的 shadowing 練習，能從最基礎、最易上手的部分切入雅思聽力備考並提升考生的專注力，雅思聽力中尤其 section 1 跟 2 雖然對話不難但很容易因為分心而錯失聽力訊息，而 section 1 和 2 是最好拿分且最好都要拿到全對的部分，整體分數才容易接近獲取聽力 7-7+，現在就一起動身，開始聽**「短對話」**！

Customer service: I am afraid all our drivers are **flat out** at the moment. I would suggest you take a taxi from the airport to the campus, but it would cost you **an arm and a leg.**	客服：很抱歉我們司機現在都很忙。我建議您自己搭計程車到學校，可是車費會很貴。
Mark: Would you refund the cost of the pickup service since I was not picked up?	馬克：那你會退我接機的費用嗎？畢竟沒有人來接我啊。

Customer service: Unfortunately, it has all been prepaid, and it is customer's responsibility to provide us the correct flight details.

Mark: That is totally unfair! I did provide the correct itinerary to my agent. It is not my fault if the information somehow got **lost in the system**. I **can't get hold of** my agent due to the time difference. If I would be charged anyway, I **would rather stick around** here for your next available driver.

客服：恐怕不行，因為接機服務都是預付的，而且提供正確的行程表是客人的責任。

馬克：這真是太不公平了，我有通知代辦中心我更改了機位，你們沒有收到正確的訂位紀錄不是我的錯。因為時差的關係我聯絡不上代辦中心。如果你們堅持要收費的話，那我情願等你們的司機有空。

影子跟讀：「短對話」

影子跟讀：「短段落」

影子跟讀：「實戰練習」

雅思聽力必考字彙

15

註冊費遲交

▶ 影子跟讀「短對話」練習 🎧 MP3 002

　　此篇為「影子跟讀短對話練習」，此章節規劃了由聽「短對話」的 shadowing 練習，能從最基礎、最易上手的部分切入雅思聽力備考並提升考生的專注力，雅思聽力中尤其 section 1 跟 2 雖然對話不難但很容易因為分心而錯失聽力訊息，而 section 1 和 2 是最好拿分且最好都要拿到全對的部分，整體分數才容易接近獲取聽力 7-7+，現在就一起動身，開始聽「短對話」！

Mark: Hi, I received this letter stating I have to pay an additional 200 dollars for the delayed student fee.	馬克：您好，我收到這封信說我的註冊費遲繳，要多交 200 美金的遲交罰金。
Sally: Well, you got that right! The tuition was late by 2 days. Unfortunately, if you wish to avoid the late fee, you got to be in time.	收銀員莎莉：你說對了，你的學費晚了兩天入帳。很遺憾地，如果你不想被罰錢的話，就要及時繳交。

Mark: That is unreasonable. You've got to understand I am an international student and my fees are wire transferred directly into the school account from overseas. My parents definitely did it before the deadline; however, we **have no control of** when the money would reach the school account. I can show you the bank receipt as the **proof of payment** it was done before the deadline. I think it should be sufficient enough for the late fees to **be waived**.

馬克：這不合理，你要知道我是留學生，我的學費是從國外直接電匯到學校的帳戶。我爸媽真的是在期限前去電匯的，只是我們無法控制要花多長的時間錢才會入帳。我有銀行水單可以做憑證，學費是在期限前匯的。這樣應該可以免去遲繳罰金了吧！

影子跟讀：「短對話」

影子跟讀：「短段落」

影子跟讀：「實戰練習」

雅思聽力必考字彙

選課錯誤

▶ 影子跟讀「短對話」練習 🎧 MP3 003

此篇為「**影子跟讀短對話練習**」，此章節規劃了由聽「**短對話**」的 shadowing 練習，能從最基礎、最易上手的部分切入雅思聽力備考並提升考生的專注力，雅思聽力中尤其 section 1 跟 2 雖然對話不難但很容易因為分心而錯失聽力訊息，而 section 1 和 2 是最好拿分且最好都要拿到全對的部分，整體分數才容易接近獲取聽力 7-7+，現在就一起動身，開始聽「**短對話**」！

Mary: I am sorry that I **screwed this up**, how could I not have realized Marketing 101 is the pre-requisite for Advance Marketing? I have **pulled out** from Advance Marketing, but all the Marketing 101 classes are full.

瑪莉：我很抱歉我搞砸了，我怎麼會不知道行銷學 101 是進階行銷學的基礎課程。我已經取消進階行銷學的選課了，可是行銷學 101 的課全是滿的。

Mr. Larson: This happens every semester. It was mentioned **over and over**, but no one **pays any attention** on what we said.

拉森先生：這種事怎麼每個學期都發生，我們說了又說可是都沒有人聽進去。很可惜地目前我幫不上你忙，最

Unfortunately, there is nothing I can do at this moment, your **best bet** would be waiting for someone to drop this unit and hopefully you can **take over** the spot. Otherwise, you would have to wait for next semester then.

好的方式就是等開學後有人要退選，希望你可以填上那個空缺，不然你就只好等下學期了。

Mary: Please do your best to **squeeze me in**; otherwise, I would have to **put off** graduation for another 6 months.

瑪莉：求求你盡力把我排進去，不然我要延六個月才能畢業。

影子跟讀：「短對話」

影子跟讀：「短段落」

影子跟讀：「實戰練習」

雅思聽力必考字彙

銀行開戶

　　此篇為「影子跟讀短對話練習」，此章節規劃了由聽「短對話」的 shadowing 練習，能從最基礎、最易上手的部分切入雅思聽力備考並提升考生的專注力，雅思聽力中尤其 section 1 跟 2 雖然對話不難但很容易因為分心而錯失聽力訊息，而 section 1 和 2 是最好拿分且最好都要拿到全對的部分，整體分數才容易接近獲取聽力 7-7+，現在就一起動身，開始聽「短對話」！

Mark: **I know what you are saying,** but I was told all I need is the letter from the university to prove I am a student which entitles me to open a student account. **I was not aware** I also need to bring a proof of address as well.

馬克：我知道你的意思，可是有人跟我説我只需要大學出的證明信函説我是學生，這樣我就可以開一個學生帳戶。我不知道我還需要地址證明。

Mary Ann: Well, because you are an overseas student, we need to verify the documents

瑪麗安：嗯，因為你是國際學生，所以我們需要小心地審核所有文件，你可以提出

carefully. Do you have anything which can prove you will be staying in the university dormitory?

你住在學校宿舍的證明嗎？

Mark: I only arrived in the country last night. All I have is a receipt to prove I paid for the accommodation for this semester. If this wasn't sufficient, I really don't know what to do. Would you consider calling the university to verify my address? Tell me what else I can do.

馬克：我昨天才抵達，我只有一張宿舍繳費的收據，證明繳了一學期。如果這樣無法接受的話，那我不知道要怎麼辦。或是你可以直接打電話給我的學校，跟他們確認我的地址，這是我唯一想到的辦法。

作業要求延遲交件

▶ 影子跟讀「短對話」練習 🎧 MP3 005

　　此篇為「影子跟讀短對話練習」，此章節規劃了由聽「短對話」的 shadowing 練習，能從最基礎、最易上手的部分切入雅思聽力備考並提升考生的專注力，雅思聽力中尤其 section 1 跟 2 雖然對話不難但很容易因為分心而錯失聽力訊息，而 section 1 和 2 是最好拿分且最好都要拿到全對的部分，整體分數才容易接近獲取聽力 7-7+，現在就一起動身，開始聽「短對話」！

Jerry: **I know you don't like to hear** about this, but I am here to ask for the deferral for the final assignment. All I am asking is just one extra week.	傑瑞：我知道你聽到這個一定不高興，但是我不得已要來跟您要求期末作業需要延期交件，只要給我多一個星期就好。
Professor Lin: Reason being?	林教授：是什麼原因？
Jerry: My parents **made it clear** that I have to be able to support myself **even if** I am a full time	傑瑞：我爸媽明確的要求我一定要自力更生，就算我是全職的學生也是一樣。我很

student. I **work my ass off jug-gling between** two part-time jobs and a full time study. You've got to **give me some credit for it.**

努力地兼了兩份差還要當全職的學生，這樣應該算是正當理由吧！

Professor Lin: That's not my problem. You should have planned it better.

林教授：那不是我的問題，你應該更有效率的安排你的時間。

Jerry: I am enrolled in 3 units this semester and how they schedule the assignments are **out of my hands.** All of the assignments are due in the same week. I just need some extra help.

傑瑞：我這學期選了三門課，我沒有辦法控制老師要怎麼安排交作業的時間表，所有的作業都需要在同一個星期交件，我只是需要多一點幫助。

科目被當見教授

▶▶ 影子跟讀「短對話」練習 🎧 MP3 006

此篇為**「影子跟讀短對話練習」**，此章節規劃了由聽**「短對話」**的 shadowing 練習，能從最基礎、最易上手的部分切入雅思聽力備考並提升考生的專注力，雅思聽力中尤其 section 1 跟 2 雖然對話不難但很容易因為分心而錯失聽力訊息，而 section 1 和 2 是最好拿分且最好都要拿到全對的部分，整體分數才容易接近獲取聽力 7-7+，現在就一起動身，開始聽**「短對話」**！

Zoe: Hi, Professor Hopkins, I am here to **have a chat** about my result.	若儀：您好，霍普金斯教授，我想來跟您談談我的成績。
Professor Hopkins: Let me **bring up** your record. Well, you are **two marks short for passing** which is a shame.	霍普金斯教授：讓我調你的資料出來看一下。嗯，你其實差兩分就可及格，真可惜。
Zoe: I wondered whether it is possible for me to redo my mid-	若儀：我想問問看是不是可以讓我重做我的期中作業，

term paper to see if I can make up for those two marks that I need. You can check my attendance, I never missed a single lecture, and I got **30 out of 40** in my final.

看看我是不是可以多得到我需要的兩分，你可以查查看我的出席率，我從來沒有缺課，我的期末考也有 75 分。

Professor Hopkins: Well, considering you did quite well in your final exam. I would **go out of my way** to help you. I will give you a week. Come and see me next Wednesday and I will **go through** your paper again.

霍普金斯教授：這麼說來你的期末考還考得不錯，我特別幫你一個忙，給你一個禮拜，下星期三帶作業來給我看看。

影子跟讀：「短對話」

影子跟讀：「短段落」

影子跟讀：「實戰練習」

雅思聽力必考字彙

買學生票沒帶證件

▶▶ 影子跟讀「短對話」練習　🎧 MP3 007

　　此篇為「影子跟讀短對話練習」，此章節規劃了由聽「短對話」的 shadowing 練習，能從最基礎、最易上手的部分切入雅思聽力備考並提升考生的專注力，雅思聽力中尤其 section 1 跟 2 雖然對話不難但很容易因為分心而錯失聽力訊息，而 section 1 和 2 是最好拿分且最好都要拿到全對的部分，整體分數才容易接近獲取聽力 7-7+，現在就一起動身，開始聽「短對話」！

Mark: Oh no! I just realized I left my student ID in the dorm. Can I still get a student ticket?	馬克：喔糟糕！我剛剛才發現我的學生證丟在宿舍裡。我還可以買學生票嗎？
Kimberly: I am sorry. I have to verify the ID before I can sell you the student ticket.	金柏莉：很抱歉我必須看過你的證件才可以賣學生票給你。
Mark: I know I should have my student ID to be able to be entitled to a student discount. Let	馬克：我知道我必須要有學生證才可以享有學生折扣，讓我看看我還有什麼，我剛

me see what else I got. I actually have a copy of my assignment, which is dated last week. I think it should be good enough to prove I am currently enrolled. Come on, I know you can **make the final call.**

好有一份作業，上面的日期是上星期。這應該足以證明我是在學學生了吧！別這樣嘛，我知道你有權力決定。

Kimberly: Well, I suppose I can **look the other way. That's good enough for me.**

金柏莉：嗯，我看我就網開一面好了，這樣就足以證明了。

Mark: **Thanks heaps! You are the best!** I am sure no one **goes this far** to **scam the system.**

馬克：太感謝你了，你真是個好人！我知道應該沒有人會為了騙一張學生票而做到這種程度的吧！

影子跟讀：「短對話」

影子跟讀：「短段落」

影子跟讀：「實戰練習」

雅思聽力必考字彙

宿舍室友吵鬧

▶ 影子跟讀「短對話」練習 🎧 MP3 008

此篇為「影子跟讀短對話練習」，此章節規劃了由聽「短對話」的 shadowing 練習，能從最基礎、最易上手的部分切入雅思聽力備考並提升考生的專注力，雅思聽力中尤其 section 1 跟 2 雖然對話不難但很容易因為分心而錯失聽力訊息，而 section 1 和 2 是最好拿分且最好都要拿到全對的部分，整體分數才容易接近獲取聽力 7-7+，現在就一起動身，開始聽「短對話」！

Mary: hey, I know you are probably still hangover, but I really need to speak to you about something. It has been bothering me for a long time.

瑪莉：我知道你可能還在宿醉，可是我真的忍無可忍了，一定要跟你説，我已經忍耐很久了。

Cameron: What is it?

卡麥倫：到底什麼事？

Mary: I've had enough of the chatting, and the loud music every night. All I want to do is

瑪莉：我真的受不了你每天晚上又是聊天又是吵鬧的音樂，我真的只想睡個好覺，

have a good night sleep, I've got to go to work in the morning and classes in the afternoon.

你要知道我早上要上班，下午還要上課。

Cameron: I am sorry but you can join us if you want.

卡麥倫：不好意思啦！你也可以加入我們啊！

Mary: I don't want to join you, and I am not telling you what to do, but every night of the week is just **too much to handle**. I can tolerate it on the weekends, but please, not the week nights.

瑪莉：我不想加入你們！我也不是告訴你該怎麼做，只是一個禮拜七天都這樣真的太過分了。如果只是週末我還可以忍受，可是拜託，一到五不要好不好。

影子跟讀：「短對話」

影子跟讀：「短段落」

影子跟讀：「實戰練習」

雅思聽力必考字彙

共同廚房誰整理

　　此篇為**「影子跟讀短對話練習」**，此章節規劃了由聽**「短對話」**的 shadowing 練習，能從最基礎、最易上手的部分切入雅思聽力備考並提升考生的專注力，雅思聽力中尤其 section 1 跟 2 雖然對話不難但很容易因為分心而錯失聽力訊息，而 section 1 和 2 是最好拿分且最好都要拿到全對的部分，整體分數才容易接近獲取聽力 **7-7+**，現在就一起動身，開始聽**「短對話」**！

Tracey: Hey Stephen, can I ask you to clean up the dishes once you are done cooking? **Just in case you didn't notice.** I have been cleaning up after you for more than a week now.

崔西：嘿，史蒂芬，我可以麻煩你在煮完飯之後把碗洗一洗嗎？你可能沒有注意到，這一個禮拜多來都是我在幫你洗碗。

Stephen: Oh.. Did I not do that? Ok..

史蒂芬：喔⋯我真的沒有洗嗎？那⋯好⋯。

Tracey: I am not trying to be a

崔西：我不是想要找你麻

pain in the ass, but I am just sick of tidying up for others. I got lots of studies to catch up. I don't mind helping you out once a while, if you got caught up with things, but not all the time.

Stephen: I am sorry I didn't realise I haven't been doing it. I guess my mind was somewhere else.

Tracey: That's all right, I am not trying to make you feel bad, I just want to draw your attention to it.

煩，可是我真的受不了一直幫人收拾善後。我自己有很多書要讀，如果你忙的話，我不介意偶爾幫一次，可是不能每次都指望我。

史蒂芬：真的很抱歉，我一直沒注意到我都沒做，可能我都在想別的事。

崔西：沒關係，我不是想讓你覺得難堪，我只是想讓你注意到這件事。

房屋修繕

▶▶ 影子跟讀「短對話」練習 🎧 MP3 010

　　此篇為「影子跟讀短對話練習」，此章節規劃了由聽「短對話」的 shadowing 練習，能從最基礎、最易上手的部分切入雅思聽力備考並提升考生的專注力，雅思聽力中尤其 section 1 跟 2 雖然對話不難但很容易因為分心而錯失聽力訊息，而 section 1 和 2 是最好拿分且最好都要拿到全對的部分，整體分數才容易接近獲取聽力 7-7+，現在就一起動身，開始聽「短對話」！

Peter: Hello Mrs. Moore. I came to see you today because I reported the problem of the leaking tap in my bathroom last month, and you promised me the plumber would be here in a few days, but till now he is **nowhere to be seen** still.

彼得：摩爾太太您好，我今天來是因為我上個月就跟你說過浴室的水龍頭在漏水。你答應我水電工這幾天就會來，可是一直都沒有人來修。

Mrs. Moore: Oh... my apologies. I will **get onto it** on Monday.

摩爾太太：不好意思，我星期一會馬上辦。

Peter: Do you realize how much we have to pay for our last water bill? It cost 50 dollars extra! I am only a student, and I don't make a lot of money and I hope you are willing to cover the extra cost until the tap is fixed. If the plumber did not **show up** on Monday, I would hire one to fix it myself and send the bill to you.

彼得：你知道我們上個月的水費繳多少錢嗎？比平常多 50 美金。我只是個學生，賺的錢不多，我希望在水龍頭修好之前你要負擔額外的水費。如果水電工星期一再不來修，我只好自己請人來修然後把帳單寄給你。

影子跟讀：「短對話」

影子跟讀：「短段落」

影子跟讀：「實戰練習」

雅思聽力必考字彙

退租押金

　　此篇為「影子跟讀短對話練習」，此章節規劃了由聽「短對話」的 shadowing 練習，能從最基礎、最易上手的部分切入雅思聽力備考並提升考生的專注力，雅思聽力中尤其 section 1 跟 2 雖然對話不難但很容易因為分心而錯失聽力訊息，而 section 1 和 2 是最好拿分且最好都要拿到全對的部分，整體分數才容易接近獲取聽力 7-7+，現在就一起動身，開始聽「短對話」！

Mr. Ferguson: I am happy with the general condition of the wall and the carpet, but the kitchen cabinet doors need to be replaced. The condition is appalling. I would have to deduct USD 150 from your bond.

佛格森先生：這房子的牆面及地毯大概的情況都還好，可是廚房儲物櫃的門需要更換，怎麼會弄得這麼糟？我必須扣你 150 美金的押金。

Claire: I do apologize. My boyfriend thought the door was jammed and he pulled it too hard. The hinges just came off. I

克萊兒：真的很抱歉，我男朋友以為櫥櫃門卡住了就用力拉，誰知道太用力了，櫃子的樞軸就掉下來了。我覺

think you can easily repair it if you get a handyman in. It would not cost USD 150, would it? I think USD 100 would be a fair price. I mean the condition of the cabinet door was not too flash when we moved in **to start with**. You can **see for yourself** we do try to **take a good care** of this place.

得如果找個雜工來處理應該很容易更換，這應該不需要150 美金吧！100 應該就可以了吧！因為我們搬進來的時候櫥櫃門本來就有點舊，你應該也看的出來我們一直都很照顧這個房子。

影子跟讀：「短對話」

影子跟讀：「短段落」

影子跟讀：「實戰練習」

雅思聽力必考字彙

安裝電話費用的紛爭

▶▶ 影子跟讀「短對話」練習 🎧 MP3 012

此篇為「**影子跟讀短對話練習**」，此章節規劃了由聽「**短對話**」的 shadowing 練習，能從最基礎、最易上手的部分切入雅思聽力備考並提升考生的專注力，雅思聽力中尤其 section 1 跟 2 雖然對話不難但很容易因為分心而錯失聽力訊息，而 section 1 和 2 是最好拿分且最好都要拿到全對的部分，整體分數才容易接近獲取聽力 7-7+，現在就一起動身，開始聽「**短對話**」！

Mark: How is your home phone going?	馬克：你的家用電話都裝好了嗎？
Jennifer: It is going ok, but I received the bill asking for the installation fee, and I remembered clearly there is no installation fee.	珍妮佛：還好，可是我收到一張帳單說要收安裝費，我記得很清楚你說過沒有安裝費的。
Mark: There is no installation fee, if you are switching from	馬克：如果你有安裝過別家公司的電話，那是沒有安裝

another phone company, but for the new client there is an installation charge.

費的。可是如果是全新用戶那就會有。

Jennifer: Well, that is not what I was told. I would not have **signed up** with you if I knew, there is going to be an installation charge. What form do I have to sign to cancel the service?

珍妮佛：可是我聽到的不是這樣，我如果知道有安裝費用我就不會選擇你們公司。那我要取消，要填什麼表格呢？

Mark: I am sorry you are **under the wrong impression**, let me check with my boss and see what I can do.

馬克：不好意思你可能誤會我的意思，讓我問一下我的上司看能怎麼處理。

Jennifer: **Now you are talking**, I am sure you don't want to lose a customer

珍妮佛：這才對，你一定也不想失去一個客戶。

影子跟讀：「短對話」

影子跟讀：「短段落」

影子跟讀：「實戰練習」

雅思聽力必考字彙

買車

▶ 影子跟讀「短對話」練習　🎧 MP3 013

　　此篇為「影子跟讀短對話練習」，此章節規劃了由聽「短對話」的 shadowing 練習，能從最基礎、最易上手的部分切入雅思聽力備考並提升考生的專注力，雅思聽力中尤其 section 1 跟 2 雖然對話不難但很容易因為分心而錯失聽力訊息，而 section 1 和 2 是最好拿分且最好都要拿到全對的部分，整體分數才容易接近獲取聽力 7-7+，現在就一起動身，開始聽「短對話」！

Carter: Hey, you sold me **a piece of crap**! The car broke down on the side of the road 3 days after I took it home. I had it checked out by the other car yard. They quoted me USD 5000 for repair. Apparently, the engine is totally **wore out.**

卡特：嘿！你賣了一台爛車給我！那台車才牽回家三天就在路邊熄火，我拿到別家車廠去檢查，他們說要花 5000 塊修理，引擎早就壞掉了！

Jennifer: Well, what do you expect when you buy a used car, you got to be prepared and un-

珍妮佛：嗯，你買的是二手車還想怎麼樣，你應該有心理準備遲早會有一些問題。

derstand there would be some problems that need to **be sorted out further down the track.**

Carter: I understand but USD 3000 should get you a **half decent** car. You know paying USD 3000 for the car and USD 5000 to get the engine replaced is just ridiculous. If I knew this early, I would not touch this car. You can take the car. I just want my money back.

卡特：我懂，可是三千塊應該可以買到還可以的車。你說花了三千元買車再花五千元換引擎是不是很蠢。早知道是這樣我才不會碰這台車。你把車拿回去，我只要把錢拿回來就好。

車窗被砸

　　此篇為**「影子跟讀短對話練習」**，此章節規劃了由聽**「短對話」**的 shadowing 練習，能從最基礎、最易上手的部分切入雅思聽力備考並提升考生的專注力，雅思聽力中尤其 section 1 跟 2 雖然對話不難但很容易因為分心而錯失聽力訊息，而 section 1 和 2 是最好拿分且最好都要拿到全對的部分，整體分數才容易接近獲取聽力 7-7+，現在就一起動身，開始聽**「短對話」**！

Jennifer: I knew that was you. I saw you walking up and down the street after I parked the car.	珍妮佛：我知道是你幹的！我停好車之後有看到你在街上閒逛。
Roy: It wasn't me! I didn't **do it. How** dare you **accuse me for** something like that, I do have a problem with you but I am not that nasty.	羅伊：真的不是我，我沒有做！你怎麼可以誣賴我會做這樣的事。我是跟你有過節可是我沒有這麼惡劣。
Jennifer: Why were you being	珍妮佛：那你為什麼鬼鬼祟

sneaky then?

Roy: What sneaky! I was just taking a walk, **what's that got to do with** you?

Jennifer: **Cut the crap**! I don't believe anything comes out of your mouth. You think I got no proof, let me call the police and pull out the footage of the surveillance camera. Let's see what else you got to say. Just let me tell you, if you were caught doing it, you'd better **watch your ass**.

崇的？

羅伊：我哪有鬼鬼祟祟！我只是在散步，這干你什麼事？

珍妮佛：少來！我才不相信你講的話。你以為我沒有證據，等我叫警察來調出監視器的畫面，到時候看你有什麼好說。我跟你說，如果真的抓到是你做，你就給我小心一點！

影子跟讀：「短對話」

影子跟讀：「短段落」

影子跟讀：「實戰練習」

雅思聽力必考字彙

預約看醫生

▶ 影子跟讀「短對話」練習 🎧 MP3 015

　　此篇為「影子跟讀短對話練習」，此章節規劃了由聽「短對話」的 shadowing 練習，能從最基礎、最易上手的部分切入雅思聽力備考並提升考生的專注力，雅思聽力中尤其 section 1 跟 2 雖然對話不難但很容易因為分心而錯失聽力訊息，而 section 1 和 2 是最好拿分且最好都要拿到全對的部分，整體分數才容易接近獲取聽力 7-7+，現在就一起動身，開始聽「短對話」！

Tony: Hello, I am calling to check whether there is a vacancy for Dr. Howard to see me this morning. **I am not feeling 100 %**.	湯尼：您好，我想問一下能不能掛哈沃醫生今天早上的門診？我覺得非常不舒服。
Nurse Chelsea: Hang on a second, I will check his availability. Well, I am sorry he is **fully booked** today.	護士雀兒喜：請等一下，我查一下預約紀錄。嗯，不好意思他今天都約滿了。
Tony: What about other doc-	湯尼：那其他醫生呢？查一

tors? Maybe Dr. Abbott?

下亞伯特醫生好嗎？

Nurse Chelsea: He is also fully booked unfortunately.

護士雀兒喜：很可惜他也約滿了。

Tony: **Can I ask for a huge favour please**? I know you don't normally do this, but would you please take my contact details and call me back if **any of the vacancies come up?** I would be home all day. Any time is a good time as long as I get to see a doctor today. I live very close, I can be there within 10 mins.

湯尼：我可以請您幫個大忙嗎？我知道你們通常不會這樣做，可是您是不是可以留下我的聯絡方式，如果有人取消請通知我好嗎？我整天都會在家，所以什麼時間都可以，只要看的到醫生就好。我住得很近，十分鐘就能到。

影子跟讀：「短對話」

影子跟讀：「短段落」

影子跟讀：「實戰練習」

雅思聽力必考字彙

有人插隊

▶ 影子跟讀「短對話」練習　🎧 MP3 016

　　此篇為「影子跟讀短對話練習」，此章節規劃了由聽「短對話」的 shadowing 練習，能從最基礎、最易上手的部分切入雅思聽力備考並提升考生的專注力，雅思聽力中尤其 section 1 跟 2 雖然對話不難但很容易因為分心而錯失聽力訊息，而 section 1 和 2 是最好拿分且最好都要拿到全對的部分，整體分數才容易接近獲取聽力 7-7+，現在就一起動身，開始聽「短對話」！

Campbell: Hey, **are you done yet?** Just pick one and **move out of the way**, I am trying to get through here.	坎伯：嘿！你有完沒完，隨便選一個然後趕快讓開，我要過去。
Carrie: Excuse me, **mind your language!** I am sorry my trolley **got in your way,** I will move it for you, but you don't have to be so rude. I am just doing my shopping here.	凱莉：什麼！你講話好聽一點好嘛！很抱歉我推車擋到你的路，我會讓路給你可是你也不用這麼沒禮貌，我也只不過是來買東西。

Campbell: I am sorry if I **came across** as rude. **I am just not myself** today. Things **are not exactly going my way** today, now I've made it worse. My apologies.

坎伯：對不起如果你覺得我是個很無理的人，我今天不知道是怎麼回事，做什麼事都不順利，現在更糟了。請接受我的道歉。

Carrie: Apology accepted. **I feel for you,** but it is not my fault. Now I am having a bad day because I got yelled at by a complete stranger.

凱莉：沒關係。我很同情你，可是你不順並不是我的錯，我無端端被一個不認識的人罵，那不是換我倒楣嗎？

影子跟讀：「短對話」

影子跟讀：「短段落」

影子跟讀：「實戰練習」

雅思聽力必考字彙

申請表填錯

▶▶ 影子跟讀「短對話」練習 🎧 MP3 017

　　此篇為「影子跟讀短對話練習」，此章節規劃了由聽「短對話」的 shadowing 練習，能從最基礎、最易上手的部分切入雅思聽力備考並提升考生的專注力，雅思聽力中尤其 section 1 跟 2 雖然對話不難但很容易因為分心而錯失聽力訊息，而 section 1 和 2 是最好拿分且最好都要拿到全對的部分，整體分數才容易接近獲取聽力 7-7+，現在就一起動身，開始聽「短對話」！

Christine: I am sorry I just realized I made a mistake on the application. I **meant to** take General training, but I accidently picked Academic. Is it possible for me to change now?

克莉絲汀：不好意思我剛才發現我的申請表填錯了，我應該要選一般訓練組，可是我誤選了學術組。請問可以更換嗎？

Mark: Well, you should have been more careful while you are **filling it out**.

馬克：嗯，你填表的時候應該小心一點。

Christine: I am really sorry, but I really do need to take General training, because there is **no hope in hell** I would pass Academic.

克莉絲汀：我真的很抱歉，可是我真的需要考一般訓練組，因為我絕對不可能通過學術組的考試。

Mark: I would suggest you check in as is and if we have any cancellations from General training, we can **swap you over**. Often we do have a few no-shows, but **there is no guarantee**.

馬克：我會建議你先以學術組的身分入場，如果有一般訓練組的考生沒來，我們再把你換過去。通常都會有人缺考，但這無法保證。

Christine: Well, thanks for the advice. I think I would **go ahead** and get checked in for now, but please **keep it in mind** that I need a swap. That will be much appreciated.

克莉絲丁：嗯，謝謝你的建議，我就照這樣先入場，再麻煩你記得我需要更換。真的很感謝你。

上網購物收到錯誤商品

▶▶ 影子跟讀「短對話」練習 🎧 MP3 018

　　此篇為「**影子跟讀短對話練習**」，此章節規劃了由聽「**短對話**」的 shadowing 練習，能從最基礎、最易上手的部分切入雅思聽力備考並提升考生的專注力，雅思聽力中尤其 section 1 跟 2 雖然對話不難但很容易因為分心而錯失聽力訊息，而 section 1 和 2 是最好拿分且最好都要拿到全對的部分，整體分數才容易接近獲取聽力 7-7+，現在就一起動身，開始聽「**短對話**」！

Alison: Hi, I ordered a pair of shoes, but what I received is the wrong size.

艾利森：您好，我有訂購一雙鞋，可是我收到的尺寸是錯的。

Timothy: Sure I can organise an exchange for you. What size are you after?

提摩西：好的，我立刻幫您換貨，請問您要哪一個尺寸？

Alison: Oh perhaps I didn't **make myself clear. What I was trying to say** is, there is a **mix up,** I ordered a size 24 and on the documentation it also stat-

艾利森：哦，我可能沒有說清楚，我是想說，我訂的是 24 號，文件上也是 24 號，可是實際上我收到的是 22 號。我的訂單號碼是：

ed size 24, but I actually received size 22 instead. My order number is #332448.

Timothy: Right, sorry for the inconvenience caused. If you can organize the item and the paperwork to be sent back to us, we will organize the exchange for you.

Alison: Do I have to pay for the postage?

Timothy: Yes, that's **correct, but you** will not be charged again the postage for us to send the right one for you.

Alison: I don't **think it is fair, because** it was negligence on your side. Why am I **liable for** the return postage? **That's a scam.**

332448。

提摩西：好的，對您造成的不便很抱歉，如果你可以連鞋子還有文件一起寄回來的話，我們會幫您換貨。

艾利森：那我要付郵資嗎？

提摩西：是的，可是你不需要付我們寄回去的郵資。

艾利森：這不公平吧！因為這是你們的疏忽為什麼我要付寄回去的郵資？這是搶人吧！

影子跟讀：「短對話」

影子跟讀：「短段落」

影子跟讀：「實戰練習」

雅思聽力必考字彙

找工作

▶ 影子跟讀「短對話」練習 🎧 MP3 019

此篇為**「影子跟讀短對話練習」**，此章節規劃了由聽「**短對話**」的 shadowing 練習，能從最基礎、最易上手的部分切入雅思聽力備考並提升考生的專注力，雅思聽力中尤其 section 1 跟 2 雖然對話不難但很容易因為分心而錯失聽力訊息，而 section 1 和 2 是最好拿分且最好都要拿到全對的部分，整體分數才容易接近獲取聽力 **7-7+**，現在就一起動身，開始聽「**短對話**」！

Jennifer: Yes, we are looking for **seasonal workers** for cucumber picking, have you done any farm work before?

珍妮佛：是的，我們有在徵採小黃瓜的臨時工，你有做過農場的工作嗎？

Arthur: **I am afraid not,** but I am very hardworking. I was wondering how much do you pay and whether the **room and board** are included?

亞瑟：不好意思沒有，可是我很認真，我想請問時薪是多少？有包吃住嗎？

Jennifer: Well, it is $22 an hour **before tax.** There is a shed on the farm where you can stay for free, but you have to **supply your own** food. How soon can you start?

珍妮佛：嗯，扣稅之前是每個小時 22 塊，農場上有一個農舍你要的話可以免費住，可是食物要自己買。你什麼時候可以開始上班？

Arthur: I can start anytime but the problem is, I **don't have a clue** how to get there, I am in Brisbane right now, and I **rely on** public transportation.

亞瑟：我隨時都可以開始，可是有一個問題，我不知道要怎麼去那裡，我目前在布里斯本，我只能搭大眾交通工具。

Jennifer: My suggestion is to **hop on** a greyhound bus to Bundaberg. Give me a call before you arrive. I can pick you up from the terminal.

珍妮佛：我建議你搭灰狗巴士到邦達堡，你到之前先打電話給我，我到車站去接你。

影子跟讀：「短對話」

影子跟讀：「短段落」

影子跟讀：「實戰練習」

雅思聽力必考字彙

住宿

▶影子跟讀「短對話」練習 🎧 MP3 020

　　此篇為**「影子跟讀短對話練習」**，此章節規劃了由聽**「短對話」**的 shadowing 練習，能從最基礎、最易上手的部分切入雅思聽力備考並提升考生的專注力，雅思聽力中尤其 section 1 跟 2 雖然對話不難但很容易因為分心而錯失聽力訊息，而 section 1 和 2 是最好拿分且最好都要拿到全對的部分，整體分數才容易接近獲取聽力 7-7+，現在就一起動身，開始聽**「短對話」**！

Mark: I understand you do not welcome a smoker, but I think having a good tenant is **far more** important.	馬克：我知道你不歡迎抽菸的人，可是我覺得找到一個好的房客才是最重要的。
Ann: I know what you are trying to say, but I really don't want to ruin the new carpet. We only just **had it put in** last year.	安：我懂你的意思，可是我真的不想把我的新地毯給毀了，我們去年才換過。
Mark: Well, what about if I **keep**	馬克：嗯，那如果我不在房

the smoke away from the room, I will only smoke when I am outside of the house. Would you consider to **take me in under that condition**?

間抽菸呢？我只在房子外面抽，這樣的話你會考慮讓我搬進來嗎？

Ann: I personally would be **happy with it**, but I need to speak to my husband before I can confirm with you.

安：我個人來說是可以接受，可是我還是要問一下我先生，才能跟你確認。

Mark: I promise you can **count on me**. Plus I am only here for a short time, I would try to **stay out of your way**.

馬克：我保證我會守信用。何況我只是租短期，我盡量不讓你添麻煩。

影子跟讀：「短對話」

影子跟讀：「短段落」

影子跟讀：「實戰練習」

雅思聽力必考字彙

沒拿到薪水

▶▶ 影子跟讀「短對話」練習 🎧 MP3 021

　　此篇為「影子跟讀短對話練習」，此章節規劃了由聽「短對話」的 shadowing 練習，能從最基礎、最易上手的部分切入雅思聽力備考並提升考生的專注力，雅思聽力中尤其 section 1 跟 2 雖然對話不難但很容易因為分心而錯失聽力訊息，而 section 1 和 2 是最好拿分且最好都要拿到全對的部分，整體分數才容易接近獲取聽力 7-7+，現在就一起動身，開始聽「短對話」！

Erin: Hey Felice, just **a quick word.** I was **under the assumption** the pay day is every Thursday, but I still haven't received my pay **for the past two weeks.**	艾倫：嗨，菲莉絲，我可以跟你談一下嗎？我們不是每個星期四發薪水嗎？可是我到現在都還沒收到前兩個禮拜的薪水。
Felice: Is that right? The pay period is actually every two weeks, but you should have received it **by now.** I am pretty sure I have **signed it off** to payroll last week. Let me check with them	菲莉絲：是嗎？我們都是兩個星期才發一次，可是你也應該收到了才對。我記得我上星期已經簽出去給薪資部了，我幫你查一下。

for you.

Erin: Thanks for that. I really need the money to pay the bills.

艾倫：謝謝你，我真的急著用錢。

Felice: I just spoke to payroll, apparently your bank detail is incorrect, and the payment has been **bounced back**. If you can **head over there** to **fix that up** today, the payment should be in your account by next Thursday.

菲莉絲：我剛跟薪資部門確認過，你的銀行帳號不正確，所以錢被退回來了。如果你今天過去那裡修改的話，應該下星期四就會進你的帳戶了。

被騙

▶ 影子跟讀「短對話」練習　🎧 MP3 022

　　此篇為「**影子跟讀短對話練習**」，此章節規劃了由聽「**短對話**」的 shadowing 練習，能從最基礎、最易上手的部分切入雅思聽力備考並提升考生的專注力，雅思聽力中尤其 section 1 跟 2 雖然對話不難但很容易因為分心而錯失聽力訊息，而 section 1 和 2 是最好拿分且最好都要拿到全對的部分，整體分數才容易接近獲取聽力 7-7+，現在就一起動身，開始聽「**短對話**」！

Freddy: Hey Jennifer, can I quickly check my last time sheet, please? The payment **doesn't seem to add up**.	佛瑞迪：嘿，珍妮佛，我可以看一下我上一次的班表嗎？薪水怪怪的。
Jennifer: **What's wrong with it?**	珍妮佛：是怎麼樣怪？
Freddy: I **kept a record** for the hours I worked since I started, I should get 1800 dollars this pay, but I only got 1750 dollars. I	佛瑞迪：我從第一天就有紀錄上班的時數，我這次的薪水應該是１８００元，可是怎麼只有 1750 元，我真的

don't **get it**.

不懂。

Jennifer: The 50 dollars were deducted for the utility bill.

珍妮佛：50 塊是拿來扣水電費的。

Freddy: You told me I can stay for free. You should have **made it clear** before I started. **I feel like a fool**.

佛瑞迪：你說我可以免費住的，我開工前你應該講清楚，我真的覺得被耍了！

Jennifer: Well, **there's no such thing as a free lunch**. **Take it or leave it**.

珍妮佛：嗯，你應該知道天下沒有白吃的午餐，要不要隨便你。

Freddy: I have no problem paying for what I used, but I do have problems with you not **being upfront with me**.

佛瑞迪：要我付水電費是沒問題，可是我的問題是你不坦白跟我說。

換工作

▶ 影子跟讀「短對話」練習　🎧 MP3 023

此篇為**「影子跟讀短對話練習」**，此章節規劃了由聽**「短對話」**的 shadowing 練習，能從最基礎、最易上手的部分切入雅思聽力備考並提升考生的專注力，雅思聽力中尤其 section 1 跟 2 雖然對話不難但很容易因為分心而錯失聽力訊息，而 section 1 和 2 是最好拿分且最好都要拿到全對的部分，整體分數才容易接近獲取聽力 7-7+，現在就一起動身，開始聽**「短對話」**！

Teddy: I don't know **a better way** to **bring this up**. Well, I've got a job **lined up** in Melbourne and I need to **jump on** the next available flight. So tomorrow will be my last day.

泰迪：我不知道該怎樣開口，嗯，我在墨爾本找到工作，我需要馬上離開，所以明天是我的最後一天。

Jennifer: You can't **do this to me,** I need people here, too. You were told that you need to give me at least **two weeks notice** if you are leaving.

珍妮佛：你怎麼可以這樣，我這裡也需要人，我跟你說過如果你要走，至少要給我兩個星期的通知。

Teddy: What can I do? They want me to start next week!

泰迪：我能怎麼辦，他們叫我下星期就開工！

Jennifer: They would have to wait then. I really don't **appreciate people screwing me over.**

珍妮佛：你叫他們等，我最不喜歡別人來這套。

Teddy: **What if** I just leave tomorrow?

泰迪：那我如果明天就走怎麼辦？

Jennifer: You won't see a cent of your pay.

珍妮佛：那你就別想拿到薪水。

Teddy: Well, **if that's the case,** I will stay for two weeks. Please take this as my resignation.

泰迪：好吧，如果是這樣的話，我也只能等兩個星期了，那這樣就算你有收到我的離職通知了吧！

影子跟讀：「短對話」

影子跟讀：「短段落」

影子跟讀：「實戰練習」

雅思聽力必考字彙

車禍

▶ 影子跟讀「短對話」練習　🎧 MP3 024

　　此篇為「影子跟讀短對話練習」，此章節規劃了由聽「短對話」的 shadowing 練習，能從最基礎、最易上手的部分切入雅思聽力備考並提升考生的專注力，雅思聽力中尤其 section 1 跟 2 雖然對話不難但很容易因為分心而錯失聽力訊息，而 section 1 和 2 是最好拿分且最好都要拿到全對的部分，整體分數才容易接近獲取聽力 7-7+，現在就一起動身，開始聽「短對話」！

Paul: What do you think you are doing? You can't just **cut in** like this without indicating! Look you made a dent on the panel. Luckily, no one was injured, but you **freaked me out!**	保羅：你在幹嘛！你不能沒有打燈就切進來！你看板金都凹進去了，還好沒有人受傷，可是我嚇到了！
Kirsten: I didn't **see you there. You** were at my **blind spot**!	柯絲汀：我沒有看到你，你在我的盲點。
Paul: There is **no excuse**. You	保羅：哦，這不是藉口，你

should be more careful when you are driving! Focus on the road! I am **in a rush** and the car is still drivable, I think I will just grab your contact details and let the insurance company **deal with it.**

開車的時候本來就要小心！注意路況！我現在趕著要走，車也還能開，不然我就先拿你的聯絡資料再請保險公司處理。

Kirsten: There is a problem, I am only a traveler here and this car is not insured. I don't **know what to do. I** think we need to call the police.

柯絲汀：這有點問題，我只是觀光客，車還沒有保險。我真不知道該怎麼辦，我看還是叫警察吧！

Paul: Well, you are **in deep trouble** then. You will have to pay for it with your own money. This will **teach you a lesson.**

保羅：嗯，你糟了你，你要用你自己的錢付，這會讓你學到教訓的。

Kirsten: it might not be my fault. Let's get the police involved.

柯絲汀：這不一定是我的錯，讓警察處理吧！

影子跟讀：「短對話」

影子跟讀：「短段落」

影子跟讀：「實戰練習」

雅思聽力必考字彙

租車

▶ 影子跟讀「短對話」練習　🎧 MP3 025

此篇為**「影子跟讀短對話練習」**，此章節規劃了由聽**「短對話」**的 shadowing 練習，能從最基礎、最易上手的部分切入雅思聽力備考並提升考生的專注力，雅思聽力中尤其 section 1 跟 2 雖然對話不難但很容易因為分心而錯失聽力訊息，而 section 1 和 2 是最好拿分且最好都要拿到全對的部分，整體分數才容易接近獲取聽力 7-7+，現在就一起動身，開始聽**「短對話」**！

Oscar: Hi, this is Oscar and I meant to **bring back** the Ford Focus by **close of business** today, but we are **caught in traffic** at the moment, **there is no way** I will **make it** there in time.

奧斯卡：嗨！你好，我本來今天下班之前要把福特的 Focus 還回去，可是我們現在卡在車陣中，我不可能及時趕到。

Jennifer: Thanks for letting us know, in that case you will be charged for an extra day.

珍妮佛：謝謝你跟我們說，那樣的話你必須多付一天的錢。

Oscar: I know, that's what I am calling for. I will only be a few hours late. Is there some kind of late fee that I can pay instead of paying for the entire day?

奧斯卡：我知道，這也是我打電話給你的理由，我只是遲幾個小時而已，有沒有可能我們付遲到的費用就好？不要收我們一天的錢？

Jennifer: Unfortunately, there will be no one here after 5pm.

珍妮佛：不好意思，我們 5 點下班之後就沒有人在辦公室了。

Oscar: **Is it possible to** return the car at your other office at the airport since it's open **24/7**?

奧斯卡：那我們能不能把車改到你機場的辦公室還，因為是開 24 小時的？

Jennifer: **That can be arranged**, but you still will be paying for the late fee and the location charge.

珍妮佛：這我們可以安排，可是你還是要付遲到的費用，還有乙地還車的費用。

影子跟讀：「短對話」

影子跟讀：「短段落」

影子跟讀：「實戰練習」

雅思聽力必考字彙

分擔油錢

▶▶ 影子跟讀「短對話」練習 🎧 MP3 026

　　此篇為**「影子跟讀短對話練習」**，此章節規劃了由聽**「短對話」**的 shadowing 練習，能從最基礎、最易上手的部分切入雅思聽力備考並提升考生的專注力，雅思聽力中尤其 section 1 跟 2 雖然對話不難但很容易因為分心而錯失聽力訊息，而 section 1 和 2 是最好拿分且最好都要拿到全對的部分，整體分數才容易接近獲取聽力 7-7+，現在就一起動身，開始聽**「短對話」**！

Scott: Hi, I saw your message that you are looking for someone to **chip in** the petrol to go to Perth. I was wondering when are you going exactly?

史考特：你好，我有看到你的貼文說要找人分擔油錢一起開車到伯斯？我想請問你什麼時候要去？

Jennifer: I am **aiming to** get there before middle of next month, but I am **pretty flexible** if the timing doesn't **suit you.**

珍妮佛：我計畫下個月中前要到，可是我蠻彈性的，如果時間不適合你的話，我們可以再談。

Scott: How long are you planning to be on the road? I still got work to do for the next week and a half. I can leave on the 10th **if that's ok with you.**

史考特：你打算要開幾天？我目前還要在工作一個半星期。如果你同意的話，我可以 10 號出發。

Jennifer: I would prefer to depart earlier, but I guess I can wait for you. I am **in no hurry.**

珍妮佛：我是希望早一點出發可是沒關係，我可以等你，反正我也不急。

Scott: So the petrol will be 50-50?

史考特：那油錢是一人一半？

Jennifer: Well, that**'s one thing I want** to **point out,** I think it would be fair if you could cover 60 and I cover 40 since the car is mine. Would this **work for you**?

魯賓：嗯，我想跟你先說清楚，我覺得既然車也是我出得化的話，我出四成你出六成比較公平，這樣你可以接受嗎？

影子跟讀：「短對話」

影子跟讀：「短段落」

影子跟讀：「實戰練習」

雅思聽力必考字彙

開車被臨檢

▶ 影子跟讀「短對話」練習 🎧 MP3 027

　　此篇為「**影子跟讀短對話練習**」，此章節規劃了由聽「**短對話**」的 shadowing 練習，能從最基礎、最易上手的部分切入雅思聽力備考並提升考生的專注力，雅思聽力中尤其 section 1 跟 2 雖然對話不難但很容易因為分心而錯失聽力訊息，而 section 1 和 2 是最好拿分且最好都要拿到全對的部分，整體分數才容易接近獲取聽力 7-7+，現在就一起動身，開始聽「**短對話**」！

Jim: I have been signaling you to stop, why didn't you stop?	吉姆：我一直指示你要停下來，你為什麼還一直開？
Carla: Sorry, I wasn't sure you are **after me**.	卡拉：抱歉我不知道你是在追我。
Jim: You almost **caused an accident** back there, why were you doing 50 at a 70 zone? Are you **under the influence**?	吉姆：你知道你剛差點造成車禍嗎？為什麼你在限速 70 的路段開 50? 你是嗑藥還是喝酒？

Carla: No, of course not! I thought I was being careful by driving slowly.

卡拉：不，當然沒有！我只是覺得開慢一點會比較安全。

Jim: You were **holding up** traffic, and people were trying to overtake you, that is rather dangerous. Can I have your license please?

吉姆：你造成交通堵塞，大家都不斷地超車，這很危險。請給我看你的駕照？

Carla: **Here you go**. This is my international license and passport.

卡拉：拿去，這是我的國際駕照還有護照。

Jim: I suppose the road rules are similar in your country. You've got to **keep up with** the traffic and don't slow down **all of a sudden**. Just **be more aware** from now on.

吉姆：我想交通規則在每個國家應該都差不多，你一定要跟上車流，不要突然慢下來，麻煩你從現在開始要多注意。

影子跟讀：「短對話」

影子跟讀：「短段落」

影子跟讀：「實戰練習」

雅思聽力必考字彙

看醫生沒有保險

▶▶ 影子跟讀「短對話」練習　🎧 MP3 028

　　此篇為「**影子跟讀短對話練習**」，此章節規劃了由聽「**短對話**」的 shadowing 練習，能從最基礎、最易上手的部分切入雅思聽力備考並提升考生的專注力，雅思聽力中尤其 section 1 跟 2 雖然對話不難但很容易因為分心而錯失聽力訊息，而 section 1 和 2 是最好拿分且最好都要拿到全對的部分，整體分數才容易接近獲取聽力 7-7+，現在就一起動身，開始聽「**短對話**」！

Miranda: Hello, I am **feeling sick** and I would like to see a doctor.	米蘭達：你好，我不太舒服，我想看醫生。
Gayle: **Have you been here before?**	蓋兒：你以前來過嗎？
Miranda: No, I am a tourist and I don't have travel insurance, can you tell me roughly how much it would cost?	米蘭達：沒有，我是觀光客，我沒有旅遊保險，你可以跟我說這樣大概要多少錢嗎？
Gayle: Seeing a doctor would be expensive without insurance,	蓋兒：看醫生沒有保險是很貴的。

Miranda: I developed a fever last night, and my body is aching, I just don't know what to do.

米蘭達：我昨天晚上開始發燒，我全身痠痛，我不知道要怎麼辦？

Gayle: I would suggest if it is not a **life threatening condition,** you can try to go to the drugstore and get the **over the counter medication**. I mean, you are **heading back** in a few days, aren't you?

蓋兒：我會建議你，如果不是攸關性命的症狀，你可以先去藥局買成藥。我是說，你應該沒幾天就會回國了吧？不是嗎？

Miranda: Thanks, I will **give it a try.** I think it is just a cold, and it will **go away** in a few days.

米蘭達：謝謝，我去試試看，我想應該是感冒，希望它幾天就會好了。

影子跟讀：「短對話」

影子跟讀：「短段落」

影子跟讀：「實戰練習」

雅思聽力必考字彙

沒趕上飛機

▶ 影子跟讀「短對話」練習　🎧 MP3 029

　　此篇為**「影子跟讀短對話練習」**，此章節規劃了由聽「短對話」的 shadowing 練習，能從最基礎、最易上手的部分切入雅思聽力備考並提升考生的專注力，雅思聽力中尤其 section 1 跟 2 雖然對話不難但很容易因為分心而錯失聽力訊息，而 section 1 和 2 是最好拿分且最好都要拿到全對的部分，整體分數才容易接近獲取聽力 7-7+，現在就一起動身，開始聽**「短對話」**！

Colin: **Hi, I was meant to be on the 12:**30 flight to Miami. I am running really late, can you please check in for me?

柯林：您好，我應該是要搭 **12:**30 的飛機到邁阿密，我已經遲到了，您可不可以讓我先登記？

Janet: **Come with me** to the counter.

珍娜：請跟我到這個櫃台。

Colin: Thanks, **you are my saviour!**

柯林：太感謝了，你真是我的救星！

Janet: Don't **speak too soon.** The gate is about to close in 10

珍娜：話別說得太早，登機門在十分鐘就要關了，基本

mins, and the check-in for that flight was just closed. I have to check with my supervisor to see if we are allowed to check you in.

Colin: Please help me out, I really have to make this flight because I've **got a cruise booked** in Miami departing tomorrow morning. I know that I am to **be blamed for it**. I **should have** been here earlier. But let's just **look at** the situation now.

Janet: I can't say **you are safe** now. I will do my best to help you.

上這班飛機的登記櫃台已經關了，我需要跟我的經理談一下是不是能夠讓你搭這班飛機。

柯林：求求你幫幫我，我真的必須搭上那班飛機，因為我明天早上還要從邁阿密出發搭郵輪。我知道遲到是我的錯，我真的應該早點來，可是先不要追究，重點是專注在現在的情況。

珍娜：我不敢保證一定可以幫你，可是我會盡力。

影子跟讀：「短對話」

影子跟讀：「短段落」

影子跟讀：「實戰練習」

雅思聽力必考字彙

飯店換房間

▶影子跟讀「短對話」練習　🎧 MP3 030

此篇為「**影子跟讀短對話練習**」，此章節規劃了由聽「**短對話**」的 shadowing 練習，能從最基礎、最易上手的部分切入雅思聽力備考並提升考生的專注力，雅思聽力中尤其 section 1 跟 2 雖然對話不難但很容易因為分心而錯失聽力訊息，而 section 1 和 2 是最好拿分且最好都要拿到全對的部分，整體分數才容易接近獲取聽力 7-7+，現在就一起動身，開始聽「**短對話**」！

Anita: Hi, I am the guest in Room 305. I **made a complaint not long ago** to complain the guest next door has been very noisy, but they still keep going, **nothing has been done.**

安妮塔：您好，我是 305 房的客人，我剛剛打過電話來抱怨隔壁的房客實在太吵了，可是他們到現在還在狂歡，沒有人去解決。

Sean: We are truly sorry. We did **send someone over** to speak to the guests. They promised that they will **keep the volume down.** We will send some-

西恩：我們真的很抱歉，我們的確有派人過去跟房客勸說了，他們有答應要小聲一點，我們馬上再派人過去。

one over again shortly.

Anita: I don't know how effective that would be. It is late and I am exhausted, all I want to do is **get some sleep.** Why don't you look up whether there is another room that you can move me to. I am happy to change the room.

安妮塔：我不覺得會有什麼用，現在已經很晚了，我也很累了，我只想休息。你可以看看你們有沒有其他房間可以讓我換過去嗎？我情願換房間。

Sean: **Sure thing**, you can have Room 505. Anything else I can **help you with**?

西恩：沒問題，你可以換到 505 號房。還有其他事我們可以幫你服務的嗎？

影子跟讀：「短對話」

影子跟讀：「短段落」

影子跟讀：「實戰練習」

雅思聽力必考字彙

取消訂房

▶ **影子跟讀「短對話」練習** 🎧 MP3 031

此篇為**「影子跟讀短對話練習」**，此章節規劃了由聽**「短對話」**的 shadowing 練習，能從最基礎、最易上手的部分切入雅思聽力備考並提升考生的專注力，雅思聽力中尤其 section 1 跟 2 雖然對話不難但很容易因為分心而錯失聽力訊息，而 section 1 和 2 是最好拿分且最好都要拿到全對的部分，整體分數才容易接近獲取聽力7-7+，現在就一起動身，開始聽**「短對話」**！

Lucas: Hello, I've got a room **reserved for** today under the name of Lucas Chow, but I am stuck in the Grand Canyon at the moment. I won't get in until tomorrow. My room has been **pre-paid,** but I was wondering whether I could push the booking by a day late.

路卡斯：您好，我今天有訂房，是以路卡斯州的名義。可是我現在卡在大峽谷，我要明天才會到。我的房間已經付清了，可是我想問問看我是不是可以把日期延後一天在入住？

Jodi: Let me check the details of your booking. Well, unfortu-

僑蒂：讓我看一下你的訂房資料，嗯，不好意思你訂的

nately you booked the **early bird deal** which is non-refundable and non-transferrable. I am afraid that if you don't **check in** today, you will still be charged.

是早鳥專案，是不能退款或轉讓的。如果你今天沒有入住的話，恐怕就浪費了。

Lucas: But I was **caught out** by the bad weather. The highway is **shut down** and there is nothing I can do.

路卡斯：可是我是被壞天氣困住，公路都封路了，這不是我能控制的。

Jodi: I am really **sorry to hear** that, I will suggest you **bring this up** to your insurance company. Some of travel **insurance policy** would cover it.

僑蒂：真的很抱歉，我只能建議你跟你的保險公司談談，有些旅行保險是有包含這種損失的。

不滿意旅行團的服務

▶▶ 影子跟讀「短對話」練習　🎧 MP3 032

　　此篇為「影子跟讀短對話練習」，此章節規劃了由聽「短對話」的 shadowing 練習，能從最基礎、最易上手的部分切入雅思聽力備考並提升考生的專注力，雅思聽力中尤其 section 1 跟 2 雖然對話不難但很容易因為分心而錯失聽力訊息，而 section 1 和 2 是最好拿分且最好都要拿到全對的部分，整體分數才容易接近獲取聽力 7-7+，現在就一起動身，開始聽「短對話」！

Heather: I like the tourist attractions we visited, but in general I think there is definitely **room for improvement.**	海瑟：我喜歡我們去的那些景點，可是整體來說是還有很大的改善空間。
Maurice: How so?	毛利斯：怎麼說呢？
Heather: **You've got to admit it,** the hotel that we stayed in last night was so dated, and the mattress was so uncomfortable.	海瑟：你必須要承認，昨天晚上我們待的那個飯店好舊，而且床墊好不舒服。

Maurice: I know the hotel **can do with** a makeover, but it is still functional.

毛利斯：我知道那間飯店外觀需要整修一下，可是還是可以使用。

Heather: **Don't get me started on** the food. It is so basic, even our **so called** deluxe seafood BBQ last night. There were only a **handful of** the shrimps and some squid rings which is barely enough **to go around.** There is nothing fancy about it this tour, you should rename it a budget tour. I know I signed up for a **midrange** comfort tour, but this is definitely more a budget one.

海瑟：更不要說餐點了，全部都好基本，就連昨天晚上所謂的海鮮總匯燒烤也只不過有幾隻蝦跟魷魚圈，根本都不夠吃。整趟旅程下來沒什麼特別的，應該更名為廉價旅行團。我知道，我參加的是中等的舒適團，可是這感覺上就像廉價團。

影子跟讀：「短對話」

影子跟讀：「短段落」

影子跟讀：「實戰練習」

雅思聽力必考字彙

迷路

▶ 影子跟讀「短對話」練習 🎧 MP3 033

此篇為「影子跟讀短對話練習」，此章節規劃了由聽「短對話」的 shadowing 練習，能從最基礎、最易上手的部分切入雅思聽力備考並提升考生的專注力，雅思聽力中尤其 section 1 跟 2 雖然對話不難但很容易因為分心而錯失聽力訊息，而 section 1 和 2 是最好拿分且最好都要拿到全對的部分，整體分數才容易接近獲取聽力 7-7+，現在就一起動身，開始聽「短對話」！

Mary: Hello, I am having trouble to find the Metropolitan museum, would you be able to point out the **general direction** for me, please?	瑪莉：你好，我一直找不到大都會博物館，你可以跟我說大概的方向在哪裡嗎？
Eason: Metropolitan museum!? You are **a long way away** from it. I guess you got off the subway too early. It will take you at least half an hour to get there **on foot.**	伊森：大都會博物館？！還很遠唉！我猜你應該是太早下地鐵了，如果走過去也至少要半個小時。

Mary: Right, what would you suggest I do?

瑪莉：那你會建議我怎麼做？

Eason: I think the easiest way would be **cut through** Central Park until you **run into** 5th Ave then turn right. You should **have no trouble** finding it once you are on 5th Ave.

伊森：我覺得最容易的方式就是切過中央公園，一直到第五大道，在第五大道右轉。如果你到了第五大道，你就一定找的到。

Mary: Thanks for your help, I have been **running around in circles** for the past twenty minutes trying to **find my way**. I should have asked someone sooner.

瑪莉：謝謝你的幫忙，我已經原地打轉二十分鐘了還找不到。我應該早點問人的。

影子跟讀：「短對話」

影子跟讀：「短段落」

影子跟讀：「實戰練習」

雅思聽力必考字彙

錯過該搭的車

▶▶ 影子跟讀「短對話」練習 🎧 MP3 034

　　此篇為「影子跟讀短對話練習」，此章節規劃了由聽「短對話」的 shadowing 練習，能從最基礎、最易上手的部分切入雅思聽力備考並提升考生的專注力，雅思聽力中尤其 section 1 跟 2 雖然對話不難但很容易因為分心而錯失聽力訊息，而 section 1 和 2 是最好拿分且最好都要拿到全對的部分，整體分數才容易接近獲取聽力 7-7+，現在就一起動身，開始聽「短對話」！

Mark: Look what happened! We just missed the bus!	馬克：你看看！我們真的錯過巴士了！
Sandy: That's **ok, I am sure the next** one will be here soon.	珊蒂：沒關係，我想下一班應該馬上就來了。
Mark: I think you really need to **manage your time a bit better.**	馬克：我覺得你應該善用你的時間。
Sandy: What do you mean?	珊蒂：你是什麼意思？

Mark: Well, if it wasn't for you **taking your time** curling your hair, we would have been on the bus **as we speak.**

馬克：嗯，如果不是因為你還在那邊慢慢捲頭髮，我們早就在巴士上了。

Sandy: Missing a bus is just a **minor issue,** but I really don't appreciate you criticising me like that. You can go to Universal studio **on your own**, I much prefer to **spend time with** my hair curler.

珊蒂：沒搭上巴士只不過是件小事，但我真的很不喜歡你這樣批評我。你可以自己去環球影城，我情願回去慢慢捲我的頭髮。

Mark: I don't mean to **offend you**, but I only have a few days here in LA. I really want to **make the most of it.**

馬克：我不是故意要得罪你，可是我在洛杉磯只有幾天的時間，我真的想好好利用。

影子跟讀：「短對話」

影子跟讀：「短段落」

影子跟讀：「實戰練習」

雅思聽力必考字彙

折扣算錯

▶ 影子跟讀「短對話」練習 🎧 MP3 035

　　此篇為「**影子跟讀短對話練習**」，此章節規劃了由聽「**短對話**」的 shadowing 練習，能從最基礎、最易上手的部分切入雅思聽力備考並提升考生的專注力，雅思聽力中尤其 section 1 跟 2 雖然對話不難但很容易因為分心而錯失聽力訊息，而 section 1 和 2 是最好拿分且最好都要拿到全對的部分，整體分數才容易接近獲取聽力 7-7+，現在就一起動身，開始聽「**短對話**」！

Troy: The total **comes to** 51.75.

特洛伊：總共是 51.75 美金。

Melinda: Well, it **doesn't seem right.** My **combo** is 25 and the BBQ ribs **on its own** is 25. That should be 50 dollars, and we got a coupon for 10 percent off the total bill. I don't understand how did you get the total of 51.75?

瑪琳達：嗯，好像不太對，我的套餐是 25 元，單點碳烤肋排是 25 元。我有一張總價打九折的折價券，這樣怎麼會是 51.75 元呢？

Troy: Yes, we did take 10 percent off, but there is a 15 percent service charge applied to the total bill.

特洛伊：是的，我們已經把折扣算進去了，可是還要另外加一成五的服務費。

Melinda: **Where did it say that?**

瑪琳達：怎麼會，我沒有看到。

Troy: That's mentioned in the **fine print.**

特洛伊：明細裡有註明。

Melinda: Right, I didn't realize that. That's a lot!

瑪琳達：是嗎？我怎麼沒發現，這金額其實很大。

Troy: This must be your first time in the US. You will **get your head around** it pretty soon.

特洛伊：這你一定是第一次到美國。你很快就會知道的。

Melinda: I don't like the rule but **what can I do!**

瑪琳達：我並不喜歡這個規定，但我又能怎樣呢？

影子跟讀：「短對話」

影子跟讀：「短段落」

影子跟讀：「實戰練習」

雅思聽力必考字彙

83

機場退稅

▶▶ 影子跟讀「短對話」練習 🎧 MP3 036

　　此篇為**「影子跟讀短對話練習」**，此章節規劃了由聽**「短對話」**的 shadowing 練習，能從最基礎、最易上手的部分切入雅思聽力備考並提升考生的專注力，雅思聽力中尤其 section 1 跟 2 雖然對話不難但很容易因為分心而錯失聽力訊息，而 section 1 和 2 是最好拿分且最好都要拿到全對的部分，整體分數才容易接近獲取聽力 7-7+，現在就一起動身，開始聽**「短對話」**！

Marcie: Hi, here is the receipt for the refund.	瑪西：嗨！這是申請退稅的收據。
Joe: Thanks, can I look at the items please?	喬：謝謝，我可以看一下物品嗎？
Marcie: Oh no, I don't **have them with me**. I packed them all in my **check-in.**	瑪西：喔！糟糕！我沒有隨身帶著，我全部包在行李裡面。

Joe: We actually need to see the things you bought to **verify against** the receipt.

喬：我們需要核對一下收據和商品。

Marcie: I am so sorry, I was not aware that I need to present them to you. I got my computer to carry and there is **not much room** left in my **carry-on**. Plus, **one of the** items is 100 ml of perfume, I am not allowed to have it as carry-on anyway. I **swear to God** I am a genuine tourist, I was just not aware of the rules. Please **make an exception** for me this time. I will remember it in the future.

瑪西：我真的很抱歉，我不知道我需要拿商品給你看。我有一台電腦要帶，所以隨身行李沒什麼位子的。還有，我其中的一個商品是一瓶 100ml 的香水，我也沒辦法放進隨身行李裡。我發誓我真的只是單純的觀光客，我不清楚退稅的規定，是不是可以請您這次放我一馬，我以後一定會記得的。

影子跟讀：「短對話」

影子跟讀：「短段落」

影子跟讀：「實戰練習」

雅思聽力必考字彙

上班遲到

▶▶ 影子跟讀「短對話」練習 🎧 MP3 037

此篇為**「影子跟讀短對話練習」**，此章節規劃了由聽**「短對話」**的 shadowing 練習，能從最基礎、最易上手的部分切入雅思聽力備考並提升考生的專注力，雅思聽力中尤其 section 1 跟 2 雖然對話不難但很容易因為分心而錯失聽力訊息，而 section 1 和 2 是最好拿分且最好都要拿到全對的部分，整體分數才容易接近獲取聽力 7-7+，現在就一起動身，開始聽**「短對話」**！

Mary: **Where the hell have you been?** You are an hour late! | 瑪莉：你跑到哪裡去了？遲到一個小時了。

Samuel: Hmmm....There was an accident on the highway, and the traffic was really **backed up**. | 山姆：嗯，高速公路上出了車禍，所以很塞車。

Mary: Why didn't you call? You could have called and let us know. You know the orders have to go out by 7 am other- | 瑪莉：為什麼你不打個電話來通知？你可以早點通知我們的！你知道訂單在七點前全部都要送出去，不然來不

wise it won't get there in time. I had customers calling the whole morning to complain. I am really **fed up** with this.

及。我正個早上都在接客戶抱怨的電話，我受夠了。

Samuel: I am really sorry. I promise **it won't happen again**.

山姆：我很抱歉。我保證不再犯了。

Mary: This is getting ridiculous now. I can't **put our reputation at risk.**

瑪莉：這現在越來越可笑。我不能讓我們名聲蒙受風險。

Samuel: I know, I know. I haven't been reliable lately, but I promise I will be on time **from now on**. My orders will go out **first thing in the morning**.

山姆：我知道，我知道，我最近一直出狀況，我保證我現在開始一定會準時。訂單我一定優先處理。

Mary: Well, **actions speak louder than words**, prove it to me.

瑪莉：嗯！不要空口說白話，證明給我看。

忘記上司交代的事

▶▶ 影子跟讀「短對話」練習 🎧 MP3 038

　　此篇為「**影子跟讀短對話練習**」，此章節規劃了由聽「**短對話**」的 shadowing 練習，能從最基礎、最易上手的部分切入雅思聽力備考並提升考生的專注力，雅思聽力中尤其 section 1 跟 2 雖然對話不難但很容易因為分心而錯失聽力訊息，而 section 1 和 2 是最好拿分且最好都要拿到全對的部分，整體分數才容易接近獲取聽力 7-7+，現在就一起動身，開始聽「**短對話**」！

Perry: I got my 2nd warning from Greg Johnson today, what a terrible way to start a day.

派瑞：我今天收到桂格強 森給的警告信，已經是第二份了。今天怎麼一早就這麼倒楣。

Mary: You've got to be kidding, **what for**?

瑪莉：開玩笑地吧！是為了什麼？

Perry: He asked me to **look after** the client last Friday, but I forgot to organize the pick-up

派瑞：他叫我負責上星期五的客戶拜訪，可是我忘了安排接機。客戶真的很不高

for him. The client was upset and Greg is really **pissed off** with me right now.

興，所以桂格現在很氣我。

Mary: Oh, no. That**'s terrible. You** know how much Greg values client relations. You are lucky you didn**'t get** fired **on the spot.** You really need to **get your act together.**

瑪莉：喔，那真的很慘，你知道桂格很注重客戶關係的，你算很幸運，沒有當場被炒魷魚。你真的要用心一點。

Perry: It was a silly mistake. But I need to be **on my best behaviour** and **lay low** for a while. I can**'t afford** to make any more mistakes, otherwise I will be gone **in no time.**

派瑞：這真的是很蠢的錯誤，我真的要發條上緊一點，暫時低調行事。不能再犯錯了，不然我應該很快就被炒了。

護照弄丟重新申請

▶▶ 影子跟讀「短對話」練習 🎧 MP3 039

　　此篇為「影子跟讀短對話練習」，此章節規劃了由聽「短對話」的 shadowing 練習，能從最基礎、最易上手的部分切入雅思聽力備考並提升考生的專注力，雅思聽力中尤其 section 1 跟 2 雖然對話不難但很容易因為分心而錯失聽力訊息，而 section 1 和 2 是最好拿分且最好都要拿到全對的部分，整體分數才容易接近獲取聽力 7-7+，現在就一起動身，開始聽「短對話」！

Jamie: Hello, I would like to **file a police report** about some stolen property.	傑米：您好，我想要報案，我的東西被偷了。
Mary: I can sort it out for you. Just need to **get a few details off you**. Can you **talk me through** about what happened?	瑪莉：我可以幫你，只是需要你的一些資料，可以告訴我發生什麼事嗎？
Jamie: Someone **cut my backpack open** and stole my pass-	傑米：有人把我的背包割開，偷了我的護照還有相

port and camera, and I am **not exactly sure** when it happened, but I can tell you the last time I saw my camera was about lunch time in Times Square.

機。我不確定是什麼時候發生的，可是我可以跟你説我最後一次看到我的相機是大概中午的時候，在時代廣場。

Mary: Ok, I must tell you **the chance is slim** for the items to be found, but if you can fill out this form, then I will **put it through** to our system. Your report number is TR00201653.

瑪莉：好的，我必須老實跟你說東西不太可能找的回來，可是如果你可以填完這張表格，我可以輸入在我們的系統內建檔，你的報案號碼是：TR00201653。

Jamie: Can I have a **hard copy** of the report, please? I need it for the embassy to issue a passport replacement for me.

傑米：可以印一張報案紀錄出來給我嗎？我需要紙本報告來申請新的護照。

影子跟讀：「短對話」

影子跟讀：「短段落」

影子跟讀：「實戰練習」

雅思聽力必考字彙

銷售能力

▶▶ 影子跟讀「短對話」練習 🎧 MP3 040

　　此篇為「影子跟讀短對話練習」，此章節規劃了由聽「短對話」的 shadowing 練習，能從最基礎、最易上手的部分切入雅思聽力備考並提升考生的專注力，雅思聽力中尤其 section 1 跟 2 雖然對話不難但很容易因為分心而錯失聽力訊息，而 section 1 和 2 是最好拿分且最好都要拿到全對的部分，整體分數才容易接近獲取聽力 7-7+，現在就一起動身，開始聽「短對話」！

Mary: You know what bothers me the most?	Mary：你知道有一件事讓我不舒服嗎？
Jack: What is it?	Jack：什麼事？
Mary: As important as we are to the company, I can't believe there are sales reps that make more than us.	Mary：我們對公司這麼重要，竟然還有業務賺得比我們多。

Jack: Who makes more than us?

Jack：誰賺得比我們多？

Mary: I think Luther makes more than us.

Mary：好像 Luther 賺得比我們多。

Jack: You know that Luther can **sell ice to Eskimos** right? His selling skill is insane! I'm fine with him making more than us if he's the only one.

Jack：你知道 Luther 有能力賣冰塊給愛斯基摩人吧？他的銷售能力太強了！他賺得比我多我一點問題都沒有。

Mary: Yeah....but he is a sales rep!

Mary：是沒錯…可是他是個業務啊！

Jack: I am okay with it. We make the products and he sells them. The company won't be profitable unless both of us are good at our jobs. So I think it is fair.

Jack：我覺得還好，我們做產品他們銷售。如果有一方做不好公司都不能賺錢，所以我覺得公平。

影子跟讀：「短對話」

影子跟讀：「短段落」

影子跟讀：「實戰練習」

雅思聽力必考字彙

動手不動口的人太多了

▶ 影子跟讀「短對話」練習 🎧 MP3 041

　　此篇為**「影子跟讀短對話練習」**，此章節規劃了由聽**「短對話」**的 shadowing 練習，能從最基礎、最易上手的部分切入雅思聽力備考並提升考生的專注力，雅思聽力中尤其 section 1 跟 2 雖然對話不難但很容易因為分心而錯失聽力訊息，而 section 1 和 2 是最好拿分且最好都要拿到全對的部分，整體分數才容易接近獲取聽力 7-7+，現在就一起動身，開始聽**「短對話」**！

Mark: Just because I'm in charge of administration does not make me a servant. It seems like everyone can just walk into my office and tell me to do this or that. This company just has **too many chiefs and not enough Indians**!

馬克：就因為我是負責行政的不代表我是他們的僕人。好多時候這幫人隨意就走進我的辦公室，要我做這做那的，這家公司動嘴的人很多，但是做事的人太少了！

Tina: I'm so sorry, did you talk to your boss about it？

蒂娜：真是抱歉，你有跟老闆提起這件事嗎？

Mark: Yes I did and he said he will assign office assistants to every department, so I won't be the only one.

馬克：有，他說他會安排每一個部門有自己的行政同事，就不會一直找我了。

Tina: That sounds like a good plan！

蒂娜：這聽起來是個好方法！

影子跟讀：「短對話」

影子跟讀：「短段落」

影子跟讀：「實戰練習」

雅思聽力必考字彙

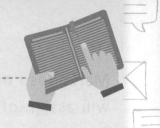

搞砸生意

▶▶影子跟讀「短對話」練習　🎧 MP3 042

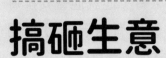

　　此篇為**「影子跟讀短對話練習」**，此章節規劃了由聽**「短對話」**的 shadowing 練習，能從最基礎、最易上手的部分切入雅思聽力備考並提升考生的專注力，雅思聽力中尤其 section 1 跟 2 雖然對話不難但很容易因為分心而錯失聽力訊息，而 section 1 和 2 是最好拿分且最好都要拿到全對的部分，整體分數才容易接近獲取聽力 7-7+，現在就一起動身，開始聽**「短對話」**！

Mary: Hey! Frank. Why the sad face?	Mary：嘿！Frank，臉色為什麼這麼糟？
Frank: I just **blew a huge deal** with this company, I was so close, but then they ran a final check on our product quality report and decided not to sign with us.	Frank：我剛剛搞砸了一個生意，我就差那麼一點點，但是最後他們再看了一次我們的產品質量報告後就決定不簽了。
Mary: Ouch! What is wrong	Mary：唉呀！那報告有什

with the report? Maybe it's not too late to **salvage** the crisis?

麼問題嗎？也許我們還有挽救的機會？

Frank: I think it's hard because apparently the inspector described our facility more like a lab than manufacturing. That turned them off instantly.

Frank：我想有點難，那審核我們的人在報告上說我們的工廠比較像實驗室，不像生產廠房。這一點馬上就讓他們打退堂鼓了。

Mary: You could invite them to come take a look themselves and maybe they will change their minds.

Mary：你可以邀請他們自己來看一次啊！也許這會改變他們的想法。

Frank: Yeah, I suppose I can give it a shot. There really is no downside for asking.

Frank：我想也是，反正問一下也沒有壞處。

影子跟讀：「短對話」

影子跟讀：「短段落」

影子跟讀：「實戰練習」

雅思聽力必考字彙

勝任團隊合作

▶▶ 影子跟讀「短對話」練習 🎧 MP3 043

　　此篇為**「影子跟讀短對話練習」**，此章節規劃了由聽**「短對話」**的 shadowing 練習，能從最基礎、最易上手的部分切入雅思聽力備考並提升考生的專注力，雅思聽力中尤其 section 1 跟 2 雖然對話不難但很容易因為分心而錯失聽力訊息，而 section 1 和 2 是最好拿分且最好都要拿到全對的部分，整體分數才容易接近獲取聽力 7-7+，現在就一起動身，開始聽**「短對話」**！

Mary: How should I prepare for a job interview?	Mary：我要怎麼準備面試呢？
Brandon: Studying some of the common questions asked in an interview helps a lot.	Brandon：找一些很常出現的面試問題，這樣準備很有幫助。
Mary: How do I make sure that it's an answer they like?	Mary：我怎麼知道他們想要聽到什麼答案？

Brandon: There are a couple of things that all companies like to hear during an interview. For example, all companies like to hear that you are a team player and you work well in a team setting. So if they ask you what your strengths are, besides mentioning what you are good at also try to include that you are a good team player.

Mary: Okay thanks!

Brandon：許多公司都喜歡聽到一些差不多的答案，比如說所有的公司都喜歡聽你說你是一個以團隊為優先的人，而在任何團隊裡你都可以勝任。所以如果他們問你的強項是甚麼，除了講你專業上的東西，也可以順便提說你是一個以團隊為主的人。

Mary：了解了，謝謝！

影子跟讀：「短對話」

影子跟讀：「短段落」

影子跟讀：「實戰練習」

雅思聽力必考字彙

做事抄捷徑

▶▶ 影子跟讀「短對話」練習 🎧 MP3 044

　　此篇為「影子跟讀短對話練習」，此章節規劃了由聽「短對話」的 shadowing 練習，能從最基礎、最易上手的部分切入雅思聽力備考並提升考生的專注力，雅思聽力中尤其 section 1 跟 2 雖然對話不難但很容易因為分心而錯失聽力訊息，而 section 1 和 2 是最好拿分且最好都要拿到全對的部分，整體分數才容易接近獲取聽力 7-7+，現在就一起動身，開始聽「短對話」！

Mark: Cindy's way of doing things bothers me sometimes.	Mark：Cindy 做事的方法讓我有點感冒。
Laura: Really? I don't work with her enough to notice anything. What does she do that bothers you?	Laura：真的啊？我跟她不夠熟，她做了甚麼嗎？
Mark: It's the little things. She always **cuts corners** and tries to do things the fastest way but	Mark：都是一些小事情啦，她總是走捷徑想用最快，但不是最正確的方法來

not necessarily the right way. She doesn't know that it might save her time now, but in the future we might not be able to find the proper data or file.

處理事情。她不知道雖然現在省了點時間,但是現在沒做好,以後可能會讓公司找不到檔案或數據。

Laura: I see. Did you talk to her about it? After all, she's just an intern. It is good for her if we tell her now to help her career.

Laura:我懂了,你有跟她溝通過嗎?她畢竟只是個實習生,現在跟她講對她的未來發展也比較好。

Mark: Good idea. I will do it this afternoon.

Mark:有道理,那我下午跟她講。

生意談成的機會不高

▶▶ 影子跟讀「短對話」練習 🎧 MP3 045

　　此篇為「**影子跟讀短對話練習**」，此章節規劃了由聽「**短對話**」的 shadowing 練習，能從最基礎、最易上手的部分切入雅思聽力備考並提升考生的專注力，雅思聽力中尤其 section 1 跟 2 雖然對話不難但很容易因為分心而錯失聽力訊息，而 section 1 和 2 是最好拿分且最好都要拿到全對的部分，整體分數才容易接近獲取聽力 7-7+，現在就一起動身，開始聽「**短對話**」！

Linda: What do you think about that company?	Linda：你覺得剛剛那家公司怎麼樣？
Sean: They are growing fast and just by looking at the office, their structure is solid and well-organized.	Sean：他們成長很快，剛剛看了一下他們辦公室感覺好像也很有制度。
Linda: I agree, they seem to have all the right elements of a good start-up company, but	Linda：對啊，一家好的初創公司要有的元素好像他們都有，不過我覺得他們好像

somehow I don't feel like they like our products too much.

對我們的產品不太感興趣。

Sean: I don't know about that, I think they try not to show too much interest to give us pressure on pricing.

Sean：我不知道。我認為他們是為了給我們談價上的壓力，才表現得沒那麼有興趣。

Linda: That is true, and they don't seem to be in a hurry to make the decision. Do you think we can get this business?

Linda：嗯，他們好像也沒有要那麼快做決定。你覺得我們這筆生意會談成嗎？

Sean: I think it's a **long shot**, but definitely possible.

Sean：有可能，但是現在看起來機率不高。

共識

▶ 影子跟讀「短對話」練習　🎧 MP3 046

　　此篇為**「影子跟讀短對話練習」**，此章節規劃了由聽**「短對話」**的 shadowing 練習，能從最基礎、最易上手的部分切入雅思聽力備考並提升考生的專注力，雅思聽力中尤其 section 1 跟 2 雖然對話不難但很容易因為分心而錯失聽力訊息，而 section 1 和 2 是最好拿分且最好都要拿到全對的部分，整體分數才容易接近獲取聽力 7-7+，現在就一起動身，開始聽**「短對話」**！

Jennifer: So what exactly is difficult about working for your boss?

Jennifer：所以到底哪裡讓你覺得幫你老闆做事很困難？

Mark: We can never be **on the same page**, whatever I say he will always interpret the other way. It's driving me crazy!

Mark：我們從來沒辦法互相了解，他總是誤解我想要表達的意思。

Jennifer: That is strange. Did you try to talk to him about it?

Jennifer：喔！那真奇怪，你有試著跟他溝通過這件事

影子跟讀：「短對話」

影子跟讀：「短段落」

影子跟讀：「實戰練習」

雅思聽力必考字彙

嗎？

Mark: I tried, but there is really a communication problem between us. Do you think I can ask for a transfer?

Mark：有啊！但是我們中間就是有溝通上的問題，你覺得我有辦法申請調到別的部門嗎？

Jennifer: Yes, you always can, but that it really depends on whether there is an opening in other divisions.

Jennifer：可以啊，可是那也要別的部門有空缺才行。

Mark: Thanks I will look into it.

Mark：謝謝，我會找找。

搞砸了

▶▶ 影子跟讀「短對話」練習 🎧 MP3 047

此篇為「影子跟讀短對話練習」，此章節規劃了由聽「短對話」的 shadowing 練習，能從最基礎、最易上手的部分切入雅思聽力備考並提升考生的專注力，雅思聽力中尤其 section 1 跟 2 雖然對話不難但很容易因為分心而錯失聽力訊息，而 section 1 和 2 是最好拿分且最好都要拿到全對的部分，整體分數才容易接近獲取聽力 7-7+，現在就一起動身，開始聽「短對話」！

Mary: Why does Francine look so sad this morning?

Mary：為什麼 Francine 今天看起來很難過啊？

Clark: Oh you haven't heard? Remember she was in charge of this company acquisition? She really **dropped the ball** on this one.

Clark：喔！你還沒聽說嗎？記不記得她是負責購買這一家公司的人？她在這過程中犯大錯了。

Mary: So what exactly happened?

Mary：所以到底發生甚麼事？

Clark: Well, what happened was that this company made a slight adjustment to the payment method, and Francine did not catch it. Now instead of paying them with 30% cash we have to pay 45% cash which is a big deal. The boss was very upset!

Mary: Oh, yes I bet.

Clark：她沒發現那家公司在購買條款上動了手腳，所以我們現在要付對方 45%的現金而不是原來的 30%。老闆很不高興呢！

Mary：喔！那是肯定的。

影子跟讀：「短對話」

影子跟讀：「短段落」

影子跟讀：「實戰練習」

雅思聽力必考字彙

燒錢

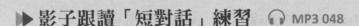

▶▶ 影子跟讀「短對話」練習 🎧 MP3 048

　　此篇為「影子跟讀短對話練習」，此章節規劃了由聽「短對話」的 shadowing 練習，能從最基礎、最易上手的部分切入雅思聽力備考並提升考生的專注力，雅思聽力中尤其 section 1 跟 2 雖然對話不難但很容易因為分心而錯失聽力訊息，而 section 1 和 2 是最好拿分且最好都要拿到全對的部分，整體分數才容易接近獲取聽力 7-7+，現在就一起動身，開始聽「短對話」！

Josh: Oh I feel like there is a million things to do and 24 hours in a day is not enough!	Josh：我覺得一天 24 小時根本不夠用，我每天都有做不完的事！
Mary: Well you are working more than 12 hours a day, so I can see that you are really busy.	Mary：我看得出你很忙，因為你一天工作超過 12 個小時。
Josh: The investor is after me on when will I launch my first product and the timeline he ex-	Josh：投資人在盯緊我要趕快把產品推出來，但是他給的時間表根本就不可能達

pects is just not possible.

到。

Luke: What is the big deal about delaying the launch? Just talk to your investor and explain to him that it's not realistic.

Luke：延後一下有甚麼關係呢？就解釋給他聽為什麼這個時間表達不到啊？

Josh: The thing is he calculated our **burn rate** precisely and gave us just enough money to survive until we can generate income from the new product. If I delayed more than one month I have no money to pay my staff and every other cost.

Josh：他根據他的時間表算準了我們需要用多少錢，然後只給我們夠用的錢到產品推出那時候。如果我遲一個月再推出產品，我可能就沒有足夠的錢付員工跟其它開銷了。

Luke: Wow that doesn't sound good.

Luke：喔！這聽起來很糟。

影子跟讀：「短對話」

影子跟讀：「短段落」

影子跟讀：「實戰練習」

雅思聽力必考字彙

時機

▶▶ 影子跟讀「短對話」練習 🎧 MP3 049

此篇為**「影子跟讀短對話練習」**，此章節規劃了由聽**「短對話」**的 shadowing 練習，能從最基礎、最易上手的部分切入雅思聽力備考並提升考生的專注力，雅思聽力中尤其 section 1 跟 2 雖然對話不難但很容易因為分心而錯失聽力訊息，而 section 1 和 2 是最好拿分且最好都要拿到全對的部分，整體分數才容易接近獲取聽力 7-7+，現在就一起動身，開始聽**「短對話」**！

Mark: Hey Lori you should really look at this start-up company. The idea is very innovative, and I think it has a lot of room for growth.

Mark：嘿！Lori，你應該來看看這家初創公司。他們的想法非常有創意，我覺得他們很有成長空間。

Lori: Many companies have good ideas, but only a few of them can thrive and grow. It takes the right combination of people, products, and timing to market to create a rapid growth

Lori：很多公司都有好的想法，但是只有少數可以真的成長。創造一家可以快速成長的公司需要對的人、產品、及市場的時機。

company.

Leslie: Sure, but I think this company's idea is so disruptive that it can become a **cash cow** like Google. Its initial investment is low, but it creates a good platform for mobile users.

Leslie：當然，但是我覺得這家公司的想法非常有破壞性，我覺得它可以成為一家像 Google 一樣可以印鈔票的公司。它的前期投資很低，但是卻創造出一個對所有手機用戶都很實用的平台。

Lori: Okay in that case, let me take a look at its portfolio.

Lori：好，那讓我來看看它的檔案。

影子跟讀：「短對話」

影子跟讀：「短段落」

影子跟讀：「實戰練習」

雅思聽力必考字彙

無法共事

▶ 影子跟讀「短對話」練習 🎧 MP3 050

　　此篇為「**影子跟讀短對話練習**」，此章節規劃了由聽「**短對話**」的 shadowing 練習，能從最基礎、最易上手的部分切入雅思聽力備考並提升考生的專注力，雅思聽力中尤其 section 1 跟 2 雖然對話不難但很容易因為分心而錯失聽力訊息，而 section 1 和 2 是最好拿分且最好都要拿到全對的部分，整體分數才容易接近獲取聽力 7-7+，現在就一起動身，開始聽「**短對話**」！

Nicole: Ellison does nothing but **lip service**. I never want to work with her again.	Nicole: Ellison 只會動嘴都不做事！我以後不想要再跟她共事了！
Larry: Really? I didn't recall working with her being that miserable.	Larry：真的嗎？我不記得跟她合作那麼糟糕啊？
Nicole: I don't know, maybe she just does that to me? Or maybe she acts differently toward	Nicole：我不知道，也許她是只對我這樣子？或也許她對男生的態度不一樣？

guys.

Larry: That could be true. She seems eager for the spotlight, but I think in general she is still a genuine and likable person.

Larry：那有可能，她是那種想要在舞台燈光下的人。但是我覺得大致來講她還算是一個真誠也滿討人喜歡的人。

Nicole: I actually thought she was a good person until I worked with her. I guess she's the type that I can be friends with but not coworker!

Nicole：我原本也覺得她是位好人直到我跟她共事，也許她是那種可以跟我當朋友，但是不能一起工作的人吧！

Larry: That could be!

Larry：有可能喔！

影子跟讀：「短對話」

影子跟讀：「短段落」

影子跟讀：「實戰練習」

雅思聽力必考字彙

兩種車型的比較

▶ 影子跟讀「短對話」練習 🎧 MP3 051

此篇為「**影子跟讀短對話練習**」，此章節規劃了由聽「**短對話**」的 shadowing 練習，能從最基礎、最易上手的部分切入雅思聽力備考並提升考生的專注力，雅思聽力中尤其 section 1 跟 2 雖然對話不難但很容易因為分心而錯失聽力訊息，而 section 1 和 2 是最好拿分且最好都要拿到全對的部分，整體分數才容易接近獲取聽力 7-7+，現在就一起動身，開始聽「**短對話**」！

Trainer: Remember, never value one type of car over another one. For example, if the customer asks whether a sports car is better than a Sedan. Do not pick a choice but instead say both have their strong suits.

Trainer：記住永遠不要把一種車子說得比另外一種好。就像如果客人問跑車好還是房車好，不要做一個選擇，要說各有好壞。

Christopher: Can you give an example on how exactly you would answer that question?

Christopher：能不能示範一下實際上你會怎麼說？

Trainer: Sure, I can say something like comparing these two types of cars are like **comparing apples and oranges** because it depends on the users' need. Sedans are more family oriented, and Sports cars obviously are for drivers with enthusiasm for style.

Christopher: Okay, thank you.

Trainer：可以，我可以說比較這兩種車型就像是比較蘋果跟橘子，主觀成分比較重。房車是比較適合家庭開的，而跑車比較受喜歡有個性及潮流的人歡迎。

Christopher：好，謝謝。

影子跟讀：「短對話」

影子跟讀：「短段落」

影子跟讀：「實戰練習」

雅思聽力必考字彙

擴張業務部門

▶ 影子跟讀「短對話」練習　🎧 MP3 052

　　此篇為「影子跟讀短對話練習」，此章節規劃了由聽「短對話」的 shadowing 練習，能從最基礎、最易上手的部分切入雅思聽力備考並提升考生的專注力，雅思聽力中尤其 section 1 跟 2 雖然對話不難但很容易因為分心而錯失聽力訊息，而 section 1 和 2 是最好拿分且最好都要拿到全對的部分，整體分數才容易接近獲取聽力 7-7+，現在就一起動身，開始聽「短對話」！

Craig: What do you think of taking up a sales role? We really need to **boost up** our sales figures.

奎格：你覺得調到業務部怎麼樣？我們真的需要增加我們的銷售額。

Mary: Me!? Doing sales? You've got to be kidding. Sales is really **not my thing**. You know I am not a people person. I **freak out whenever I need to speak to someone I don't know**. I can't do it. It is too full on.

瑪莉：你說我嗎？當業務？不要開玩笑了！我真的不適合，你知道我不會跟人家相處。我只要跟陌生人講話就會緊張，我沒辦法啦！壓力太大了！

Craig: I think as long as you **come out of your shell** a bit more, you will be fine! You know we will train you.

奎格：我覺得只要你放開一點，你就可以了！我們也會提供訓練的。

Mary: Honestly, this is not what I signed **up for Craig. Can't you just let me be?**

瑪莉：說實話，這真的不是我想要的，你不能讓我做我現在的職務就好了嗎？

Craig: **You don't have to rush into** any decision right now. Go home and **sleep on it**, trust me it is not all that bad. You will be on base salary plus commission.

奎格：你不用現在急著決定，回家好好想一想，相信我這真的沒有那麼糟。你是領底薪加傭金。

Mary: I think you should talk to Tina about it. She would make a wonderful sales.

瑪莉：我覺得你應該跟緹娜談談，她會很適合當業務。

影子跟讀：「短對話」

影子跟讀：「短段落」

影子跟讀：「實戰練習」

雅思聽力必考字彙

熱臉貼冷屁股

▶ 影子跟讀「短對話」練習 🎧 MP3 053

此篇為「**影子跟讀短對話練習**」，此章節規劃了由聽「**短對話**」的 shadowing 練習，能從最基礎、最易上手的部分切入雅思聽力備考並提升考生的專注力，雅思聽力中尤其 section 1 跟 2 雖然對話不難但很容易因為分心而錯失聽力訊息，而 section 1 和 2 是最好拿分且最好都要拿到全對的部分，整體分數才容易接近獲取聽力 7-7+，現在就一起動身，開始聽「**短對話**」！

Mary: Gordon I've been struggling reaching my sales quota. Can you give me any pointers on how to improve?	Mary：Gordon，我一直在掙扎達不到銷售目標。你可不可以幫助我進步？
Gordon: What area do you struggle with the most?	Gordon：你哪方面最有困難？
Lenny: I can't **make cold calls**. I have yet to get customers to sign a deal with me over the	Lenny：我不知道怎麼打銷售電話，我到現在還沒有成功在電話上跟客戶簽約過。

影子跟讀：「短對話」

影子跟讀：「短段落」

影子跟讀：「實戰練習」

雅思聽力必考字彙

phone.

Gordon: Yeah so that's a problem. Are you intimidated by the person on the other end of line because 95% of those people hate getting cold calls?

Gordon：嗯！那是一個問題。你有沒有因為 95%的人都討厭接到銷售電話這件事，而害怕面對電話那一頭的人呢？

Lenny: Yes, I am always afraid and feel bad I am interrupting their lives!

Lenny：有啊！我總是很害怕，而且我會因為覺得打擾了他們生活，而有罪惡感。

Gordon: Okay! let's start working on getting rid of the guilt!

Gordon：好吧！那第一件事就是要把這個罪惡感拿掉！

估算一個數字

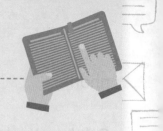

▶▶ 影子跟讀「短對話」練習 🎧 MP3 054

　　此篇為**「影子跟讀短對話練習」**，此章節規劃了由聽**「短對話」**的 shadowing 練習，能從最基礎、最易上手的部分切入雅思聽力備考並提升考生的專注力，雅思聽力中尤其 section 1 跟 2 雖然對話不難但很容易因為分心而錯失聽力訊息，而 section 1 和 2 是最好拿分且最好都要拿到全對的部分，整體分數才容易接近獲取聽力 7-7+，現在就一起動身，開始聽**「短對話」**！

Sherry: What are you doing? I don't have anything to present!

Sherry：你在幹嘛啊？我又沒有東西要報告！

Gerald: They are asking for some detailed numbers. I got all my numbers from you and you have to help me out now.

Gerald：他們再問一些比較細的數字，我所有的數字都是你給的，所以你要幫幫我。

Sherry: Everything I know is in your presentation. If they want more, I can't help!

Sherry：我已經把我所有的數字給你了，如果他們要更多我沒辦法幫忙！

Gerald: They are only asking for **ballpark numbers,** so just reason out a good estimate and they will take it. They understand we are doing this on the fly, so it doesn't have to be a precise number.

Sherry: Okay, I will try.

Gerald：他們只是要估一個數字，只要推算出一個大概的就可以了。他們知道我們是臨時做得，不會要求很精準。

Sherry：好吧！我試試看。

尋找有經驗的創業者

▶ 影子跟讀「短對話」練習　🎧 MP3 055

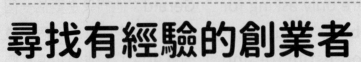

　　此篇為「影子跟讀短對話練習」，此章節規劃了由聽「短對話」的 shadowing 練習，能從最基礎、最易上手的部分切入雅思聽力備考並提升考生的專注力，雅思聽力中尤其 section 1 跟 2 雖然對話不難但很容易因為分心而錯失聽力訊息，而 section 1 和 2 是最好拿分且最好都要拿到全對的部分，整體分數才容易接近獲取聽力 7-7+，現在就一起動身，開始聽「短對話」！

Amanda: I have this idea that I want to build around, but I don't know how to **get the ball rolling**!

Amanda：我想要以我的這個想法為基礎來開公司，可是我不知道怎麼開始！

Benson: Yes, starting a business is not as easy as you think.You need to write a good business plan to start. While you are writing the plan it will force you to think about a lot of things you have not thought of before.

Benson：是啊，開一家公司不是那麼簡單的。你需要寫一份商業計畫，在寫計畫的同時會逼你去想一些你還沒想的事情。

Amanda: Can you please help me with the plan?

Benson: I can give you the ones I did with my old business. Try to follow my train of thought.

Amanda: Okay. Thank you!

Amanda：你能幫我一起寫計畫嗎？

Benson：我可以給妳我以前的檔案，試著用相同邏輯寫看看。

Amanda：好，謝謝！

影子跟讀：「短對話」

影子跟讀：「短段落」

影子跟讀：「實戰練習」

雅思聽力必考字彙

拍馬屁

此篇為**「影子跟讀短對話練習」**，此章節規劃了由聽**「短對話」**的 shadowing 練習，能從最基礎、最易上手的部分切入雅思聽力備考並提升考生的專注力，雅思聽力中尤其 section 1 跟 2 雖然對話不難但很容易因為分心而錯失聽力訊息，而 section 1 和 2 是最好拿分且最好都要拿到全對的部分，整體分數才容易接近獲取聽力 7-7+，現在就一起動身，開始聽**「短對話」**！

Mark: I'm trying to make the boss like me more. What should I do?

Mark：我想要讓我老闆更喜歡我一點，我應該怎麼做？

Miranda: Are you trying to get some **brownie points**?

Miranda：你是想拍他馬屁嗎？

Mark: No not at all! I just hope we can have a natural conversation, so it's not that awkward in the office. Honestly, I never see

Mark：不是的！我只是希望可以跟他有比較自然的對話，這樣在辦公室裡的氣氛就不會那麼尷尬。講實在

him smile.

Miranda: Everybody is different. You are a person that emphasizes relationships, so this might feel awkward for you, but maybe for him this is pretty natural. At the end of the day, as long as you do a good job at work, he will recognize your effort.

Mark: Okay, I see. Thanks for the advice!

的，我從來沒看他笑過。

Miranda：每一個人都不太一樣。你是一個注重關係的人，所以現在這相處模式可能對你有點奇怪，但是可能你老闆很習慣這種方式。總之我覺得，只要你好好努力工作，老闆還是會肯定你的。

Mark：好的，我了解了，謝謝你的意見。

影子跟讀：「短對話」

影子跟讀：「短段落」

影子跟讀：「實戰練習」

雅思聽力必考字彙

好的創意都支持

▶▶ 影子跟讀「短對話」練習 🎧 MP3 057

　　此篇為**「影子跟讀短對話練習」**，此章節規劃了由聽**「短對話」**的 shadowing 練習，能從最基礎、最易上手的部分切入雅思聽力備考並提升考生的專注力，雅思聽力中尤其 section 1 跟 2 雖然對話不難但很容易因為分心而錯失聽力訊息，而 section 1 和 2 是最好拿分且最好都要拿到全對的部分，整體分數才容易接近獲取聽力 7-7+，現在就一起動身，開始聽**「短對話」**！

Mary: What do you think of this new CEO? How is he different than our old boss?	Mary：你覺得這個新執行長怎麼樣？他跟我們舊老闆有甚麼不一樣？
Chad: Well, our old boss was very dominant and likes to give a very specific direction. This new boss is willing to listen to us and tries to discover good ideas from us.	Chad：嗯，舊老闆個性上比較強勢，很喜歡給一個明確的方向。現在的比較會聽我們的看法來試圖從我們中間挖掘出好的想法。

Mary: Yes, our boss is like Steve Jobs who al located all of Apple's resources to just make a few products and this new guy is like Larry Page who uses a **shotgun approach** in Google to launch all the good ideas they can think of.

Chad: That's a good comparison.

Mary：對，舊老闆像賈伯斯用蘋果所有的資源就做少數產品，而新老闆像賴瑞配吉一樣用散彈槍的方式，只要是好的創意都願意支持。

Chad：這個比喻很不錯。

炒魷魚

▶▶ 影子跟讀「短對話」練習 🎧 MP3 058

　　此篇為**「影子跟讀短對話練習」**，此章節規劃了由聽**「短對話」**的 shadowing 練習，能從最基礎、最易上手的部分切入雅思聽力備考並提升考生的專注力，雅思聽力中尤其 section 1 跟 2 雖然對話不難但很容易因為分心而錯失聽力訊息，而 section 1 和 2 是最好拿分且最好都要拿到全對的部分，整體分數才容易接近獲取聽力 7-7+，現在就一起動身，開始聽**「短對話」**！

Mark: Patty, why are you putting away your stuff?

Mark：Patty，你為什麼要收拾妳的東西呢？

Patty: I got a **pink slip** this morning...

Patty：我今天早上被炒了。

Mark: Oh no! Are you okay?

Mark：喔！不，那你還好嗎？

Patty: Yeah, I will take a short

Patty：嗯，我會先放自己

vacation first before I start looking for the next job.

一個假，等回來再找下一份工作。

Mark: Did Ted (Patty's manager) say why?

Mark: Ted（Patty 的主管）有沒有說為什麼呢？

Patty: He said it is nothing personal, but my group is cutting costs and because I'm the newest member so...

Patty：他說跟我沒什麼關係，只是我的團隊要縮小，既然我是最後加入的，要走的就是我囉。

Mark: I will ask around to see if there are any openings!

Mark：我會到處問問看看有沒有公司在找人！

Patty: Okay, thanks!

Patty：好的，謝謝！

影子跟讀：「短對話」

影子跟讀：「短段落」

影子跟讀：「實戰練習」

雅思聽力必考字彙

營運作業上有豐富經驗

▶▶ 影子跟讀「短對話」練習　🎧 MP3 059

此篇為「影子跟讀短對話練習」，此章節規劃了由聽「短對話」的 shadowing 練習，能從最基礎、最易上手的部分切入雅思聽力備考並提升考生的專注力，雅思聽力中尤其 section 1 跟 2 雖然對話不難但很容易因為分心而錯失聽力訊息，而 section 1 和 2 是最好拿分且最好都要拿到全對的部分，整體分數才容易接近獲取聽力 7-7+，現在就一起動身，開始聽「短對話」！

Mary: How did you get in touch with John?	Mary：你是怎麼跟 John 聯絡上的呢？
Eric: I knew John a long time ago and when you mentioned to me about this opening. I immediately thought about him. He is the perfect candidate.	Eric：我認識 John 很久了，這次當你說需要一位人選的時候我馬上想到他。John 絕對是你最好的人選。
Mary: Why do you think so highly of him?	Mary：你為什麼這麼推薦他呢？

Eric: John has a strong **track record** of setting up operation structures within both start-ups and large public companies. He knows how to customize the operation to match the uniqueness of the company. He's just the guy you are looking for.

Mary: Okay, sounds good. Let's set up an interview then.

Eric: John 在營運作業上有豐富的經驗，不管是初創公司或是有規模的大公司他都有做過，而且他非常擅長於根據公司的特色來調整營運模式。

Mary：聽起來不錯，那我們就安排一個面試吧。

影子跟讀：「短對話」

影子跟讀：「短段落」

影子跟讀：「實戰練習」

雅思聽力必考字彙

131

折扣和優惠討論

▶▶ 影子跟讀「短對話」練習 🎧 MP3 060

　　此篇為**「影子跟讀短對話練習」**，此章節規劃了由聽**「短對話」**的 shadowing 練習，能從最基礎、最易上手的部分切入雅思聽力備考並提升考生的專注力，雅思聽力中尤其 section 1 跟 2 雖然對話不難但很容易因為分心而錯失聽力訊息，而 section 1 和 2 是最好拿分且最好都要拿到全對的部分，整體分數才容易接近獲取聽力 7-7+，現在就一起動身，開始聽**「短對話」**！

Tim: Did we reach our goal on revenue this quarter?	Tim：我們這一季銷售有達到目標嗎？
Amber: We have exceeded our goals by 20%, but that is due in large part to discounts and pro-motions.	Amber：我們超過了我們預期的 **20%**，但那是因為我們的折扣跟優惠策略。
Tim: Did the move hurt our **bot-tom line**?	Tim：有沒有影響到我們的盈利？

Amber: We are still **in the black**, but next quarter is not looking as good as competition gets fierce and; therefore, the discount effect might be diluted.

Amber: 我們還是賺錢，可是下一季前景不是很好，因為競爭越來越激烈，也讓折扣策略的效果減低。

Tim：Okay that is fine because next quarter we should have new products come in to provide us the margins that we need.

Tim：沒關係，下一季我們會有新產品上架，新產品會提供我們需要的毛利。

影子跟讀：「短對話」

影子跟讀：「短段落」

影子跟讀：「實戰練習」

雅思聽力必考字彙

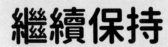

繼續保持

▶▶ 影子跟讀「短對話」練習 🎧 MP3 061

　　此篇為「影子跟讀短對話練習」，此章節規劃了由聽「短對話」的 shadowing 練習，能從最基礎、最易上手的部分切入雅思聽力備考並提升考生的專注力，雅思聽力中尤其 section 1 跟 2 雖然對話不難但很容易因為分心而錯失聽力訊息，而 section 1 和 2 是最好拿分且最好都要拿到全對的部分，整體分數才容易接近獲取聽力 7-7+，現在就一起動身，開始聽「短對話」！

Josh: Inventory of raw materials is running low, but the supplier cannot promise to deliver within our time.	Josh：我們原材料的庫存已經很少了，但是供應商可能沒辦法在我們要求的時間內給我們。
Lisa: What is the problem?	Lisa：是什麼問題呢？
Josh: Their factory had a small fire last week, and a lot of products were destroyed.	Josh：他們的工廠上禮拜有一個小火災，燒掉了很多產品。

Lisa: That is the main supplier right? What about the other suppliers? Can they increase their usual product ion and meet our target?

Lisa：這是最主要的廠家對不對？聯繫一下第二跟第三家廠商，看看他們能不能提高平常的量來滿足我們的需求。

Josh: We never really developed the 2nd and 3rd suppliers as the main supplier was always good until now.

Josh：我們沒有其他的供應商，因為這家直到今天以前一直很穩定。

Lisa: Josh, this was one of the **action items** from last quarter. I can't believe you have not done it. I need you to get **on top of this** right now!

Lisa: Josh，找更多供應商是上一季的結論，我不敢相信你還沒做。你現在趕快去做！

Josh: Okay I'll get right on it.

Josh：好的，我這就去。

簽約

▶ 影子跟讀「短對話」練習 🎧 MP3 062

　　此篇為「影子跟讀短對話練習」，此章節規劃了由聽「短對話」的 shadowing 練習，能從最基礎、最易上手的部分切入雅思聽力備考並提升考生的專注力，雅思聽力中尤其 section 1 跟 2 雖然對話不難但很容易因為分心而錯失聽力訊息，而 section 1 和 2 是最好拿分且最好都要拿到全對的部分，整體分數才容易接近獲取聽力 7-7+，現在就一起動身，開始聽「短對話」！

Emily: Andy, I don't think we should agree to the terms they are offering. We are straining ourselves, if we sign with them because we don't have the manpower to take on the next possible more lucrative case.

Emily: Andy，我不覺得他們給的條件很好。我們跟他們簽約只是綁住我們自己，讓我們沒有足夠的人力來接下一個更賺錢的專案。

Andy: I'm sorry Emily, but **that ship has sailed**. We signed the contract with them this morning and I won't risk the compa-

Andy：對不起 Emily，但是現在討論這件事已經太晚了。我們今天早上已經跟這家公司簽約了，而為了我們

ny's reputation to change course now.

公司的形象我也不會在現在毀約。

Emily: I didn't know we had already signed. Let's just focus on doing the work and forget what I said then.

Emily：我不知道已經簽約了，那就當我什麼都沒講，專心把這件事做完吧！

Andy: Thank you for your understanding Emily.

Andy: Emily，謝謝你的諒解。

重新獲得產品優勢

▶ 影子跟讀「短對話」練習 🎧 MP3 063

　　此篇為**「影子跟讀短對話練習」**，此章節規劃了由聽**「短對話」**的 shadowing 練習，能從最基礎、最易上手的部分切入雅思聽力備考並提升考生的專注力，雅思聽力中尤其 section 1 跟 2 雖然對話不難但很容易因為分心而錯失聽力訊息，而 section 1 和 2 是最好拿分且最好都要拿到全對的部分，整體分數才容易接近獲取聽力 7-7+，現在就一起動身，開始聽**「短對話」**！

Paul: Now that we are clear that we **started off on the wrong foot** Last year, we needed to change our course and regain our edge this year. So please think creatively to help the next product design.

Paul：我們現在很清楚去年我們的方向是錯的，我們今年得要改變方向來使我們重新獲得產品優勢。現在請你們發揮想像力來幫助下一個產品的構想。

Daniel: To prevent us from making the same mistake again, what we should do is really focus on what the users will enjoy

Daniel：為了不重蹈覆轍，我們要學習如何從使用者的角度去思考，不是只要是有創意的點子都是好的。

using, and not just random creative ideas.

Matt: Daniel made a great point, I think a lot of times, our engineers get caught up in what is so called the latest, fastest, or coolest technology, but overlook what users really want.

Matt: Daniel 講得很好，很多時候我們工程師很容易迷上最新、最酷或是最有想像力的發明，可是常常忘記使用者想要甚麼樣的功能。

Mary: Good start. Let's start our session.

Mary：很好的開始，請大家開始進行腦力激盪。

我的想法

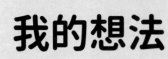

▶▶ 影子跟讀「短對話」練習 🎧 MP3 064

此篇為「**影子跟讀短對話練習**」，此章節規劃了由聽「**短對話**」的 shadowing 練習，能從最基礎、最易上手的部分切入雅思聽力備考並提升考生的專注力，雅思聽力中尤其 section 1 跟 2 雖然對話不難但很容易因為分心而錯失聽力訊息，而 section 1 和 2 是最好拿分且最好都要拿到全對的部分，整體分數才容易接近獲取聽力 7-7+，現在就一起動身，開始聽「**短對話**」！

Mary: Is there any feedback that you would like to make to help improve our company?

Mary：你們有沒有什麼意見可以幫助公司再進步呢？

Eric: **Here's my two cents**, I feel there is room for improvement regarding operational efficiency. I notice that sometimes project managers have only the title but don't have actual authority and power to do many things because none of the team

Eric：我有一個想法，我覺得在公司運作上還有進步的空間，比如說我發現很多時候專案經理只是空有頭銜，但是沒有實質的權力，因為下面的人都是從其他專屬部門借來的。這樣子很多時候都沒有辦法把優先權放在他

members really report to him or her. They are borrowing people from other groups and therefore the priority sometimes is not there for them.

們的專案上。

Mary: Interesting and valid point, I think you need to communicate with HR and devise a new structure for project manager to make life easier on them. Nathan, can you talk to Jack about this?

Mary：嗯！很有道理，這一方面你需要跟人事溝通好，以幫助專案經理有新的架構定位來讓他們能更有效率。Mary，你能不能跟 Jack 討論這件事？

Nathan: Yes, Mary I will.

Nathan：是的，瑪莉，我會的。

咬緊牙關

▶▶ 影子跟讀「短對話」練習　🎧 MP3 065

此篇為「影子跟讀短對話練習」，此章節規劃了由聽「短對話」的 shadowing 練習，能從最基礎、最易上手的部分切入雅思聽力備考並提升考生的專注力，雅思聽力中尤其 section 1 跟 2 雖然對話不難但很容易因為分心而錯失聽力訊息，而 section 1 和 2 是最好拿分且最好都要拿到全對的部分，整體分數才容易接近獲取聽力 7-7+，現在就一起動身，開始聽「短對話」！

Tim: We need to restructure our system so that we utilize all our manpower to the best efficiency.	Tim：我們需要一個新的架構，好讓我們可以把每個員工的效率都帶出來。
Mary: Yes, last time Eric's proposal regarding the project managers is already underway for change.	Mary：嗯，上次 Eric 提出有關專案經理的制度調整已經在做改變了。
Tim: That is just one area. Let's	Tim：這只是一部分，我們

look at all the possible improvements we can make with a new structure. I know restructuring is always hard for employees and for the company, but let's **bite the bullet** and make this right from the beginning.

需要看看每一塊可以改進的地方。我知道安排新架構總是對員工及公司很難,但是讓我們咬緊牙關撐過去,做一次就到位。

Mary: Okay, I sure will get on top of this.

Mary:好的,我會開始執行這件事。

裁員

▶▶ 影子跟讀「短對話」練習　🎧 MP3 066

　　此篇為「影子跟讀短對話練習」，此章節規劃了由聽「短對話」的 shadowing 練習，能從最基礎、最易上手的部分切入雅思聽力備考並提升考生的專注力，雅思聽力中尤其 section 1 跟 2 雖然對話不難但很容易因為分心而錯失聽力訊息，而 section 1 和 2 是最好拿分且最好都要拿到全對的部分，整體分數才容易接近獲取聽力 7-7+，現在就一起動身，開始聽「短對話」！

Mary: How much cost do we need to slash to **keep heads above the water**?	Mary：我們要減少多少開銷才能讓公司生存？
Jeremy: We need to reduce operational cost by $460,000 a quarter.	Jeremy：我們每一季需要減少 460,000 元。
Mary: Wow if we reduce all that from staff that's a lot of salaries.	Mary：如果全從員工薪水那邊省的話，是很多人要走的。

Jeremy: Yes, but I think we can trim down our costs in some other areas, I think we just need to let go 10 people.

Jeremy：對！但是我們還可以從別的方面省錢，我估計大概要裁掉 10 個員工。

Mary: Okay let's hold the meeting with all directors to see if we can get a list of people we can terminate.

Mary：好吧！那我們找所有主管來開會，看看能不能列出可裁掉的員工。

影子跟讀：「短對話」

影子跟讀：「短段落」

影子跟讀：「實戰練習」

雅思聽力必考字彙

扭轉劣勢

此篇為**「影子跟讀短對話練習」**，此章節規劃了由聽**「短對話」**的 shadowing 練習，能從最基礎、最易上手的部分切入雅思聽力備考並提升考生的專注力，雅思聽力中尤其 section 1 跟 2 雖然對話不難但很容易因為分心而錯失聽力訊息，而 section 1 和 2 是最好拿分且最好都要拿到全對的部分，整體分數才容易接近獲取聽力 7-7+，現在就一起動身，開始聽**「短對話」**！

Mark: This company has a diverse product portfolio, and they don't care if they lose money on this particular product line. How do I **level the playing field**?

馬克：這家公司有很多不同產品，所以他們不介意在這項產品上虧一點錢。我要怎麼扭轉劣勢？

Emily: You want to avoid playing the pricing game wi th them because you have no chance to beat them. Smaller company versus big company is always

Emily：你要避免跟他們在價格上競爭，因為這方面你輸定了。小公司要跟大公司競爭總是不容易，但是就像大衛打倒歌利亞一樣，這個

hard, like **David fights Goliath**, but if the moral of the story teaches us anything it is that big companies will react slower to the market. They lack your mobility, so you have to use that to your advantage.

故事教我們大公司的反應不會有你這麼快。你要用這一點跟他打。

Mark: Okay, that's good advice. I will go dwell on what I can do.

馬克：好的，這個建議很好我會回去想想看要怎麼做。

討論訂單

▶▶ 影子跟讀「短對話」練習 🎧 MP3 068

此篇為「**影子跟讀短對話練習**」，此章節規劃了由聽「**短對話**」的 shadowing 練習，能從最基礎、最易上手的部分切入雅思聽力備考並提升考生的專注力，雅思聽力中尤其 section 1 跟 2 雖然對話不難但很容易因為分心而錯失聽力訊息，而 section 1 和 2 是最好拿分且最好都要拿到全對的部分，整體分數才容易接近獲取聽力 7-7+，現在就一起動身，開始聽「**短對話**」！

Shane: About the company you visited last week, do you think you can close the deal?	Shane：你們可以拿到上週你們去拜訪的那家公司的訂單嗎？
Linda: Yes it should be **low-hanging fruit**, The owners are very pleased with our products, and; therefore, I don't see any reason why this deal would fall through.	Linda：嗯，這應該很容易。那家老闆對我們的產品很滿意，我想不出任何能讓這生意跑走的原因。

Shane: Are there any other competitors that have approached them?

Shane：有別家競爭對手去拜訪嗎？

Linda: Yes but we offer much better product quality at about the same price, so it should be an easy pick for the owner.

Linda：有，但是我們產品的品質要好很多，而且也沒有比較貴，對於那家老闆來說應該不難做這決定。

Shane: Okay. Good let's close the deal as soon as possible.

Shane：Okay 很好！那就盡快把這個單子拿到。

影子跟讀：「短對話」

影子跟讀：「短段落」

影子跟讀：「實戰練習」

雅思聽力必考字彙

請假代班

▶ 影子跟讀「短對話」練習 🎧 MP3 069

　　此篇為**「影子跟讀短對話練習」**，此章節規劃了由聽**「短對話」**的 shadowing 練習，能從最基礎、最易上手的部分切入雅思聽力備考並提升考生的專注力，雅思聽力中尤其 section 1 跟 2 雖然對話不難但很容易因為分心而錯失聽力訊息，而 section 1 和 2 是最好拿分且最好都要拿到全對的部分，整體分數才容易接近獲取聽力 7-7+，現在就一起動身，開始聽**「短對話」**！

Robert: Hey Annie, I will be gone for 2 weeks on vacation. If there are urgent matters, you can reach me by phone and email. You get to make the less important decisions.	Robert：嘿！Annie，我準備要請兩週的假。如果有甚麼緊急的事就打電話或 Email 給我，不重要的事情你可以決定。
Annie: Cool! Does that mean I get to **call the shots**?	Annie：太好了，你是説我可以作主喔！
Robert: I have to emphasize	Robert：我必須要強調是在

that your authority is for non-urgent matters only.

非重要的事情上你可以做主。

Annie: Sure, but there are a lot of non-urgent matters which means I can act like a boss for 2 weeks without taking on any responsibilities. I like that!

Annie：我了解，但是有很多非重要的事啊，就是說我可以當老闆但是又不用擔壓力。

Robert: I'm glad you like your temporary role.

Robert：我很高興你喜歡你這暫時的角色。

影子跟讀：「短對話」

影子跟讀：「短段落」

影子跟讀：「實戰練習」

雅思聽力必考字彙

卸責

▶ 影子跟讀「短對話」練習 MP3 070

　　此篇為「**影子跟讀短對話練習**」，此章節規劃了由聽「**短對話**」的 shadowing 練習，能從最基礎、最易上手的部分切入雅思聽力備考並提升考生的專注力，雅思聽力中尤其 section 1 跟 2 雖然對話不難但很容易因為分心而錯失聽力訊息，而 section 1 和 2 是最好拿分且最好都要拿到全對的部分，整體分數才容易接近獲取聽力 7-7+，現在就一起動身，開始聽「**短對話**」！

Dean: Your careless mistake has cost us. You need to give me a reason and write a report on how you will not make the same mistake next time.

狄恩：你的粗心大意讓我們花了大錢。你要給我一個理由加上一份報告講說你要怎麼注意，下次才不會再犯錯。

Mary: I am only partially responsible for this. The engineer told me to modify the recipe and I made a mistake along the way. If the engineers had modified it themselves then there

瑪莉：我只應該負一半責任。工程師叫我改製成參數，在過程中我弄錯了，如果工程師自己改的話就不會有事了。

would not be any problem.

Dean: And now you are trying to **pass the buck** to the engineers? I want to see the report by tomorrow.

狄恩：所以你現在要把責任推給工程師？我明天要看到那份報告。

影子跟讀：「短對話」

影子跟讀：「短段落」

影子跟讀：「實戰練習」

雅思聽力必考字彙

電視的發展❶

▶▶ 影子跟讀「短段落」練習　🎧 MP3 071

此篇為「**影子跟讀短段落練習**」，此章節規劃了由聽「**短段落**」的 shadowing 練習，從最基礎、最易上手的部分切入雅思聽力備考並提升考生的專注力，雅思聽力中尤其 section 3 跟 4 雖然話題不難，且很多時候不是考生程度沒到某個分數段，但確實很容易因為**定位錯誤**而錯失聽力訊息或誤判題本的上該題訊息已經唸過了，強化這部分能提升 section 3 和 4 的得分，整體分數要 7+或 7.5+其實這部分要很費心喔!，現在就一起動身，開始聽「**短段落**」!

From the number of TV audiences in each American household, televisions not only provide entertainments and all kinds of information, but also have become a daily necessity.

從每個美國家庭電視收看觀眾的數量來看，電視不只提供娛樂和各種訊息，而且成了每日必需品。

The word television comes from the Greek prefix "tele" and the Latin word "vision". It converts images into electrical impulses along cables, or by radio waves or satellite to a receiver, and then they are changed back into a picture.

電視這個字源自於希臘語字首的「遠程」和拉丁字「願景」的組合。它將圖像轉換成電脈衝沿著電纜，或通過無線電波或衛星到接收器，然後將它們再變回為圖像。

As most inventions, more than one individual contributed to the development of television. The earliest development was recorded in the late 1800s. A German student, Paul Gottlieb Nipkow, developed the first mechanical module for television.

如同大部分的發明，許多人都對電視的發展有所貢獻。最早的發展記錄是在 19 世紀末期。一位德國學生，保羅・戈特利布–尼普可夫研製了第一台電視的機械模塊。

影子跟讀：「短對話」

影子跟讀：「短段落」

影子跟讀：「實戰練習」

雅思聽力必考字彙

▶▶ 影子跟讀「短段落」練習　🎧 MP3 071

此部分為**「影子跟讀短段落練習❷」**，請重新播放音檔並完成試題，除了能提升並修正拼寫能力外，也可以藉由音檔注意自己專注力和定位聽力訊息部份，短段落聽力的提升能強化 section1 和 2 答題的正確性，現在就一起動身，開始完成**「短段落練習❷」**吧！

From the 1._____ of TV 2._____ in each American 3._____, televisions not only provide 4._____ and all kinds of 5._____, but also have become a daily 6._____.

The word television comes from the Greek 7._____ "tele" and the Latin word "vision". It converts 8._____ into 9._____ along cables, or by 10._____ or 11._____ to a 12._____, and then they are changed back into a picture.

As most 13._____, more than one 14._____ contributed to the development of television. The earliest development was recorded in the late 1800s. A 15._____ student, Paul Gottlieb Nipkow, developed the first 16._____ for television.

▶▶ 參考答案

1. number	2. audiences
3. household	4. entertainments
5. information	6. necessity
7. prefix	8. images
9. electrical impulses	10. radio waves
11. satellite	12. receiver
13. inventions	14. individual
15. German	16. mechanical module

影子跟讀：「短對話」

影子跟讀：「短段落」

影子跟讀：「實戰練習」

雅思聽力必考字彙

電視的發展❷

▶ 影子跟讀「短段落」練習 🎧 MP3 072

　　此篇為「**影子跟讀短段落練習**」，此章節規劃了由聽「**短段落**」的 shadowing 練習，從最基礎、最易上手的部分切入雅思聽力備考並提升考生的專注力，雅思聽力中尤其 section 3 跟 4 雖然話題不難，且很多時候不是考生程度沒到某個分數段，但確實很容易因為**定位錯誤**而錯失聽力訊息或誤判題本的上該題訊息已經唸過了，強化這部分能提升 section 3 和 4 的得分，整體分數要 7+或 7.5+其實這部分要很費心喔!，現在就一起動身，開始聽「**短段落**」!

　　He sent images through wires with the help of a rotating metal disk. It only had 18 lines of resolution. In 1926, a Scottish amateur scientist, John Logie Baird, transmitted the first moving pictures through the mechanical disk system. In 1934, all television systems had converted into the electronic system, which is what is being used today.

　　他透過電線與旋轉金屬盤發送圖像。它只有 18 線的分辨率。1926 年，蘇格蘭業餘科學家，約翰・勞基・貝瑞德透過機械磁盤系統發送出第一個動畫。1934 年，所有的電視系統已轉換成電子系統，這即是今天被使用的系統。

An American inventor, Philo Taylor Farnsworth first had the idea of electronic television at the age of 14. By the time he was 21, he created the first electronic television system which is the basis of all TV we have today. Until the 1990s , all TVs were monochrome. In 1925, color television was just conceptualized, but had never been built. It was not until 1953 that color television became available to the public.

　　美國發明家，菲洛−泰勒−法恩斯沃思在 14 歲時便有了電子電視的想法。在 21 歲時，他創造了第一個電子電視系統，這是所有我們今天所擁有的所有電視的基礎。直到 1900 年代，所有的電視都還是黑白的。1925 年時彩色電視都還只是概念，從來沒有被製造過。直到 1953 年，彩色電視才被提供給一般消費者。

▶▶ 影子跟讀「短段落」練習 🎧 MP3 072

此部分為「**影子跟讀短段落練習❷**」，請重新播放音檔並完成
試題，除了能提升並修正拼寫能力外，也可以藉由音檔注意自己專注
力和定位聽力訊息部份，短段落聽力的提升能強化 section1 和 2 答
題的正確性，現在就一起動身，開始完成「**短段落練習❷**」吧！

He sent 1.＿＿＿＿＿＿ through 2.＿＿＿＿＿＿ with the
help of a rotating 3.＿＿＿＿＿＿. It only had 18 lines of
4.＿＿＿＿＿＿. In 1926, a Scottish 5.＿＿＿＿＿＿, John
Logie Baird, transmitted the first moving 6.＿＿＿＿＿＿
through the 7.＿＿＿＿＿＿ disk system. In 1934, all television systems had converted into the 8.＿＿＿＿＿＿,
which is what is being used today.

An American 9.＿＿＿＿＿＿, Philo Taylor Farnsworth
first had the idea of 10.＿＿＿＿＿＿ television at the age
of 14. By the time he was 21, he created the first electronic
television system which is the basis of all TV we have today.
Until the 1990s , all TVs were 11.＿＿＿＿＿＿. In 1925,
12.＿＿＿＿＿ was just 12.＿＿＿＿＿＿, but had
never been built. It was not until 1953 that color television
became 14.＿＿＿＿＿ to the 15.＿＿＿＿.

▶▶ 參考答案

1. images	2. wires
3. metal disk	4. resolution
5. amateur scientist	6. pictures
7. mechanical	8. electronic system
9. inventor	10. electronic
11. monochrome	12. color television
13. conceptualized	14. available
15. public	

影子跟讀：「短對話」

影子跟讀：「短段落」

影子跟讀：「實戰練習」

雅思聽力必考字彙

印刷術 ❶

▶▶ 影子跟讀「短段落」練習 🎧 MP3 073

　　此篇為**「影子跟讀短段落練習」**，此章節規劃了由聽**「短段落」**的 shadowing 練習，從最基礎、最易上手的部分切入雅思聽力備考並提升考生的專注力，雅思聽力中尤其 section 3 跟 4 雖然話題不難，且很多時候不是考生程度沒到某個分數段，但確實很容易因為**定位錯誤**而錯失聽力訊息或誤判題本的上該題訊息已經唸過了，強化這部分能提升 section 3 和 4 的得分，整體分數要 7+或 7.5+其實這部分要很費心喔!，現在就一起動身，開始聽**「短段落」**!

The mechanization of bookmaking led to the first mass production of books in Europe. It could produce 3,600 pages per day which is much more productive than the typographic block type.

　　造書的機械化帶領了歐洲書籍的大規模生產。它可以每天生產 3,600 頁，它比印刷塊的類型有更高的生產力。

The demand for printing presses kept expanding throughout Europe. By 1500, more than twenty million volumes were produced. And the number kept doubling every year. The operation of a printing press became synonymo u s with the enterprise of printing and lent its name to a new branch of media, the press.

　　印刷機的需求在整個歐洲不斷增加。到 1500 年代，超過兩千萬本書被製作出來。而數字每年保持翻倍成長。印刷機更與印刷企業劃上等號，因此新媒體的分支新聞界也分用同一個名詞「The-Press」。

In the 19th century, steam-powered rotary presses re-placed the hand- operated presses. It allowed high volume industrial scale printing.

　　在 19 世紀時，蒸汽動力輪轉印刷機取代了手工操作的印刷機。它實現了大批量的工業規模印刷。

▶▶ 影子跟讀「短段落」練習 🎧 MP3 073

此部分為「**影子跟讀短段落練習❷**」，請重新播放音檔並完成試題，除了能提升並修正拼寫能力外，也可以藉由音檔注意自己專注力和定位聽力訊息部份，短段落聽力的提升能強化 section1 和 2 答題的正確性，現在就一起動身，開始完成「**短段落練習❷**」吧！

The 1.＿＿＿＿＿＿＿＿ of 2.＿＿＿＿＿＿＿＿ led to the first 3.＿＿＿＿＿＿＿＿ of books in 4.＿＿＿＿＿＿＿＿. It could produce 5.＿＿＿＿＿＿ per day which is much more 6.＿＿＿＿ than the 7.＿＿＿＿＿＿＿ block type.

The 8.＿＿＿＿＿＿＿＿ for printing presses kept 9.＿＿＿＿＿ throughout Europe. By1500, more than 10.＿＿＿＿＿＿ were produced. And the number kept doubling every year. The 11.＿＿＿＿＿ of a printing press became synonymous with the 12.＿＿＿＿＿＿ of printing and lent its name to a new branch of media, 13.＿＿＿＿＿.

In the 19th century, 14.＿＿＿＿＿＿＿＿ rotary presses replaced the 15.＿＿＿＿＿＿＿ presses. It allowed high volume 16.＿＿＿＿＿＿＿ scale printing.

▶▶ 參考答案

1. mechanization	2. bookmaking
3. mass production	4. Europe
5. 3,600 pages	6. productive
7. typographic	8. demand
9. expanding	10. twenty million volumes
11. operation	12. enterprise
13. the press	14. steam-powered
15. hand-operated	16. industrial

影子跟讀：「短對話」

影子跟讀：「短段落」

影子跟讀：「實戰練習」

雅思聽力必考字彙

印刷術❷

▶ 影子跟讀「短段落」練習　🎧 MP3 074

　　此篇為「**影子跟讀短段落練習**」，此章節規劃了由聽「**短段落**」的 shadowing 練習，從最基礎、最易上手的部分切入雅思聽力備考並提升考生的專注力，雅思聽力中尤其 section 3 跟 4 雖然話題不難，且很多時候不是考生程度沒到某個分數段，但確實很容易因為**定位錯誤**而錯失聽力訊息或誤判題本的上該題訊息已經唸過了，強化這部分能提升 section 3 和 4 的得分，整體分數要 7+或 7.5+其實這部分要很費心喔!，現在就一起動身，開始聽「**短段落**」!

Because of the invention of the printing press, the entire classical canon was reprinted and promulgated throughout Europe.

由於印刷術的發明，整個古典經文已被重印並廣傳整個歐洲。

It was a very important step towards the democratization of knowledge. Also because of the invention of printing press, it helped unify and standardize the spelling and syntax of vernaculars. Johannes Gutenberg was born in an upper-class family in Mainz Germany, most likely in 1398.

這也是對知識民主化來説非常重要的一步。印刷術發明的同時，它也幫助統一和規範俗語的拼寫和語法。約翰‧古騰堡出生於德國美因茨的一個上流家庭。

He had been a blacksmith, a goldsmith, and printer, and even a publisher. Gutenberg's understanding of the trade of goldsmithing and possessing of the knowledge and technical skills in metal working originated from his father's working at ecclesiastic mint.

他當過鐵匠、金匠和印刷商，甚至出版商。因為他的父親在傳教士的造幣廠工作過，因此古騰堡在長大過程中就了解金匠的行業，並擁有金屬加工的知識和技術技能。

影子跟讀：「短對話」

影子跟讀：「短段落」

影子跟讀：「實戰練習」

雅思聽力必考字彙

此部分為「**影子跟讀短段落練習❷**」，請重新播放音檔並完成試題，除了能提升並修正拼寫能力外，也可以藉由音檔注意自己專注力和定位聽力訊息部份，短段落聽力的提升能強化 section1 和 2 答題的正確性，現在就一起動身，開始完成「**短段落練習❷**」吧！

Because of the 1.＿＿＿＿＿＿ of the printing press, the entire 2.＿＿＿＿＿＿ was reprinted and 3.＿＿＿＿＿ throughout Europe.

It was a very 4.＿＿＿＿ towards the 5.＿＿＿＿＿ of 6.＿＿＿＿＿＿. Also because of the invention of printing press, it helped 7.＿＿＿＿＿＿ and 8.＿＿＿＿＿＿ the spelling and 9.＿＿＿＿＿＿ of 10.＿＿＿＿＿＿. Johannes Gutenberg was born in an 11.＿＿＿＿＿＿ family in Mainz 12.＿＿＿＿＿, most likely in 1398.

He had been a 13.＿＿＿＿＿＿, a goldsmith, and printer, and even a 14.＿＿＿＿＿. Gutenberg's understanding of the 15.＿＿＿＿ of goldsmithing and possessing of the knowledge and 16.＿＿＿＿＿ in metal working 17.＿＿＿＿ from his father's working at 18.＿＿＿＿.

▶▶ 參考答案

1. invention	2. classical canon
3. promulgated	4. important step
5. democratization	6. knowledge
7. unify	8. standardize
9. syntax	10. vernaculars
11. upper-class	12. Germany
13. blacksmith	14. publisher
15. trade	16. technical skills
17. originated	18. ecclesiastic mint

銀行的演變

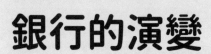

此篇為**「影子跟讀短段落練習」**，此章節規劃了由聽**「短段落」**的 shadowing 練習，從最基礎、最易上手的部分切入雅思聽力備考並提升考生的專注力，雅思聽力中尤其 section 3 跟 4 雖然話題不難，且很多時候不是考生程度沒到某個分數段，但確實很容易因為**定位錯誤**而錯失聽力訊息或誤判題本的上該題訊息已經唸過了，強化這部分能提升 section 3 和 4 的得分，整體分數要 7+或 7.5+其實這部分要很費心喔!，現在就一起動身，開始聽**「短段落」**！

In today's highly technical world, banks are no longer a brick-and-mortar financial institution. From remittance to investment, people nowadays only need to go thru online banking to finish all their work. The concept of online banking has been simultaneously evolving with the development of the World Wide Web, and has actually been accessible around since the early 1980s.

在當今高科技的世界裡，銀行不再是實體的金融機構。從匯款到投資，人們現在只需要上網路銀行就可以完成所有的工作。網路銀行這一概念與全球資訊網一同發展演變，而且自 **1980** 年代初期就

已經出現。

In 1981, the four biggest banks in New York City Citibank, Chase Manhattan, Chemical and Manufacturers Hanover, made the home banking access available to their customers. However, customers didn't really take to the initiative. This innovative way of doing business was too advanced and failed to gain momentum until the mid 1990s.

在 1981 年，紐約的四大銀行，花旗銀行、大通曼哈頓銀行、化工銀行和製造漢諾威銀行提供了家庭銀行給他們的客戶。但客戶並沒有真正採取行動。這個生意方式的創新太過先進，直到 1990 年代中期都沒能獲得新的動力。

In October, 1994, Stanford Federal Credit Union offered online banking to all its customers, and about a year later, Presidential Bank offered its customers online account accesses. These were the start of online banking, and soon other banks followed.

1994 年 10 月，史丹佛的聯邦信貸聯盟提供了所有的客戶網上銀行，大約一年後，總統銀行提供客戶網銀的服務。這就是網路銀行的開始。不久後其他銀行隨即跟進。

影子跟讀：「短對話」

影子跟讀：「短段落」

影子跟讀：「實戰練習」

雅思聽力必考字彙

▶▶ 影子跟讀「短段落」練習 🎧 MP3 075

　　此部分為「**影子跟讀短段落練習❷**」，請重新播放音檔並完成試題，除了能提升並修正拼寫能力外，也可以藉由音檔注意自己專注力和定位聽力訊息部份，短段落聽力的提升能強化 section1 和 2 答題的正確性，現在就一起動身，開始完成「**短段落練習❷**」吧！

　　In today's highly 1.＿＿＿＿＿＿ world, 2.＿＿＿＿＿＿ are no longer a brick-and-mortar 3.＿＿＿＿＿＿. From 4.＿＿＿＿＿＿ to 5.＿＿＿＿＿＿, people nowadays only need to go thru 6.＿＿＿＿＿＿ banking to finish all their work. The 7.＿＿＿＿＿＿ of online banking has been simultaneously evolving with the 8.＿＿＿＿＿＿ of the World Wide Web, and has actually been 9.＿＿＿＿＿＿ around since the early 1980s.

　　In 1981, the four biggest banks in New York City Citibank, Chase 10.＿＿＿＿＿＿, Chemical and Manufacturers Hanover, made the home banking access available to their 11.＿＿＿＿＿＿. However, they didn't really take to the initiative. This 12.＿＿＿＿＿＿ way of doing business was too 13.＿＿＿＿ and failed to gain 14.＿＿＿＿＿＿ until the mid 1990s.

　　In October, 1994, 15.＿＿＿＿＿＿ Federal Credit Union offered online banking to all its customers, and about

a year later, Presidential Bank offered its customers online
16.＿＿＿＿＿＿＿. These were the start of online banking, and
soon other banks followed.

▶▶ 參考答案

1. technical	2. banks
3. financial institution	4. remittance
5. investment	6. online
7. concept	8. development
9. accessible	10. Manhattan
11. customers	12. innovative
13. advanced	14. momentum
15. Stanford	16. account accesses

電話的發展

此篇為**「影子跟讀短段落練習」**，此章節規劃了由聽**「短段落」**的 shadowing 練習，從最基礎、最易上手的部分切入雅思聽力備考並提升考生的專注力，雅思聽力中尤其 section 3 跟 4 雖然話題不難，且很多時候不是考生程度沒到某個分數段，但確實很容易因為**定位錯誤**而錯失聽力訊息或誤判題本的上該題訊息已經唸過了，強化這部分能提升 section 3 和 4 的得分，整體分數要 7+或 7.5+其實這部分要很費心喔!，現在就一起動身，開始聽**「短段落」**！

The paper cup telephone is a great childhood memory for most of us. Centuries ago, acoustic telephone, the first mechanical telephone was based on the same theory which utilized sound transmission through pipes. It connects two diaphragms with a string or wire and transmits sound by mechanical vibrations from one side to another. Two hundred years later in 1876, Alexander Graham Bell was granted the first U.S. patent for the invention of the electrical telephone.

紙杯電話對我們大多數人來說是一個偉大的童年記憶。基於同

樣的理論，聲覺電話幾百年前利用管線傳送聲音，是最早的機械電話。它是英國物理學家羅伯特・胡克於 1667 年利用細繩或金屬絲連接兩個隔膜，由機械振動的原理從一側傳送聲音到另一端。200 年後的 1876 年，亞歷山大・格雷厄姆・貝爾獲得他第一個發明電話的專利。

Although the credit for the invention of the electric telephone is frequently disputed. Many other inventors, such as Charles Bourseul, Antonio Meucci, and others have all been credited with the telephone invention. By 1904 over three million phones were reconnected by manual switchboard in the United States. The US became the world leader in telephone density. The telephone with bell and induction coil which we are familiar with was introduced in the 1930s. Another 30 years later, the touch-tone signaling replaced the rotary dial.

雖然這個電話發明的榮譽經常有爭議。許多其他的發明家，如查爾斯・布爾瑟，安東尼奧・穆齊，和其他人都被認為發明了電話。到 1904 年，美國人工總機總共有超過三百萬個連結。美國的電話密度領先全球。我們所熟悉，有鈴聲和感應線圈的電話在 1930 年代引入。30 年後，按鍵信號取代旋轉撥號。

此部分為「**影子跟讀短段落練習❷**」，請重新播放音檔並完成試題，除了能提升並修正拼寫能力外，也可以藉由音檔注意自己專注力和定位聽力訊息部份，短段落聽力的提升能強化 section1 和 2 答題的正確性，現在就一起動身，開始完成「**短段落練習❷**」吧！

The paper cup 1._____ is a great childhood 2._____ for most of us. 3._____ ago, acoustic telephone, the first 4._____ telephone was based on the same 5._____ which utilized 6._____ through 7._____. It connects two 8._____ with a string or wire and transmits sound by mechanical 9._____ from one side to another. Two hundred years later in 1876, Alexander Graham Bell was 10._____ the first U.S. 11._____ for the invention of the electrical telephone.

Although the credit for the invention of the electric telephone is frequently disputed. Many other inventors, such as Charles Bourseul, Antonio Meucci, and others have all been 12._____ with the telephone invention. By 1904 over three million phones were reconnected by manual 13._____ in the United States. The US became the world leader in telephone 14._____. The telephone with bell and induction 15._____ which we are familiar with was introduced in the 1930s. Another 30 years later, the touch-tone signaling replaced the 16.＿＿＿＿＿＿＿.

▶▶ 參考答案

1. telephone	2. memory
3. Centuries	4. mechanical
5. theory	6. sound transmission
7. pipes	8. diaphragms
9. vibrations	10. granted
11. patent	12. credited
13. switchboard exchanges	14. density
15. coil	16. rotary dial

臉書的普及和沿革

▶ 影子跟讀「短段落」練習 🎧 MP3 077

　　此篇為**「影子跟讀短段落練習」**，此章節規劃了由聽**「短段落」**的 shadowing 練習，從最基礎、最易上手的部分切入雅思聽力備考並提升考生的專注力，雅思聽力中尤其 section 3 跟 4 雖然話題不難，且很多時候不是考生程度沒到某個分數段，但確實很容易因為**定位錯誤**而錯失聽力訊息或誤判題本的上該題訊息已經唸過了，強化這部分能提升 section 3 和 4 的得分，整體分數要 7+或 7.5+其實這部分要很費心喔!，現在就一起動身，開始聽**「短段落」**!

　　The popularity of Facebook started to grow in 2007. Most of the youngsters back then joined Facebook in 2007. Late in 2007, Facebook had 100,000 business pages which allowed companies to attract potential customers and introduce themselves.

　　臉書於 2007 年開始普及。當時大部分的年輕人都是在 2007 年加入臉書。2007 年的下半年，臉書開始有企業專頁，使得企業可以介紹自己的企業並吸引潛在客戶。

　　The business potential of this social network just kept

blooming, and on October 2008, Facebook set up its international headquarters in Dublin, Ireland. Statistics from October 2011 showed that over 100 billion photos are shared on Facebook, and over 350 million users accessed Facebook through their mobile phones which is only about 33% of all Facebook traffic.

社會網絡的商業潛力不停地綻放。2008 年 10 月，臉書在愛爾蘭的都柏林設立了國際總部。從 2011 年 10 月的統計顯示，超過一兆的照片在臉書上共享，而超過 350 萬的用戶利用手機查閱臉書，這大概只是 33%的臉書的總流量。

Born in 1984, Mark Zuckerberg was born in White Plains, New York. Zuckerberg began using computers and writing software in middle school. His father taught him Atari BASIC Programming in the 1990s, and later hired software developer David Newman to tutor him privately. Zuckerberg took a graduate course in the subject at Mercy College near his home while still in high school. He enjoyed developing computer programs, especially communication tools and games.

1984 年，馬克‧扎克伯格出生於紐約的懷特普萊恩斯。扎克伯格在中學時期就開始使用電腦和編寫的軟體。他的父親教他寫 90 年代的 AtariBASIC 編程，後來又聘請了軟體開發者大衛‧ 紐曼私下指導他。扎克伯格在高中時便在他家附近的慈悲學院選修研究生的課程。他喜歡開發電腦軟體，特別是通訊工具和遊戲。

影子跟讀：「短對話」

影子跟讀：「短段落」

影子跟讀：「實戰練習」

雅思聽力必考字彙

▶▶ 影子跟讀「短段落」練習 🎧 MP3 077

此部分為「**影子跟讀短段落練習❷**」，請重新播放音檔並完成試題，除了能提升並修正拼寫能力外，也可以藉由音檔注意自己專注力和定位聽力訊息部份，短段落聽力的提升能強化 section1 和 2 答題的正確性，現在就一起動身，開始完成「**短段落練習❷**」吧！

The 1._____ of Facebook started to grow in 2007. Most of the 2._____ back then joined Facebook in 2007. Late in 2007, Facebook had 3._____ which allowed 4._____ to attract 5._____ and introduce themselves. The 6._____ of this 7._____ just kept blooming, and on 8._____, Facebook set up its international 9._____ in Dublin, 10._____. Statistics from 11._____ showed that over 12._____ are shared on Facebook, and over 13._____ accessed Facebook through their 14._____ which is only about 33% of all 15._____.

Born in 1984, Mark Zuckerberg was born in White Plains, 16._____. Zuckerberg began using computers and writing software in middle school. His father taught him Atari BASIC Programming in the 1990s, and later hired 17._____ David Newman to tutor him privately. Zuckerberg took a 18._____ in the subject at

Mercy College near his home while still in high school. He enjoyed developing 19._____, especially 20._____ tools and games.

▶▶ 參考答案

1. popularity	2. youngsters
3. 100,000 business pages	4. companies
5. potential customers	6. business potential
7. social network	8. October 2008
9. headquarters	10. Ireland
11. October 2011	12. 100 billion photos
13. 350 million users	14. mobile phones
15. Facebook traffic	16. New York
17. software developer	18. graduate course
19. computer programs	20. communication

Google 的成立

▶▶ 影子跟讀「短段落」練習 🎧 MP3 078

　　此篇為「**影子跟讀短段落練習**」，此章節規劃了由聽「**短段落**」的 shadowing 練習，從最基礎、最易上手的部分切入雅思聽力備考並提升考生的專注力，雅思聽力中尤其 section 3 跟 4 雖然話題不難，且很多時候不是考生程度沒到某個分數段，但確實很容易因為**定位錯誤**而錯失聽力訊息或誤判題本的上該題訊息已經唸過了，強化這部分能提升 section 3 和 4 的得分，整體分數要 7+或 7.5+其實這部分要很費心喔!，現在就一起動身，開始聽「**短段落**」！

　　The headquarters of Google is located in Mountain Valley, California. They named it Googleplex. They moved into the facility the same year when the company went IPO in 2004. The company offered 19,605,052 shares at a price of $85 per share. By January 2014, its market capitalization had grown to $397 billion dollars. Larry Page: Being a child of two computer experts, Larry Page was born in an environment that led him to who he is today. Born in 1973, Page grew up in a standard home that was filled with computers and technical and science magazines in Michigan. He first played with a computer at the age of six and immediately got attracted to it. He was the first kid who utilized a word processor to do his homework.

　　谷歌的總部設在加州山景城。他們把它命名為 Googleplex。他們在 2004 年搬進了這棟建築，同時並首次公開發行。該公司以 85 美元美股的金額提供了 19605052 股。到 2014 年 1 月，其市值已增長到 3970 億美元。拉里・佩奇：父母皆為電腦專家，拉里・佩奇出生的環境造就了他。出生於 1973 年，佩琪在密西根一個充滿電腦和技術及科學雜誌的標準家庭中長大。

He was also encouraged by his family to take things apart to see how they work. Maybe that's why he got interested in inventing things. Page earned his Bachelor degree in engineering from the University of Michigan and concent rated on computer engineering at Stanford University where he met his partner Sergey Brin.

　　在他六歲的時候，他開始玩他的第一台電腦，並立即被吸引。他是在他上的小學裡第一個利用文字處理器做功課的小孩。他的家人也鼓勵他拆解東西來看看是如何運作的。也許這就是為什麼他對發明創造有興趣。佩琪從密歇根大學得到了他的工程學位。之後，他便在史丹佛大學專心於他的資訊工程學位。在那裡他遇到了他的搭檔謝爾蓋・布林。

▶▶ 影子跟讀「短段落」練習 🎧 MP3 078

　　此部分為「**影子跟讀短段落練習❷**」，請重新播放音檔並完成試題，除了能提升並修正拼寫能力外，也可以藉由音檔注意自己專注力和定位聽力訊息部份，短段落聽力的提升能強化 section1 和 2 答題的正確性，現在就一起動身，開始完成「**短段落練習❷**」吧！

　　The 1._____ of Google is located in Mountain Valley, 2._____. They named it 3._____. They moved into the 4._____ the same year when the company went IPO in 2004. The company offered 5._____ shares at a price of $85 per share. By 6._____, its market 7._____ had grown to $397 billion dollars. Larry Page: Being a child of two 8._____, Larry Page was born in an 9._____ that led him to who he is today. Born in 1973, Page grew up in a 10._____ home that was filled with computers and technical and 11._____ in Michigan. He first played with a computer at the age of 12._____ and immediately got attracted to it. He was the 13._____ who utilized a 14._____ to do his homework.

　　He was also 15._____ by his family to take things apart to see how they work. Maybe that's why he got interested in inventing things. Page earned his Bachelor degree in 16._____ from the University of Michigan and concent rated on computer engineering at 17._____ where he met his 18._____ Sergey Brin.

▶▶ 參考答案

1. headquarters	2. California
3. Googleplex	4. facility
5. 19,605,052	6. January 2014
7. capitalization	8. computer experts
9. environment	10. standard
11. science magazines	12. six
13. first kid	14. word processor
15. encouraged	16. engineering
17. Stanford University	18. partner

影子跟讀：「短對話」

影子跟讀：「短段落」

影子跟讀：「實戰練習」

雅思聽力必考字彙

條碼的沿革

▶ 影子跟讀「短段落」練習 🎧 MP3 079

　　此篇為「影子跟讀短段落練習」，此章節規劃了由聽「短段落」的 shadowing 練習，從最基礎、最易上手的部分切入雅思聽力備考並提升考生的專注力，雅思聽力中尤其 section 3 跟 4 雖然話題不難，且很多時候不是考生程度沒到某個分數段，但確實很容易因為**定位錯誤**而錯失聽力訊息或誤判題本的上該題訊息已經唸過了，強化這部分能提升 section 3 和 4 的得分，整體分數要 7+或 7.5+其實這部分要很費心喔!，現在就一起動身，開始聽「**短段落**」!

　　An infinite amount of information is being stored by these lines or dots. They limited human errors and sped the transition of information. But when we are doing the easy scanning, have we even considered this-What exactly is a barcode? How does it work? A barcode is an optical machine readable representation of data relating to the object to which it is attached. We see it on almost all products. Ori g i n a l l y, barcodes systematically represented data by varying the widths and spacing of parallel lines.

　　無限量的信息被存儲在這些線或點裡。他們將人為錯誤減到最

低並加快了訊息的傳訊。但是，當我們在做這簡單的掃描時，我們是否有想過 - 到底什麼是條碼？它是如何作業的？條碼是一個光學儀器可讀取有關連結對象的數據。我們幾乎可以在所有產品上看到它。最初是通過改變寬度和平行線間距的條碼系統來表示數據。

Now we even have the two dimensional barcodes that evolved into rectangles, dots, hexagons and other patterns. Also nowadays, we no longer require special optical scanners to read the barcodes. They can be read by smartphones as well.

現在，我們甚至有利用矩形、點、六邊形等所演變出的二維條碼。而且現在，我們不再需要特殊的光學掃描儀讀取條碼。它們可以通過智能電話被讀取。

影子跟讀：「短對話」

影子跟讀：「短段落」

影子跟讀：「實戰練習」

雅思聽力必考字彙

此部分為「**影子跟讀短段落練習❷**」，請重新播放音檔並完成試題，除了能提升並修正拼寫能力外，也可以藉由音檔注意自己專注力和定位聽力訊息部份，短段落聽力的提升能強化 section1 和 2 答題的正確性，現在就一起動身，開始完成「**短段落練習❷**」吧！

An infinite amount of 1.＿＿＿＿＿＿＿ is being stored by these 2.＿＿＿＿＿＿＿. They limited 3.＿＿＿＿＿＿＿ and sped the transition of information. But when we are doing the 4.＿＿＿＿＿＿, have we even considered this-What exactly is 5.＿＿＿＿＿＿？ How does it work? A barcode is an 6.＿＿＿＿＿＿ machine readable representation of 7.＿＿＿＿＿＿ relating to the object to which it is attached. We see it on almost 8.＿＿＿＿＿＿＿. Originally, barcodes systematically represented data by varying the 9.＿＿＿＿ and spacing of 10.＿＿＿＿＿＿＿.

Now we even have the two 11.＿＿＿＿＿ barcodes that evolved into 12.＿＿＿＿＿＿, dots, 13.＿＿＿＿＿＿ and other patterns. Also nowadays, we no longer require 14.＿＿＿＿＿＿ to read the barcodes. They can be read by 15.＿＿＿＿＿＿ as well.

▶▶ **參考答案**

1. information	2. lines or dots
3. human errors	4. easy scanning
5. a barcode	6. optical
7. data	8. all products
9. widths	10. parallel lines
11. dimensional	12. rectangles
13. hexagons	14. special optical scanners
15. smartphones	

塑膠工業之父

▶ 影子跟讀「短段落」練習 🎧 MP3 080

此篇為**「影子跟讀短段落練習」**，此章節規劃了由聽**「短段落」**的 shadowing 練習，從最基礎、最易上手的部分切入雅思聽力備考並提升考生的專注力，雅思聽力中尤其 section 3 跟 4 雖然話題不難，且很多時候不是考生程度沒到某個分數段，但確實很容易因為**定位錯誤**而錯失聽力訊息或誤判題本的上該題訊息已經唸過了，強化這部分能提升 section 3 和 4 的得分，整體分數要 7+或 7.5+其實這部分要很費心喔!，現在就一起動身，開始聽**「短段落」**！

What are plastics exactly? The majority of the polymers are based on chains of carbon atoms along with oxygen, sulfur, or nitrogen. Most plastics contain other organic or inorganic compounds blended in.

塑膠到底是什麼？大多數聚合物都基於碳原子和氧、硫、或氮的鏈。大多數塑膠混有其他有機或無機化合物。

The amount of additives ranges from zero percentage to more than 50% for certain electronic applications. The invention of plastic was a great success but also brought us a serious environmental concerns regarding its slow decom-position rate after being discarded. One way to help with the environment is to practice recycling or use other envi-ronmental friendly materials instead. Another approach is to speed up the development of biodegradable plastic.

在一些電子應用上，添加劑的量從零至 50%以上。塑膠的發明獲得了巨大的成功，但也給我們帶來了關於其被丟棄後緩慢分解所造成嚴重的環境問題。練習回收或改用其他對環境友好的材料是幫助環境的一種方法。另一種方法是，加快生物分解性塑料的開發。

The father of the Plastics Industry, Leo Baekeland, was born in Belgium on November 14th, 1863. He was best known for his invention of Bakelite which is an inexpensive, nonflammable and versatile plastic. Because of his inven-tion, the plastic industry started to bloom and became a popular material in many different industries.

塑膠工業之父，利奧‧ 貝克蘭，於 1863 年 11 月 14 日出生於比利時。他最為人知的是酚醛塑的發明，這是一種廉價，不可燃和通用的塑膠。由於他的發明，塑料行業開始盛行，在許多不同的行業成為一個受歡迎的材料。

影子跟讀：「短對話」

影子跟讀：「短段落」

影子跟讀：「實戰練習」

雅思聽力必考字彙

此部分為「影子跟讀短段落練習❷」，請重新播放音檔並完成試題，除了能提升並修正拼寫能力外，也可以藉由音檔注意自己專注力和定位聽力訊息部份，短段落聽力的提升能強化 section1 和 2 答題的正確性，現在就一起動身，開始完成「**短段落練習❷**」吧！

What are plastics exactly? The majority of the 1.＿＿＿＿＿ are based on chains of 2.＿＿＿＿＿ along with 3.＿＿＿＿＿, sulfur, or 4.＿＿＿＿＿. Most plastics contain other organic or 5.＿＿＿＿＿ blended in.

The amount of 6.＿＿＿＿＿ ranges from 7.＿＿＿＿＿ percentage to more than 50% for certain 8.＿＿＿＿＿. The 9.＿＿＿＿＿ of plastic was a great 10.＿＿＿＿＿ but also brought us a serious 11.＿＿＿＿＿ concerns regarding its 12.＿＿＿＿＿ rate after being discarded.

One way to help with the environment is to practice 13.＿＿＿＿＿ or use other 14.＿＿＿＿＿ materials instead. Another approach is to speed up the development of 15.＿＿＿＿＿.

The father of the Plastics Industry, Leo Baekeland, was

born in 16._____ on November 14th, 1863. He was best known for his invention of 17._____ which is an inexpensive, 18._____ and versatile plastic. Because of his invention, the plastic industry started to 19._____ and became a popular material in many different 20._____.

▶▶ 參考答案

1. polymers
2. carbon atoms
3. oxygen
4. nitrogen
5. inorganic compounds
6. additives
7. zero
8. electronic applications
9. invention
10. success
11. environmental
12. slow decomposition
13. recycling
14. environmental friendly
15. biodegradable plastic
16. Belgium
17. Bakelite
18. nonflammable
19. bloom
20. industries

影子跟讀：「短對話」

影子跟讀：「短段落」

影子跟讀：「實戰練習」

雅思聽力必考字彙

諾貝爾的生平

▶▶ 影子跟讀「短段落」練習 🎧 MP3 081

　　此篇為**「影子跟讀短段落練習」**，此章節規劃了由聽**「短段落」**的 shadowing 練習，從最基礎、最易上手的部分切入雅思聽力備考並提升考生的專注力，雅思聽力中尤其 section 3 跟 4 雖然話題不難，且很多時候不是考生程度沒到某個分數段，但確實很容易因為**定位錯誤**而錯失聽力訊息或誤判題本的上該題訊息已經唸過了，強化這部分能提升 section 3 和 4 的得分，整體分數要 7+或 7.5+其實這部分要很費心喔!，現在就一起動身，開始聽**「短段落」**!

　　Nobel was born in Stockholm, Sweden on October 21st, 1833. His family moved to St. Petersburg in Russia in 1842. Nobel was sent to private tutoring, and he excelled in his studies, particularly in chemistry and languages. He achieved fluency in English, French, German and Russian. Throughout his life, Nobel only went to school for 18 months. In 1860, Nobel started his invention of dynamite, and it was 1866 when he first invented the dynamite successfully. Nobel never let himself take any rest. He founded Nitroglycerin AB in Stockholm, Sweden in 1864.

　　諾貝爾於 1833 年 10 月 21 日出生在瑞典斯德哥爾摩。在

1842 年時，他舉家遷往俄羅斯聖彼得堡。諾貝爾被送往私塾，他擅長於學習，特別是在化學和語言。他能精通英語，法語，德語和俄語。終其一生，諾貝爾只去了學校 18 個月。1860 年，諾貝爾開始了炸藥的發明。1866 年，他第一次成功地發明了炸藥。諾貝爾從來沒有讓自己休息。他於 1864 年在瑞典斯德哥爾摩創立硝酸甘油 AB 公司。

A year later, he built the Alfred Nobel Co. Factory in Hamburg, Germany. In 1866, he established the United States Blasting Oil Company in the U.S. And 4 years later, he established the Société général pour la fabrication de la dynamite in Paris, France. Nobel was proud to say he is a world citizen. He passed away in 1896. A year before that, he started the Nobel prize which is awarded yearly to people whose work helps humanity. When he died, Alfred Nobel left behind a nine million- dollar endowment fund.

一年後，他在德國漢堡建立了阿爾弗雷德·諾貝爾公司的工廠。1866 年，他在美國成立了美國爆破石油公司。4 年後，他又在法國巴黎成立了炸藥實驗室。諾貝爾自豪地說，他是一個世界公民。他在 1896 年過世。在他過世前，他成立諾貝爾獎以鼓勵對人類有幫助的人們。當他過世時，諾貝爾留下了九百萬美元的捐贈基金。

影子跟讀：「短對話」

影子跟讀：「短段落」

影子跟讀：「實戰練習」

雅思聽力必考字彙

　　此部分為「**影子跟讀短段落練習❷**」，請重新播放音檔並完成試題，除了能提升並修正拼寫能力外，也可以藉由音檔注意自己專注力和定位聽力訊息部份，短段落聽力的提升能強化 section1 和 2 答題的正確性，現在就一起動身，開始完成「**短段落練習❷**」吧！

　　Nobel was born in Stockholm, 1.＿＿＿＿＿＿＿ on 2.＿＿＿＿＿＿＿, 1833. His family moved to St. Petersburg in 3.＿＿＿＿＿＿＿＿ in 1842. Nobel was sent to 4.＿＿＿＿＿＿＿, and he excelled in his studies, particularly in 5.＿＿＿＿＿ and languages. He achieved fluency in English, French, 6.＿＿＿＿＿＿＿＿.

　　Throughout his life, Nobel only went to school for 7.＿＿＿＿＿. In 1860, Nobel started his invention of 8.＿＿＿＿＿＿, and it was 1866 when he first invented the 9.＿＿＿＿＿＿＿. Nobel never let himself take any rest. He founded Nitroglycerin AB in Stockholm, Sweden in 1864.

　　A year later, he built the Alfred Nobel Co. Factory in Hamburg, Germany. In 1866, he established the United States Blasting 10.＿＿＿＿＿＿＿＿ in the U.S. And 4 years later, he established the Société général pour la fabrication de la dynamite in Paris, France. Nobel was proud to say he is a world citizen. He passed away in 1896. A year before that, he started the 11._____ which is awarded yearly to people whose 12._____ helps 13._____. When he died, Alfred Nobel left behind a nine million- dollar 14._____.

▶▶ 參考答案

1. Sweden	2. October 21st
3. Russia	4. private tutoring
5. chemistry	6. German and Russian
7. 18 months	8. dynamite
9. dynamite successfully	10. Oil Company
11. Nobel prize	12. work
13. humanity	14. endowment fund

直升機的發展和貢獻

▶ **影子跟讀「短段落」練習** 🎧 MP3 082

　　此篇為**「影子跟讀短段落練習」**，此章節規劃了由聽**「短段落」**的 shadowing 練習，從最基礎、最易上手的部分切入雅思聽力備考並提升考生的專注力，雅思聽力中尤其 section 3 跟 4 雖然話題不難，且很多時候不是考生程度沒到某個分數段，但確實很容易因為**定位錯誤**而錯失聽力訊息或誤判題本的上該題訊息已經唸過了，強化這部分能提升 section 3 和 4 的得分，整體分數要 7+或 7.5+其實這部分要很費心喔!，現在就一起動身，開始聽**「短段落」**!

　　Since then, the helicopter development was going on all over the world, from the United States, to England, France, Denmark and even Russia. But it was not until 1942 that a helicopter designed by Igor Sikorsky reached a full-scale production. The most common helicopter configuration had a single main rotor with antitorque tail rotor, unlike the earlier designs that had multiple rotors. Centuries of development later, the invention of the helicopter improves the transportation of people and cargo, uses for military, construction, firefighting, research, rescue, medical transport, and many others. The contributions of the helicopter are uncountable.

　　此後，直升機在世界各地不停的發展，有來自美國、英國、法國、丹麥，甚至俄羅斯。直到 1942 年由伊戈爾·西科斯基設計的直升機才達到全面性的生產。最常見的直升機配置有具有抗扭矩尾槳和單一主螺旋槳。不同於早期的設計，有多個螺旋槳。幾個世紀的發展之後，直升機的發明提高了人員和貨物的運輸，使用於軍事、建築、消防、科研、救護，醫療轉運，和許多其他地方。直升機的貢獻是不可數計的。

Some people might recognize the name of Igor Ivanovich Sikorsky from the public airport in Fairfield County, Connecticut. No doubt that due to the great contributions from Sikorsky to the aviation industry, the airport of his hometown decided to be named after him.

　　有些人可能會從康乃狄克州費爾菲爾德縣的大眾機場那裡認出「伊戈爾·伊万諾維奇·西科斯基」這個名字。毫無疑問的，由於西科斯基對航空業的巨大貢獻，家鄉的機場決定以他的名字來命名。

影子跟讀：「短對話」

影子跟讀：「短段落」

影子跟讀：「實戰練習」

雅思聽力必考字彙

▶▶ 影子跟讀「短段落」練習 🎧 MP3 082

　　此部分為「**影子跟讀短段落練習❷**」，請重新播放音檔並完成試題，除了能提升並修正拼寫能力外，也可以藉由音檔注意自己專注力和定位聽力訊息部份，短段落聽力的提升能強化 section1 和 2 答題的正確性，現在就一起動身，開始完成「**短段落練習❷**」吧！

　　Since then, the 1._____ development was going on all over the world, from the 2._____, to England, France, 3._____ and even Russia. But it was not until 1942 that a helicopter designed by Igor Sikorsky reached a 4._____. The most common helicopter 5._____ had a single main rotor with anti-torque tail rotor, unlike the 6._____ that had multiple rotors. Centuries of development later, the invention of the helicopter improves the 7._____ of people and 8._____, uses for 9._____, construction, 10._____, research, rescue, 11._____, and many others. The 12._____ of the helicopter are uncountable.

　　Some people might recognize the name of Igor Ivanovich Sikorsky from the public airport in Fairfield County, 13._____. No doubt that due to the great contributions from Sikorsky to the 14._____, the 15._____ of his 16._____ decided to be named after him.

▶▶ 參考答案

1. helicopter	2. United States
3. Denmark	4. full-scale production
5. configuration	6. earlier designs
7. transportation	8. cargo
9. military	10. firefighting
11. medical transport	12. contributions
13. Connecticut	14. aviation industry
15. airport	16. hometown

影子跟讀：「短對話」

影子跟讀：「短段落」

影子跟讀：「實戰練習」

雅思聽力必考字彙

聽診器帶來的便利性

▶▶ 影子跟讀「短段落」練習 🎧 MP3 083

　　此篇為「**影子跟讀短段落練習**」，此章節規劃了由聽「**短段落**」的 shadowing 練習，從最基礎、最易上手的部分切入雅思聽力備考並提升考生的專注力，雅思聽力中尤其 section 3 跟 4 雖然話題不難，且很多時候不是考生程度沒到某個分數段，但確實很容易因為**定位錯誤**而錯失聽力訊息或誤判題本的上該題訊息已經唸過了，強化這部分能提升 section 3 和 4 的得分，整體分數要 7+或 7.5+其實這部分要很費心喔!，現在就一起動身，開始聽「**短段落**」!

　　Graduating in medicine in 1804, Laennec became an associate at the Societe de IEcole de Medicine. He then found that tubercle lesions could be present in all organs of the body and not just the lungs. By 1816, at the age of 35, he was offered the position of a physician at the Necker Hospital in Paris. Laennec is considered to be one of the greatest doctors of all time. It was him that introduced auscultation. This method involves listening and identifying various sounds made by different body organs.

　　１８０４年畢業於醫藥，拉埃內克成為 Societe de IEcole de

Medicine 的一員。之後他發現了結節性病變可能存在於身體的所有器官，而不僅僅是肺部。到了 1816 年，在他 35 歲的時候，他得到了巴黎內克爾醫院醫生的位子。拉埃內克被認為是所有時代內最偉大的醫生之一。他引進了聽診技術。這種方法涉及聽力，並確定由不同的身體器官製成各種聲音。

Before the invention of this method, doctors needed to put their ears on patients' chests to diagnose patients' problems. He felt uncomfortable especially while he was diagnosing young women. This led to the innovation of a new device called the stethoscope which he initially termed as "chest examiner". With a stethoscope, nowadays all doctors are able to study different sounds of the heart and understand patients' condition in a much more precise way. Laennec's works were way ahead of his time and had a great impact on medical science.

這種方法發明之前，醫生需要把耳朵放在患者的胸前以診斷病人的問題。由其當他診斷年輕女性時，這個方法令他不舒服這促使了一個新的設備的發明，稱為聽診器。他最初稱這個儀器為「胸部測試器」。因為聽診器，現在所有的醫生都能夠學習心臟的不同的聲音，並以一個更精確的方式了解患者的病情。拉埃內克的作品於是遙遙領先了他所處的時代並對醫學有很大的影響。

此部分為「**影子跟讀短段落練習❷**」，請重新播放音檔並完成試題，除了能提升並修正拼寫能力外，也可以藉由音檔注意自己專注力和定位聽力訊息部份，短段落聽力的提升能強化 section1 和 2 答題的正確性，現在就一起動身，開始完成「**短段落練習❷**」吧！

Graduating in 1.＿＿＿＿＿＿ in 1804, Laennec became 2.＿＿＿＿＿＿ at the Societe de IEcole de Medicine. He then found that tubercle lesions could be present in all 3.＿＿＿＿＿ of the body and not just the 4.＿＿＿＿. By 1816, at the age of 5.＿＿＿＿, he was offered the position of a physician at the Necker 6.＿＿＿＿＿. Laennec is considered to be one of the greatest 7.＿＿＿＿＿ of all time. It was him that introduced 8.＿＿＿＿＿. This method involves 9.＿＿＿＿＿ and identifying 10.＿＿＿＿ made by different body organs.

Before the invention of this method, doctors needed to put their ears on

11.＿＿＿＿＿ to diagnose patients' problems. He felt uncomfortable especially while he was diagnosing 12.＿＿＿＿. This led to the 13.＿＿＿＿＿ of a new device called the 14.＿＿＿＿＿ which he initially termed as "chest examiner". With a stethoscope, nowadays all doctors are able to study different 15.＿＿＿＿＿

and understand patients' condition in a much more precise way. Laennec's works were way ahead of his time and had a great impact on 16._____.

▶▶ 參考答案

1. medicine	2. an associate
3. organs	4. lungs
5. 35	6. Hospital in Paris
7. doctors	8. auscultation
9. listening	10. various sounds
11. patients' chests	12. young women
13. innovation	14. stethoscope
15. sounds of the heart	16. medical science

汽車發展史

▶▶ 影子跟讀「短段落」練習　🎧 MP3 084

　　此篇為**「影子跟讀短段落練習」**，此章節規劃了由聽**「短段落」**的 shadowing 練習，從最基礎、最易上手的部分切入雅思聽力備考並提升考生的專注力，雅思聽力中尤其 section 3 跟 4 雖然話題不難，且很多時候不是考生程度沒到某個分數段，但確實很容易因為**定位錯誤**而錯失聽力訊息或誤判題本的上該題訊息已經唸過了，強化這部分能提升 section 3 和 4 的得分，整體分數要 7+或 7.5+其實這部分要很費心喔!，現在就一起動身，開始聽**「短段落」**！

　　There were many people who made a great contribution to the invention of different types of automobiles. But it was only when Karl Benz built the first petrol automobile that vehicles became practical and went into actual production. The first gasoline-powered automobile built by Karl Benz contained an internal combustion engine. He built it in 1885 in Mannheim and was granted a patent for his automobile in 1886. Two years later, he began the first production of automobiles. In 1889, Gottlied Daimler and Wilhelm May-bach also designed a vehicle from scratch in Stuttgart.

許多人都曾對發明不同類型的汽車有偉大的貢獻，但直到卡爾‧賓士製造了第一台汽油汽車，汽車才真正能被有效利用，走進實際生產。卡爾‧賓士製作了第一個汽油動力汽車內所用的內燃機。他於 1885 年製作，並在 1886 年於曼海姆取得第一台汽車的專利。2 年後他開始了第一輛汽車的生產。1889 年，古特蘭‧戴姆勒和威廉‧邁巴赫也在斯圖加特開始了汽車的設計。

In 1895, a British engineer, Frederick William Lanchester built the first fourwheeled petrol driven automobile and also patented the disc brake. Between 1895 and 1898, the first electric starter was installed on the Benz Velo. By the 1930s, most of the mechanical technology used in today's automobiles had been invented. But due to the Great Depression, the number of auto manufacturers declined sharply. Many companies consolidated and matured. After that, the automobile market was booming for decades until the 1970s.

1895 年，一名英國工程師，腓特烈‧威廉在曼徹斯特製造了第一台四輪驅動的汽油汽車，並申請了盤式制動器的專利。在 1895 年和 1898 年間，賓士在車內安裝了首款的電動起動器。到了 1930 年代，今天汽車內使用的大部分機械技術已被發明出來。但由於經濟大蕭條，汽車製造業的數量急劇下降。許多公司合併且趨於成熟。在此之後，汽車市場蓬勃發展了幾十年直到 70 年代。

▶▶ 影子跟讀「短段落」練習 🎧 MP3 084

　　此部分為「**影子跟讀短段落練習❷**」，請重新播放音檔並完成試題，除了能提升並修正拼寫能力外，也可以藉由音檔注意自己專注力和定位聽力訊息部份，短段落聽力的提升能強化 section1 和 2 答題的正確性，現在就一起動身，開始完成「**短段落練習❷**」吧！

　　There were many people who made a great 1._____ to the invention of different types of 2._____. But it was only when Karl Benz built the first 3._____ that vehicles became practical and went into 4._____. The first 5._____ automobile built by Karl Benz contained an 6._____. He built it in 1885 in Mannheim and was granted 7._____ for his automobile in 1886. Two years later, he began the first production of automobiles. In 1889, Gottlied Daimler and Wilhelm Maybach also designed a vehicle from 8._____ in Stuttgart.

　　In 1895, a 9._____, Frederick William Lanchester built the first 10._____ petrol driven automobile and also patented the disc brake. Between 1895 and 1898, the first electric starter was installed on the Benz Velo. By the 1930s, most of the 11._____ used in today's automobiles had been invented. But due to the 12._____, the number of auto manufacturers de-

clined sharply. Many 13._____ consolidated and matured. After that, the automobile 14._____ was
booming for decades until the 1970s.

▶▶ **參考答案**

1. contribution

2. automobiles

3. petrol automobile

4. actual production

5. gasoline-powered

6. internal combustion engine

7. a patent

8. scratch

9. British engineer

10. fourwheeled

11. mechanical technology

12. Great Depression

13. companies

14. market

影子跟讀：「短對話」

影子跟讀：「短段落」

影子跟讀：「實戰練習」

雅思聽力必考字彙

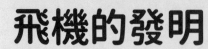

飛機的發明

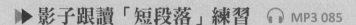

▶ 影子跟讀「短段落」練習 🎧 MP3 085

　　此篇為「**影子跟讀短段落練習**」，此章節規劃了由聽「**短段落**」的 shadowing 練習，從最基礎、最易上手的部分切入雅思聽力備考並提升考生的專注力，雅思聽力中尤其 section 3 跟 4 雖然話題不難，且很多時候不是考生程度沒到某個分數段，但確實很容易因為**定位錯誤**而錯失聽力訊息或誤判題本的上該題訊息已經唸過了，強化這部分能提升 section 3 和 4 的得分，整體分數要 7+或 7.5+其實這部分要很費心喔！，現在就一起動身，開始由聽「**短段落**」！

According to the document from IATA in 2011, 2.8 billion passengers were carried by airplane, which means on average there are 690,000 passengers in the air at any given moment. Air travel is known as the safest way to travel and it shortens the times between countries. What would the world be like today without the invention of airplane? We will never know. The first airplane was invented by Orville and Wilbur Wright in 1903.

　　據國際航空運輸協會在 2011 年的文件指出，一年中一共有 28 億的乘客搭乘飛機，這意味著無論任何時候都有平均 69 萬位乘客在

空中飛行。航空旅行號稱是最安全的旅行方式，它縮短了國與國之間的距離。如果沒有飛機的發明，今天這個世界會變如何？我們永遠不會知道。

Before the Wright's invention, many people made numerous attempts to fly like birds. In 1799, Sir George Cayley designed the first fixed-wing aircraft. In 1874, Felix duTemple made the first attempt at powered flight by hopping off the end of a ramp in a steam-driven monoplane.

在奧維爾和威爾，萊特於 1903 年發明第一架飛機以前，很多人嘗試了像鳥一樣的飛翔方式。1799 年，喬治·凱利爵士設計了第一架固定翼的飛機。1874 年，菲利克斯·杜湯普跳躍過斜坡，利用蒸汽驅動單翼，第一次嘗試動力飛行。

In 1894, the first controlled flight was made by Otto Lilienthal by shifting his body weight. Inspired by Lilienthal, the Wright brothers experimented with aerodynamic surfaces to control an airplane in flight and later on made the first airplane that was powered and controllable.

1894 年，奧托·李林塔爾利用轉移他的體重，創造出第一架可控飛行機。由於李林塔爾的啟發，萊特兄弟實驗氣動表面來控制飛行的飛機，後來提出電動並可控制的第一架飛機。

　　此部分為「**影子跟讀短段落練習❷**」，請重新播放音檔並完成試題，除了能提升並修正拼寫能力外，也可以藉由音檔注意自己專注力和定位聽力訊息部份，短段落聽力的提升能強化 section1 和 2 答題的正確性，現在就一起動身，開始完成「**短段落練習❷**」吧！

　　According to the 1.＿＿＿＿＿＿＿ from IATA in 2011, 2.＿＿＿＿＿＿＿ were carried by airplane, which means on average there are 3.＿＿＿＿＿＿＿ in the air at any given moment. 4.＿＿＿＿＿＿＿ is known as the safest way to travel and it shortens the times between 5.＿＿＿＿＿＿＿. What would the world be like today without the invention of 6.＿＿＿＿＿＿? We will never know. The first airplane was invented by Orville and Wilbur Wright in 1903.

　　Before the Wright's invention, many people made 7.＿＿＿＿＿＿ to fly like 8.＿＿＿＿＿＿. In 1799, Sir George Cayley designed the first 9.＿＿＿＿＿＿. In 1874, Felix du-Temple made the first attempt at powered flight by hopping off the end of a ramp in a steam-driven 10.＿＿＿＿＿＿.

　　In 1894, the first controlled flight was made by Otto Lilienthal by shifting his 11.＿＿＿＿＿＿＿. Inspired by Lilienthal, the Wright brothers experimented with aerodynamic 12.＿＿＿＿＿＿ to control 13.＿＿＿＿＿＿ in flight and

later on made the first airplane that was powered and
14._____.

▶▶ 參考答案

1. document	2. 2.8 billion passengers
3. 690,000 passengers	4. Air travel
5. countries	6. airplane
7. numerous attempts	8. birds
9. fixed-wing aircraft	10. monoplane
11. body weight	12. surfaces
13. an airplane	14. controllable

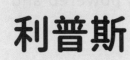

利普斯

▶ 影子跟讀「短段落」練習 🎧 MP3 086

　　此篇為「影子跟讀短段落練習」，此章節規劃了由聽「短段落」的 shadowing 練習，從最基礎、最易上手的部分切入雅思聽力備考並提升考生的專注力，雅思聽力中尤其 section 3 跟 4 雖然話題不難，且很多時候不是考生程度沒到某個分數段，但確實很容易因為定位錯誤而錯失聽力訊息或誤判題本的上該題訊息已經唸過了，強化這部分能提升 section 3 和 4 的得分，整體分數要 7+或 7.5+其實這部分要很費心喔!，現在就一起動身，開始聽「短段落」!

　　Hans Lippershey, a master lens grinder and spectacle maker was born in Wesel Germany in 1570. He then got married and settled in Middelburg in the Netherlands in 1594. Eight years later, he immigrated in the Netherlands. Lippershey filed a patent for telescope in 1607 and this was known as the earliest written record of a refracting telescope. There are several different versions of how Lippershey came up with the invention of the telescope.

　　身為一位鏡片研磨師和眼鏡製造商的漢斯·利普斯在 1570 年誕生於德國韋塞爾。爾後，在 1594 年定居於荷蘭米德爾堡，並在

同一年結婚。8 年後移民荷蘭。利普斯在 1607 年申請了望遠鏡的專利，這被稱為是折射望遠鏡最早的文字記錄。對於利普斯如何想出望遠鏡的原因有幾種不同的版本。

The most interesting one has to be the one in which Lippershey observed two kids playing with lenses and commented how they could make a far away weather-vane seem closer when looking at it through two lenses. Lippershey's original instrument consisted of either two convex lenses for an inverted image or a convex objective and a concave eyepiece lens so it would have an upright image. Lippershey remained in Middelburg until he passed away in 1619.

　　最有趣的版本是有一次利普斯觀察到兩個小孩玩耍時的對話，他們在評論如何利用鏡頭讓一個遙遠的天氣風向標看起來似乎更接近。利普斯的原始工具包括利用兩個凸透鏡以呈現出一個倒置的圖像，或利用凸物鏡和凹透鏡的眼鏡片以呈現出一個正面的圖像。利普斯終其一生留在米德爾，直到他在 1619 年去世。

影子跟讀：「短對話」

影子跟讀：「短段落」

影子跟讀：「實戰練習」

雅思聽力必考字彙

▶▶ 影子跟讀「短段落」練習　🎧 MP3 086

此部分為「**影子跟讀短段落練習❷**」，請重新播放音檔並完成試題，除了能提升並修正拼寫能力外，也可以藉由音檔注意自己專注力和定位聽力訊息部份，短段落聽力的提升能強化 section1 和 2 答題的正確性，現在就一起動身，開始完成「**短段落練習❷**」吧！

Hans Lippershey, a master 1.＿＿＿＿＿＿ and 2.＿＿＿＿＿ was born in Wesel 3.＿＿＿＿＿ in 1570. He then got married and settled in Middelburg in the 4.＿＿＿＿＿ in 1594. Eight years later, he immigrated in the Netherlands. Lippershey filed 5.＿＿＿＿＿ for 6.＿＿＿＿＿ in 1607 and this was known as the earliest 7.＿＿＿＿＿ of a refracting telescope. There are several different 8.＿＿＿＿＿ of how Lippershey came up with the invention of the telescope.

The most interesting one has to be the one in which Lippershey observed 9.＿＿＿＿＿ playing with lenses and commented how they could make a far away weather-vane seem closer when looking at it through 10.＿＿＿＿＿. Lippershey's original 11.＿＿＿＿＿ consisted of either 12.＿＿＿＿＿ for an inverted image or a convex 13.＿＿＿＿＿ and a 14.＿＿＿＿＿ eyepiece lens so it would have an 15.＿＿＿＿＿. Lippershey remained in 16.＿＿＿＿＿ until he passed away in 1619.

▶▶ 參考答案

1. lens grinder

2. spectacle maker

3. Germany

4. Netherlands

5. a patent

6. telescope

7. written record

8. versions

9. two kids

10. two lenses

11. instrument

12. two convex lenses

13. objective

14. concave

15. upright image

16. Middelburg

影子跟讀：「短對話」

影子跟讀：「短段落」

影子跟讀：「實戰練習」

雅思聽力必考字彙

打字機的發明

　　此篇為**「影子跟讀短段落練習」**，此章節規劃了由聽**「短段落」**的 shadowing 練習，從最基礎、最易上手的部分切入雅思聽力備考並提升考生的專注力，雅思聽力中尤其 section 3 跟 4 雖然話題不難，且很多時候不是考生程度沒到某個分數段，但確實很容易因為**定位錯誤**而錯失聽力訊息或誤判題本的上該題訊息已經唸過了，強化這部分能提升 section 3 和 4 的得分，整體分數要 7+或 7.5+其實這部分要很費心喔!，現在就一起動身，開始聽**「短段落」**!

　　A typewriter is a writing machine that has one character on each key press. The machine prints characters by making ink impressions on a moveable type letterpress printing. Typewriters, like other practical products such as automobiles , telephones , and refrigerators, are an invention that was developed by numerous inventors. The very first record of the typewriter invention was back in 1575.

　　打字機是一個寫作的機器，在每個按鍵上各有一個字母。機器利用活字凸版印刷通過墨水打印字符。打字機，如同其他實用的產品，如汽車、電話和冰箱，是由眾多的發明人所開發出來的。打字機

發明的第一個記錄最早在 1575 年。1575 年，意大利的版畫家，弗朗西斯，發明了「scritturatattile」，這是一台用來打字的機器。幾百年過去了，很多不同類型的打字機被開發出來。然而，沒有商業實用機的創建。直到 1829 年，美國發明家威廉・奧斯汀伯特申請了一台機器的專利稱為「字體設計」，它被列為「第一台打字機」。

In 1575, an Italian printmaker, Francesco Rampazzetto, invented the "scrittura tattile" which is a machine to impress letters on papers. Hundreds of years passed and many different types of typewriters have been developed. However, no commercially practical machine was created. It wasn't until 1829 that an American inventor William Austin Burt patented a machine called the "Typographer" which is listed as the "first typewriter". However, the design was still not practical enough for the market since it was slower than handwriting. In 1865, Rasmus Malling-Hansen from Denmark invented the first commercially sold typewriter, called the Hansen Writing Ball. It was successfully sold in Europe. In the US, the first commercially successful typewriter was invented by Christopher Latham Sholes in 1868.

然而，設計仍然不夠實用，因為它比寫字要緩慢。1865 年，來自丹麥的拉斯穆斯莫林・漢森發明了第一台在市場上銷售的打字機，叫做漢森寫作球。它成功地在歐洲銷售。在美國，第一個商業成功的打字機是在 1868 年由克里斯托弗・萊瑟姆・肖爾斯所發明的。

影子跟讀：「短對話」

影子跟讀：「短段落」

影子跟讀：「實戰練習」

雅思聽力必考字彙

此部分為**「影子跟讀短段落練習❷」**，請重新播放音檔並完成試題，除了能提升並修正拼寫能力外，也可以藉由音檔注意自己專注力和定位聽力訊息部份，短段落聽力的提升能強化 section1 和 2 答題的正確性，現在就一起動身，開始完成**「短段落練習❷」**吧！

A 1._____ is a writing 2._____ that has one character on each key press. The machine prints characters by making 3._____ on a moveable type letterpress printing. Typewriters, like other 4._____ such as automobiles , 5._____ , and 6._____ , are an invention that was developed by numerous 7._____. The very first record of the typewriter invention was back in 1575.

In 1575, an Italian printmaker, Francesco Rampazzetto, invented the"scrittura tattile" which is 8._____ to impress letters on papers. Hundreds of years passed and many different types of typewriters have been developed. However, no 9._____ machine was created. It wasn't until 1829 that an 10._____ William Austin Burt patented a machine called the"Typographer"which is listed as the "first typewriter". However, the 11._____ was still not practical enough for the market since it was slower than 12._____. In

1865, Rasmus Malling-Hansen from 13._____ invented the first commercially sold typewriter, called the Hansen Writing Ball. It was successfully sold in 14._____. In the US, the first commercially successful typewriter was invented by Christopher Latham Sholes in 1868.

▶▶ 參考答案

1. typewriter
2. machine
3. ink impressions
4. practical products
5. telephones
6. refrigerators
7. inventors
8. a machine
9. commercially practical
10. American inventor
11. design
12. handwriting
13. Denmark
14. Europe

石墨：皇室的象徵

▶▶ 影子跟讀「短段落」練習　🎧 MP3 088

　　此篇為**「影子跟讀短段落練習」**，此章節規劃了由聽**「短段落」**的 shadowing 練習，從最基礎、最易上手的部分切入雅思聽力備考並提升考生的專注力，雅思聽力中尤其 section 3 跟 4 雖然話題不難，且很多時候不是考生程度沒到某個分數段，但確實很容易因為**定位錯誤**而錯失聽力訊息或誤判題本的上該題訊息已經唸過了，強化這部分能提升 section 3 和 4 的得分，整體分數要 7+ 或 7.5+ 其實這部分要很費心喔！，現在就一起動身，開始聽**「短段落」**！

　　In 1812, a Massachusetts cabinet maker, William Monroe, made the first wooden pencil. The American pencil industry also took off during the 19th century. Starting with the Joseph Dixon Crucible Company, many pencil factories were based on the East Coast, such as New York or New Jersey.

　　1812 年，麻省的一個櫥櫃製造商，威廉·莫瑞，製作了第一個木製鉛筆。美國製筆業也是在 19 世紀起飛。由約瑟夫·狄克遜公司開始，很多鉛筆工廠都開在東岸，如紐約或新澤西州。

At first, pencils were all natural, unpainted and without printing company's names. Not until the 1890s, many pencil companies started to paint pencils in yellow and put their brand name on it. Why yellow? Red or blue would look nice, too." You might think. It was actually a special way to tell the consumer that the graphite came from China.

起初，鉛筆都是天然的，沒有油漆，沒有印刷公司的名稱。直到 1890 年代，許多鉛筆公司開始把鉛筆漆成黃色，並把自己的品牌名稱印上。你可能會認為「為什麼是黃色？紅色或藍色的也很好看。」。它實際上是用一種特殊的方式在告訴大家，石墨是來自中國。

It is because back in the 1800s, the best graphite in the world came from China. And the color yellow in China means royalty and respect. Only the imperial family was allowed to use the color yellow. Therefore, the American pencil companies began to paint their pencils bright yellow to show the regal feeling. Here we will be introducing Nicolas Jacques Conte who was credited as the inventor of the modern lead pencil from France.

這是因為早在 1800 年時，世界上最好的石墨來自中國。而在中國，黃色意味著皇室和尊重。只有皇室允許使用的黃色。因此，美國的鉛筆公司開始將自己的鉛筆漆成明亮的黃色，以顯示帝王的感覺。在這裡，我們將介紹尼古拉斯·雅克·康特，一位來自法國的現代鉛筆發明人。

▶▶ 影子跟讀「短段落」練習 🎧 MP3 088

此部分為「**影子跟讀短段落練習❷**」，請重新播放音檔並完成試題，除了能提升並修正拼寫能力外，也可以藉由音檔注意自己專注力和定位聽力訊息部份，短段落聽力的提升能強化 section1 和 2 答題的正確性，現在就一起動身，開始完成「**短段落練習❷**」吧！

In 1812, a Massachusetts 1._____, William Monroe, made the first 2._____. The American pencil industry also took off during the 19th century. Starting with the Joseph Dixon Crucible Company, many 3._____ were based on the East Coast, such as New York or 4._____.

At first, pencils were all natural, 5._____ and without printing company's names. Not until the 1890s, many pencil companies started to paint pencils in 6._____ and put their brand name on it. Why yellow? 7._____ would look nice, too." You might think. It was actually a special way to tell the 8._____ that the 9._____ came from 10._____.

It is because back in the 1800s, the best graphite in the world came from China. And the color yellow in China means 11._____. Only the imperial family was allowed to use the color yellow. Therefore, the American pencil companies began to paint their pencils bright yellow to show the 12.＿＿＿＿＿＿. Here we will be introducing Nicolas Jacques Conte who was credited as the 13.＿＿＿＿＿＿ of the modern lead pencil from 14.＿＿＿＿＿＿.

▶▶ 參考答案

1. cabinet maker	2. wooden pencil
3. pencil factories	4. New Jersey
5. unpainted	6. yellow
7. Red or blue	8. consumer
9. graphite	10. China
11. royalty and respect	12. regal feeling
13. inventor	14. France

原子筆的潛力

▶ 影子跟讀「短段落」練習　🎧 MP3 089

　　此篇為「**影子跟讀短段落練習**」，此章節規劃了由聽「**短段落**」的 shadowing 練習，從最基礎、最易上手的部分切入雅思聽力備考並提升考生的專注力，雅思聽力中尤其 section 3 跟 4 雖然話題不難，且很多時候不是考生程度沒到某個分數段，但確實很容易因為**定位錯誤**而錯失聽力訊息或誤判題本的上該題訊息已經唸過了，強化這部分能提升 section 3 和 4 的得分，整體分數要 7+或 7.5+其實這部分要很費心喔!，現在就一起動身，開始聽「**短段落**」!

　　The Birome was brought to the United States in 1945 by a mechanical pencil maker, Eversharp Co. Eversharp Co. and Eberhard Faner Co. teamed up and licensed the rights to sell the Birome ballpoint pen in the US.

　　Ｂｉrome 原子筆在 1945 年由自動鉛筆公司 Eversharp 公司聯合 Eberhard Faner 公司拿下特許權，並在美國販售 Birome 原子筆。

　　At the same time, an American entrepreneur Milton Reynolds saw the potential of the ballpoint pen, and therefore founded the Reynolds International Pen Company.

在同時，美國企業 家米爾頓–雷諾茲看到原子筆的潛力，並因此成立了雷諾國際製筆公司。

Both companies were doing great and ballpoint pen sales went rocket high in 1946, though people were still not 100% satisfied.

兩家公司都在做得非常好。原子筆銷量在 1946 年到達高峰，雖然人們仍然不是 100%滿意。

Another famous ballpoint pen maker would be Marcel Bich. Bich was the founder of the famous pen company Bic we all recognize today. The Bic ballpoint pen has a history going back to 1953. Unlike most inventors , whose inventions were appreciated by the society when they were alive, John Jacob Loud did not.

另一個著名的圓珠筆製造商是馬塞爾–畢克。畢克是著名的筆公司 Bic 的創辦人。Bi c 原子筆擁有自 1 9 5 3 年以來的歷史。與大多數發明家不同的是，約翰勞德於生前的發明並未受到社會重視。

影子跟讀：「短對話」

影子跟讀：「短段落」

影子跟讀：「實戰練習」

雅思聽力必考字彙

▶▶ 影子跟讀「短段落」練習 🎧 MP3 089

　　此部分為**「影子跟讀短段落練習❷」**，請重新播放音檔並完成試題，除了能提升並修正拼寫能力外，也可以藉由音檔注意自己專注力和定位聽力訊息部份，短段落聽力的提升能強化 section1 和 2 答題的正確性，現在就一起動身，開始完成**「短段落練習❷」**吧！

　　The Birome was brought to the 1.＿＿＿＿＿＿＿＿ in 1945 by a mechanical pencil 2.＿＿＿＿＿＿, Eversharp Co. Eversharp Co. and Eberhard Faner Co. teamed up and 3.＿＿＿＿＿＿ the rights to sell the Birome 4.＿＿＿＿＿＿＿＿ in the US.

　　At the same time, an American 5.＿＿＿＿＿＿ Milton Reynolds saw the 6.＿＿＿＿＿＿＿＿ of the ballpoint pen, and therefore founded the Reynolds 7.＿＿＿＿＿＿ Pen Company.

　　Both companies were doing great and ballpoint pen sales went 8.＿＿＿＿＿＿ high in 1946, though people were still not 9.＿＿＿＿＿＿ satisfied.

　　Another 10.＿＿＿＿＿＿ ballpoint pen maker would be Marcel Bich. Bich was the founder of the famous pen company

pany

　　Bic we all recognize today. The Bic ballpoint pen has a
11.＿＿＿＿＿＿＿ going back to 1953. Unlike most inventors,
whose inventions were appreciated by 12.＿＿＿＿＿＿＿
when they were alive, John Jacob Loud did not.

▶▶ 參考答案

1. United States	2. maker
3. licensed	4. ballpoint pen
5. entrepreneur	6. potential
7. International	8. rocket
9. 100%	10. famous
11. history	12. the society

解雇促成了立可白發明

▶ 影子跟讀「短段落」練習　🎧 MP3 090

　　此篇為**「影子跟讀短段落練習」**，此章節規劃了由聽**「短段落」**的 shadowing 練習，從最基礎、最易上手的部分切入雅思聽力備考並提升考生的專注力，雅思聽力中尤其 section 3 跟 4 雖然話題不難，且很多時候不是考生程度沒到某個分數段，但確實很容易因為**定位錯誤**而錯失聽力訊息或誤判題本的上該題訊息已經唸過了，強化這部分能提升 section 3 和 4 的得分，整體分數要 7+或 7.5+其實這部分要很費心喔!，現在就一起動身，開始聽**「短段落」**！

　　Back in the late 90's when computers were not as common, liquid paper could be found in every pencil case and on every desk. It was actually a brand name of the Newell Rubbermaid company that sold correction products. It is not a surprise that liquid paper was invented by a typist. Bette Graham who used to make many mistakes while working as a typist, invented the first correction fluid in her kitchen back in 1951. Using only paints and kitchen ware, G raham made her first generation correction fluid called Mistake Out and started to sell it to her co-workers.

在九零年代，當電腦還不普及時，你幾乎可以在每一個鉛筆盒，每一張桌子上看到立可白。它實際上是 Newell Rubbermaid 公司所銷售之修正產品的品牌名稱。立可白是由一位打字員所發明的，這並不意外。貝蒂・格雷厄姆在當打字員時經常發生錯誤。因此，在 1951 年時格雷厄姆在她的廚房裡，只利用了油漆及廚具，發明了她的第一代修正液，並且將它賣給自己的同事。

Graham for sure saw the business opportunity with her invention and founded the Mistake Out Company back in 1956 while she was still working as a typist. However, she was later fired from her job because of some silly mistakes. Just like that, she worked from her kitchen alone for 17 years. In 1961, the company name was changed to Liquid Paper and it was sold to the Gillette Corporation for $47.5 million in 1979.

格雷厄姆肯定看到了這個發明的商機，在 1956 年她還在擔任打字員時便創辦了 Mistake Out 公司。爾後，她因為一些愚蠢的原因被公司解雇。就這樣，她在廚房裡獨自工作了 17 年。在 1961 年，該公司的名稱改為立可白，並在 1979 年以$47.5 百萬美元出售給吉列特公司。

影子跟讀：「短對話」

影子跟讀：「短段落」

影子跟讀：「實戰練習」

雅思聽力必考字彙

▶▶ 影子跟讀「短段落」練習 🎧 MP3 090

　　此部分為「**影子跟讀短段落練習❷**」，請重新播放音檔並完成試題，除了能提升並修正拼寫能力外，也可以藉由音檔注意自己專注力和定位聽力訊息部份，短段落聽力的提升能強化 section1 和 2 答題的正確性，現在就一起動身，開始完成「**短段落練習❷**」吧！

　　Back in the late 90's 1.＿＿＿＿＿＿ were not as common, 2.＿＿＿＿＿＿ could be found in every pencil case and on every 3.＿＿＿＿＿＿. It was actually a 4.＿＿＿＿＿＿ of the Newell Rubbermaid company that sold 5.＿＿＿＿＿＿. It is not a surprise that liquid paper was invented by a 6.＿＿＿＿＿＿. Bette Graham who used to make many 7.＿＿＿＿＿＿ while working as a typist, invented the first correction 8.＿＿＿＿＿＿ in her 9.＿＿＿＿＿＿ back in 1951. Using only paints and 10.＿＿＿＿＿＿, G raham made her first generation correction fluid called Mistake Out and started to sell it to her 11.＿＿＿＿＿＿co-workers.

　　Graham for sure saw the 11.＿＿＿＿＿＿ with her invention and founded the Mistake Out Company back in 1956 while she was still working as a typist. However, she was later fired from her job because of some 12.＿＿＿＿＿＿. Just like that, she worked from her kitchen alone for 13.＿＿＿＿＿＿. In 1961, the company name was changed to Liquid Paper and it was sold to the Gillette Corporation for 14.＿＿＿＿＿＿ in 1979.

▶▶ 參考答案

1. when computers	2. liquid paper
3. desk	4. brand name
5. correction products	6. typist
7. mistakes	8. fluid
9. kitchen	10. kitchen ware
11. business opportunity	12. silly mistakes
13. 17 years	14. $47.5 million

紙技術傳至歐洲

▶ 影子跟讀「短段落」練習 🎧 MP3 091

　　此篇為**「影子跟讀短段落練習」**，此章節規劃了由聽**「短段落」**的 shadowing 練習，從最基礎、最易上手的部分切入雅思聽力備考並提升考生的專注力，雅思聽力中尤其 section 3 跟 4 雖然話題不難，且很多時候不是考生程度沒到某個分數段，但確實很容易因為**定位錯誤**而錯失聽力訊息或誤判題本的上該題訊息已經唸過了，強化這部分能提升 section 3 和 4 的得分，整體分數要 7+或 7.5+其實這部分要很費心喔!，現在就一起動身，開始由聽**「短段落」**!

　　For a long time, the Chinese kept the paper manufacture as a secret to ensure a monopoly. However, losing in a battle at the Talas River, the Chinese prisoners revealed the paper making technique to the Arabs which helped them built the first paper industry in Baghdad in 793 A.D.

　　長期以來，中國一直將造紙技術保密，以確保壟斷。然而公元 793 年，由於在失去塔拉斯河的戰役，中國戰俘透露製作技術並幫助阿拉伯人在巴格達建立了第一個造紙行業。

　　Interestingly, the Arabs also kept the first technique as a

secret from the European. As a result, the paper making technique did not reach Europe until hundreds of years later. Spain built the first European factory in 1150 A.D. Finally, after another 500 years, the first paper industry was built in Philadelphia in the USA. That is 1500 years after the first piece of paper was made!

有意思的是，阿拉伯人也將此技術保密。因此，造紙技術在幾百年後才傳到歐洲。西班牙在公元 1150 年時建立了第一個歐洲的造紙廠，再過 500 年後美國的費城才建立了美國的第一個造紙廠。這是從第一張紙被發明算起的 1500 年後！

Around 2000 years ago, Cai Lun wasborn in Guiyang during the Han Dynasty. Because of his father's accusation, Cai was brought to the palace and got castrated at the age of 12. Even so, Cai loved to study and was designated to study along with the Emperor's son. He was a very hard working person , so he was given several promotions under the rule of Emperor He. He was given the right to be in charge of manufacturing instruments and weapons.

大約 2000 多年前，蔡倫出生於漢朝的貴陽。由於他的父親犯罪，因此蔡被帶到了皇宮，在 12 歲時便被閹割。即便如此，蔡倫喜愛學習，所以被指定當作皇帝兒子的陪讀。他是一個很努力工作的人，因此在漢和帝的執政下被多次的升官。他被任命負責儀器及武器的製作。

影子跟讀：「短對話」

影子跟讀：「短段落」

影子跟讀：「實戰練習」

雅思聽力必考字彙

此部分為「**影子跟讀短段落練習❷**」，請重新播放音檔並完成試題，除了能提升並修正拼寫能力外，也可以藉由音檔注意自己專注力和定位聽力訊息部份，短段落聽力的提升能強化 section1 和 2 答題的正確性，現在就一起動身，開始完成「**短段落練習❷**」吧！

For a long time, 1.＿＿＿＿＿＿＿ kept the paper 2.＿＿＿＿＿＿＿ as a secret to ensure 3.＿＿＿＿＿＿＿. However, losing in 4.＿＿＿＿＿＿＿ at the Talas River, the Chinese 5.＿＿＿＿＿＿＿ revealed the paper making 6.＿＿＿＿＿＿＿ to the Arabs which helped them built the first paper 7.＿＿＿＿＿＿＿ in Baghdad in 793 A.D.

Interestingly, 8.＿＿＿＿＿＿ also kept the first technique as a secret from 9.＿＿＿＿＿＿＿＿＿. As a result, the paper making technique did not reach Europe until hundreds of years later. 10.＿＿＿＿＿＿＿ built the first European factory in 1150 A.D. Finally, after another 500 years, the first 11.＿＿＿＿＿ was built in 12.＿＿＿＿＿＿＿＿ in the USA. That is 1500 years after the first piece of paper was made!

Around 2000 years ago, Cai Lun wasborn in Guiyang during the 13.＿＿＿＿＿＿＿. Because of his father's 14.＿＿＿＿＿, Cai was brought to the 15.＿＿＿＿＿＿ and got castrated at the age of 16.＿＿＿＿＿. Even so, Cai loved to study and was designated to study along with the 17.＿＿＿＿＿＿＿＿＿＿. He was a very hard working person , so he was given several 18.＿＿＿＿＿＿＿＿＿ under the rule of Emperor He. He was given the right to be in charge of manufacturing instruments and weapons.

▶▶ 參考答案

1. the Chinese	2. manufacture
3. a monopoly	4. a battle
5. prisoners	6. technique
7. industry	8. the Arabs
9. the European	10. Spain
11. paper industry	12. Philadelphia
13. Han Dynasty	14. accusation
15. palace	16. 12
17. Emperor's son	18. promotions

影子跟讀：「短對話」

影子跟讀：「短段落」

影子跟讀：「實戰練習」

雅思聽力必考字彙

底片的進展

▶ 影子跟讀「短段落」練習　🎧 MP3 092

　　此篇為**「影子跟讀短段落練習」**，此章節規劃了由聽**「短段落」**的 shadowing 練習，從最基礎、最易上手的部分切入雅思聽力備考並提升考生的專注力，雅思聽力中尤其 section 3 跟 4 雖然話題不難，且很多時候不是考生程度沒到某個分數段，但確實很容易因為**定位錯誤**而錯失聽力訊息或誤判題本的上該題訊息已經唸過了，強化這部分能提升 section 3 和 4 的得分，整體分數要 7+或 7.5+其實這部分要很費心喔!，現在就一起動身，開始聽**「短段落」**！

　　Before digital photography became popular in the 21st century, photographic film was the dominant form of photography for hundreds of years. Without the invention of photographic film, movies would not be invented and many historical records would be much less realistic. The first flexible photographic roll of film was sold by George Eastman in 1885. It was a paper-based film. In 1889, the first transparent plastic roll film was invented. It was made of cellulose nitrate which is chemically similar to guncotton. It was quite dangerous because it was highly flammable.

在 21 世紀數位攝影開始流行前，底片是攝影數百年來的主要形式。如果沒有底片的發明，電影將不會被發明，眾多的歷史記錄也會較不真實。第一個柔性膠卷是由喬治‧伊士曼於 1885 年售出。它是一種紙基膜。在 1889 年，第一個透明的塑料筒膜被發明出來。它是利用硝酸纖維素所製造，化學性質是類似於硝化纖維素。這其實是相當危險的，因為它是高度易燃的。

Therefore, special storage was required. The first flexible movie films measured 35-mm wide and came in long rolls on a spool. Similar roll film for the camera was also invented in the mid 1920s. By the late 1920s, medium format roll film was created and had a paper backing which made it easy to handle in daylight.

因此，特殊的儲存方式是必要的。第一個柔性電影底片是 35 毫米寬，排列在長卷的捲筒上。相機類似的膠卷也在 1920 年代中期被發明出來。到了 1920 年代末期，中寬幅的底片被發明出來，它也有紙襯，使得它容易攜帶於日光下。

影子跟讀：「短對話」

影子跟讀：「短段落」

影子跟讀：「實戰練習」

雅思聽力必考字彙

▶▶▶ 影子跟讀「短段落」練習 🎧 MP3 092

此部分為「**影子跟讀短段落練習❷**」，請重新播放音檔並完成試題，除了能提升並修正拼寫能力外，也可以藉由音檔注意自己專注力和定位聽力訊息部份，短段落聽力的提升能強化 section1 和 2 答題的正確性，現在就一起動身，開始完成「**短段落練習❷**」吧！

Before digital 1.＿＿＿＿＿＿＿＿ became popular in the 21st century, 2.＿＿＿＿＿＿＿＿ was the dominant form of photography for hundreds of years. Without the invention of photographic film, 3.＿＿＿＿＿＿ would not be invented and many 4.＿＿＿＿＿＿ would be much less realistic. The first flexible photographic 5.＿＿＿＿＿ of film was sold by George Eastman in 1885. It was a 6.＿＿＿＿＿＿ film. In 1889, the first 7.＿＿＿＿＿ plastic roll film was invented. It was made of 8.＿＿＿＿＿＿ nitrate which is chemically similar to 9.＿＿＿＿＿. It was quite dangerous because it was highly flammable.

Therefore, special 10.＿＿＿＿＿ was required. The first flexible movie films measured 11.＿＿＿＿ and came in long rolls on a spool. Similar roll film for the 12.＿＿＿＿＿ was also invented in the mid 1920s. By the late 1920s, medium 13.＿＿＿＿＿ roll film was created and had 14.＿＿＿＿ backing which made it easy to handle in daylight.

▶▶ **參考答案**

1. photography
2. photographic film
3. movies
4. historical records
5. roll
6. paper-based
7. transparent
8. cellulose
9. guncotton
10. storage
11. 35-mm wide
12. camera
13. format
14. a paper

影子跟讀：「短對話」

影子跟讀：「短段落」

影子跟讀：「實戰練習」

雅思聽力必考字彙

燈泡的發展

▶ **影子跟讀「短段落」練習** 🎧 MP3 093

此篇為**「影子跟讀短段落練習」**，此章節規劃了由聽**「短段落」**的 shadowing 練習，從最基礎、最易上手的部分切入雅思聽力備考並提升考生的專注力，雅思聽力中尤其 section 3 跟 4 雖然話題不難，且很多時候不是考生程度沒到某個分數段，但確實很容易因為**定位錯誤**而錯失聽力訊息或誤判題本的上該題訊息已經唸過了，強化這部分能提升 section 3 和 4 的得分，整體分數要 7+或 7.5+其實這部分要很費心喔!，現在就一起動身，開始聽**「短段落」**！

If you think that Thomas Edison invented the first light bulb, you are technically wrong. There were several people who invented the light bulb, but Thomas Edison mostly got credit for it because he was the person who created the first practical light bulb that was available for the general public. 76 years before Thomas Edison filed the patent application for "Improvement in Electric Lights", Humphrey Davy invented an electric battery. When he connected wires to the battery and a piece of carbon, the carbon glowed. That was the first electric light ever invented.

影子跟讀：「短對話」

影子跟讀：「短段落」

影子跟讀：「實戰練習」

雅思聽力必考字彙

如果你認為愛迪生發明第一個燈泡，嚴格上來說你是錯誤的。世上有幾個人發明了電燈泡，但湯瑪斯·愛迪生得到大部分的榮耀，因為他創造了第一個可用於一般大眾的實用電燈泡。早在湯瑪斯·愛迪生提出「電燈的改善」專利的 76 年之前，漢弗萊·戴維發明了電池。當他連接了導線、電池與一塊碳，碳發光了。這是首個電燈的發明。

Though it was not ready for general use because the light didn't last long enough, and it was too bright for practical use. Years later, several other inventors tried to create light bulbs but no practical products were created. It was even made with platinum, but the cost of platinum made it impractical for commercial use.

不過，由於無法長時間維持光亮，且光線太亮，所以這個發明還沒準備好被實際應用。幾年後，其他幾個發明家也試圖創造燈泡，但沒有實用的產品被創作出來。有人甚至提出用鉑作為材料，但鉑金的成本無法作為商業用途。

▶▶▶ 影子跟讀「短段落」練習 🎧 MP3 093

　　此部分為「**影子跟讀短段落練習❷**」，請重新播放音檔並完成試題，除了能提升並修正拼寫能力外，也可以藉由音檔注意自己專注力和定位聽力訊息部份，短段落聽力的提升能強化 section1 和 2 答題的正確性，現在就一起動身，開始完成「**短段落練習❷**」吧！

　　If you think that 1.＿＿＿＿＿＿ invented the first 2.＿＿＿＿＿＿, you are technically wrong. There were several people who invented the light bulb, but Thomas Edison mostly got credit for it because he was the person who created the first 3.＿＿＿＿＿＿ that was available for the 4.＿＿＿＿＿. 76 years before Thomas Edison filed the patent 5.＿＿＿＿＿＿ for "Improvement in Electric Lights", Humphrey Davy invented an 6.＿＿＿＿＿. When he connected wires to the 7.＿＿＿＿ and a piece of carbon, the carbon glowed. That was the first 8.＿＿＿＿ ever invented.

　　Though it was not ready for general use because the light didn't last long enough, and it was too 9.＿＿＿＿ for practical use. Years later, several other 10.＿＿＿＿ tried to create light bulbs but no practical products were created. It was even made with platinum, but the 11.＿＿＿＿ of platinum made it impractical for 12.＿＿＿＿.

▶▶ 參考答案

1. Thomas Edison	2. light bulb
3. practical light bulb	4. general public
5. application	6. electric battery
7. battery	8. electric light
9. bright	10. inventors
11. cost	12. commercial use

影子跟讀：「短對話」

影子跟讀：「短段落」

影子跟讀：「實戰練習」

雅思聽力必考字彙

尿布

▶ 影子跟讀「短段落」練習 🎧 MP3 094

此篇為 **「影子跟讀短段落練習」**，此章節規劃了由聽 **「短段落」** 的 shadowing 練習，從最基礎、最易上手的部分切入雅思聽力備考並提升考生的專注力，雅思聽力中尤其 section 3 跟 4 雖然話題不難，且很多時候不是考生程度沒到某個分數段，但確實很容易因為**定位錯誤**而錯失聽力訊息或誤判題本的上該題訊息已經唸過了，強化這部分能提升 section 3 和 4 的得分，整體分數要 7+或 7.5+其實這部分要很費心喔!，現在就一起動身，開始聽 **「短段落」**！

The diaper, one of the very first items that distinguished human from animals, was found being used from the Egyptians to the Romans. Though back then, people were using animal skins, leaf wraps, and other natural resources instead of the disposable diapers we know today. The cotton "diaper like" progenitor was worn by the European and the American infants by the late 1800's. The shape of the progenitor was similar to the modern diaper but was held in place with safety pins. Back then, people were not aware of bacteria and viruses. Therefore, diapers were reused after drying in the sun. It was not until the beginning of the 20th century that people started to use boiled water in order to reduce common rash problems.

影子跟讀：「短對話」

尿布是最早區分人類與動物的項目之一。從埃及人到羅馬人都有被發現使用尿布。雖然當時人們用獸皮、樹葉和其他自然資源包裹，與我們現今所知的紙尿布有所不同。尿布的前身在 1800 年底被歐洲及美國的嬰兒所穿著。尿布前身的形狀設計非常類似現今的尿布，但卻是使用安全別針。那時，人們還沒有細菌和病毒的意識。因此，尿布曬乾後便再重複使用。

影子跟讀：「短段落」

However, due to World War II, cotton became a strategic material, so the disposable absorbent pad used as a diaper was created in Sweden in 1942. In 1946, Marion Donovan, a typical housewife from the United States invented a waterproof covering for diapers, called the "Boater." The model of the disposable diaper was made from a shower curtain. Back then, disposable diapers were only used for special occasions, such as vacations because it was considered a "luxury item."

影子跟讀：「實戰練習」

直到 20 世紀初，人們開始使用開水（燙尿布），這才減少了常見的皮疹問題。但由於第二次世界大戰，棉花成為了戰略物資，因此，拋棄式的尿布墊於 1942 年在瑞典被製作出來。1946 年，瑪麗安‧唐納文，一位來自美國的典型家庭主婦發明了一種防水的尿布，她稱之為「船工」。她利用浴簾製作了紙尿布的模型。當時，紙尿布由於是被認為是奢侈品。

雅思聽力必考字彙

▶▶ 影子跟讀「短段落」練習 🎧 MP3 094

　　此部分為「**影子跟讀短段落練習❷**」，請重新播放音檔並完成試題，除了能提升並修正拼寫能力外，也可以藉由音檔注意自己專注力和定位聽力訊息部份，短段落聽力的提升能強化 section1 和 2 答題的正確性，現在就一起動身，開始完成「**短段落練習❷**」吧！

　　The 1._____, one of the very first 2._____ that distinguished human from 3._____, was found being used from the 4._____ to the 5._____. Though back then, people were using 6._____, leaf wraps, and other 7._____ instead of the 8._____ diapers we know today. The cotton "diaper like" progenitor was worn by the European and the 9._____ by the late 1800's. The shape of the progenitor was similar to the modern diaper but was held in place with safety pins. Back then, people were not aware of 10._____. Therefore, diapers were reused after drying in the sun. It was not until the beginning of the 20th century that people started to use 11._____ in order to reduce common 12._____ problems.

　　However, due to World War II, cotton became a strategic material, so the disposable 13._____ pad used as a diaper was created in 14._____ in 1942. In 1946, Marion Donovan, a typical 15._____ from the United States invented a 16._____ covering for diapers, called the "Boater." The model of the disposable diaper was made from a 17._____. Back then, disposable diapers were only used for special occasions, such as 18._____ because it was considered a "luxury item."

▶▶ 參考答案

1. diaper	2. items
3. animals	4. Egyptians
5. Romans	6. animal skins
7. natural resources	8. disposable
9. American infants	10. bacteria and viruses
11. boiled water	12. rash
13. absorbent	14. Sweden
15. housewife	16. waterproof
17. shower curtain	18. vacations

塗鴉及凱斯・哈林

▶ 影子跟讀「實戰練習」　🎧 MP3 095

　　此篇為「**影子跟讀實戰練習**」，此章節規劃了由聽「**實際考試長度的英文內容**」的 shadowing 練習，經由先前的兩個部份的練習，已經能逐步掌握跟聽一定句數的英文內容，現在經由實際考試長度的聽力內容來練習，讓耳朵適應聽這樣長度的英文內容，提升在考場時的答題穩定度和適應性，進而獲取理想成績，現在就一起動身，開始由聽「**實戰練習**」！（如果聽這部份且跟讀練習的難度還是太高請重複前兩個部份的練習數次後再來做這部分的練習喔！）

　　Graffiti has existed for as long as written words have existed, with examples traced back to Ancient Greece, Ancient Egypt, and the Roman Empire. In fact, the word graffiti came from the Roman Empire. Some even consider cave drawings by cavemen in the Neolithic Age the earliest form of graffiti, and thus make it the longest existent art form. Basically, graffiti refers to writing or drawings that have been scrawled, painted, or sprayed on surfaces in the public domain in an illicit manner. The general functions of graffiti include expressing personal emotion, recording historical event, and conveying political messages. Nevertheless, today graffiti has found its place in mainstream art, and for many graffiti artists, their works have become highly commercialized and lucrative.

影子跟讀：「短對話」

影子跟讀：「短段落」

塗鴉的歷史就跟文字的歷史一樣久，塗鴉的例子可追溯到古希臘、古埃及和羅馬帝國。事實上，graffiti 這個字發源自羅馬帝國。有些人甚至將新石器時代的穴居人所畫的洞穴壁畫視為塗鴉最早的形式，使得塗鴉成為現存最久的藝術。基本上，塗鴉指的是未經法律許可在公共領域的壁面上潦草書寫，畫畫或噴漆形成的文字或圖案。塗鴉的主要功能包括表達個人情緒，記錄歷史事件，及傳達政治訊息。然而，今日塗鴉已經在主流藝術中取得一席之地，而且對許多塗鴉藝術家而言，他們的作品已經被高度商業化並帶來高度利潤。

影子跟讀：「實戰練習」

Contemporary artistic graffiti has just arisen in the past twenty-five years in the inner city of New York, with street artists painting and writing illegitimately on public buildings, street signs or public transportation, more commonly on the exteriors of subway trains. These artists experimented with different styles and mediums, such as sprays and stencils. The difference between artistic graffiti and traditional graffiti is that the former has evolved from scribbling on a wall to a complex and skillful form of personal and political expression.

雅思聽力必考字彙

當今的藝術性塗鴉是在過去二十五年間於紐約市中心興起的，當時街頭藝術家未經法律許可就在公共建築、馬路上的標誌或公共運輸工具上面畫畫及寫字，比較普遍的是畫在地鐵車廂的外層。這些藝

術家實驗不同的風格和媒介，例如噴漆和金屬模板。藝術性塗鴉和傳統塗鴉的差異在於前者已從在牆壁上潦草畫畫進化成表達個人和政治意涵的複雜及高技術的型式。

Graffiti artists have also collaborated with fashion designers to branch out numerous products, increasing the daily and global presence of this art form. In the U. S., many graffiti artists have extended their careers to skateboard, apparel, and shoe design for companies such as DC Shoes, Adidas, and Osiris. The most famous American graffiti artist is probably Keith Haring, who brought his art into the commercial mainstream by opening his Pop Shop in New York in 1986, where the public could purchase commodities with Haring's graffiti imageries. Keith Haring viewed his Pop Shop as an extension of his subway drawings, with his philosophy of making art accessible to the public, not just to collectors.

塗鴉藝術家也和流行服飾設計師合作拓展出許多產品，提高此藝術在日常生活和全球的能見度。在美國，許多塗鴉藝術家已經將職涯延伸到滑板、服裝及鞋子設計，他們替 DC Shoes、愛迪達和 Osiris 等品牌設計。最有名的美國塗鴉藝術家可能是凱斯・哈林。他在 1986 年於紐約開了他的普普店，將他的藝術帶入商業主流。在這間店大眾可以買到印有哈林的塗鴉圖案的商品。哈林視普普店為他的地鐵繪畫的延伸，這間店蘊含他對藝術的哲學，即藝術應該讓大眾輕易取得，而不是只針對收藏家。

Keith Haring lived a short life, yet he is probably the

most well-known graffiti artists of the late 20th century. He was born in 1958, and passed away in 1990. In his 31 years of life, he not only left a rich legacy of pop art, but also inspired numerous Americans to pay attention to the social issues that plagued them in the 1980s, including drugs, AIDS, and the destruction of nature. Even if you are not familiar with the artist's background, you must have seen his drawings reproduced on a variety of products, from clothes and shoes to key chains and suitcases.

凱斯‧哈林的生命短暫，但他可能是二十世紀末期最知名的塗鴉藝術家。他出生於 1958 年，於 1990 年逝世。在他 31 年的人生中，他不只留下豐厚的普普藝術遺產，也鼓舞許多美國人注意到 1980 年代讓他們苦惱的社會議題，包括毒品、愛滋和破壞大自然。即使你對這位藝術家的背景不熟悉，你一定看過他的繪畫，他的繪畫被重製在各種商品上，從衣服及鞋子到鑰匙圈及行李箱。

No other artists have such a unique style as Haring's. His drawings are highly recognizable, for they are always composed distinctive bold lines and convey a vibrant atmosphere. The bright colors also transmit an optimistic vibe and strong energy. The recurrent figures in his works include dancing figures, an infant emitting light, and figures with television heads, which have become his signature icons, along with a barking dog, a flying saucer, and large hearts.

沒有其他藝術家的風格能像哈林的風格那樣獨特。他的繪畫是

高度可辨識的，因為它們總是以鮮明的粗線條構圖並傳遞活躍的氣氛。明亮的色彩傳遞樂觀的氛圍及強烈的能量。他作品裡重複出現的人物包括跳舞的角色、一個散發出光的嬰兒及有電視頭型的角色，這些都變成他的獨家圖案，其他獨家圖案有吠犬、飛碟和大型心臟。

In Haring's early career in the 1980s, he was fined and arrested numerous times for his graffiti drawings in the New York subway system since the police viewed his art as vandalism. Notwithstanding, Haring considered subway drawings his responsibility of communicating art to the public. While he was drawing on the blank panels, he was often surrounded and observed by commuters. Being a prolific artist, he could produce about 40 drawings a day. Yet, most of his subway drawings were not recorded, as they were either cleaned or covered by new advertisements. It was the ephemeral nature that acted as an impetus for him to reinvent themes with easily identifiable images, such as babies, dogs, and angels, all illustrated with outlines. His themes involve sexuality, war, birth, and death, often mocking the mainstream society in caricatures.

在 1980 年代哈林早期的職涯裡，他因為在紐約市地鐵系統塗鴉被罰款和逮捕許多次，因為警察將他的藝術視為破壞公物。然而，哈林認為地鐵繪畫是他的責任，藉此他能將藝術溝通給大眾。當他在空白的長板子上繪畫時，他常常被通勤者圍觀。身為多產的藝術家，他一天可以畫大約四十幅塗鴉。但是，他大部份的地鐵繪畫沒有被記錄下來，因為它們不是被清潔掉，就是被新的廣告蓋上。正是這種稍

縱即逝的本質形成他不斷重新創作主題的動力。他的塗鴉主題運用容易辨識的圖案，例如嬰兒、小狗和天使形象，而所有的圖案都只有外觀輪廓。他的主題牽涉了性意識、戰爭、出生及死亡，且經常以諷刺漫畫嘲諷主流社會。

As Haring's reputation grew, he took on larger projects. His most notable work is the public mural titled, "Crack is Wack", inspired by his studio assistant who was addicted to crack and addressing the deteriorating drug issue in New York. The mural is representative of Haring's broad concerns for the American society in the 1980s. He was a social activist as well, heavily involved in socio-political movements, in which he participated in charitable support for children and fought against racial discrimination. Before his death at age 31, he established the Keith Haring Foundation and the Pop Shop; both have continued his legacy till today.

　　隨著哈林的名聲提高，他進行更大型的計畫。他最值得一提的作品是名為「吸毒等同發瘋」公共壁畫，這幅壁畫的靈感來自他對毒品上癮的工作室助理，同時也針對紐約市日益惡化的毒品問題。這幅壁畫代表了哈林對 1980 年代美國社會的廣泛關注。他也是位行動主義者，深度參與社會及政治方面的活動，並支援兒童慈善活動及反對種族歧視。在他 31 歲過世前，他成立了凱斯‧哈林基金會及普普店，兩者至今都延續了他的精神。

Keith Haring has become a worldwide icon of the 20th century Pop Art. His contribution is multifaceted, from changing our idea of street art to incorporating social and political messages in Pop Art. Nowadays, his works are collected by art museums around the world, but he once commented that his drawings on subway panels and those collected in museums mean the same to him, which reflects his ideology that art is inseparable from the mundane.

　　凱斯・哈林已成為二十世紀普普藝術的代表人物。他的貢獻是多方面的，從改變我們對街頭藝術的觀念到將社會及政治訊息融入普普藝術。今日世界各地的美術館都收藏他的作品，但他曾評論，對他而言，在地鐵板子上的繪畫及被博物館收藏的繪畫並沒什麼不同，這反映了他認為藝術和世俗生活是不可切割的意識形態。

▶▶ 影子跟讀「實戰練習」　🎧 MP3 095

　　此部分為「**影子跟讀實戰練習❷**」，請重新播放音檔並完成試題，除了能提升並修正拼寫能力外，也可以藉由音檔注意自己專注力和定位聽力訊息部份，走神或定位錯都會影響在實際考場中的表現，尤其在 section3 和 4 影響的得分會更明顯，現在就一起動身，開始完成「**實戰練習❷**」吧！

　　Some even consider cave drawings by 1.＿＿＿＿＿ in the Neolithic Age the earliest form of graffiti, and thus make it the longest existent art form. The general functions of graffiti include expressing 2.＿＿＿＿＿＿＿, recording 3.＿＿＿＿＿＿, and conveying 4.＿＿＿＿＿＿＿.

　　These artists experimented with different styles and mediums, such as 5.＿＿＿＿ and 6.＿＿＿＿.

　　Graffiti artists have also collaborated with 7.＿＿＿＿＿ to branch out numerous products, increasing the daily and global presence of this art form. Keith Haring viewed his Pop Shop as an extension of his 8.＿＿＿＿, with his philosophy of making art accessible to the public, not just to collectors. No other artists have such a unique style as Haring's. His drawings are highly recognizable, for they are always composed distinctive 9.＿＿＿＿＿ and convey a 10.＿＿＿＿＿.

In Haring's early career in the 1980s, he was fined and arrested numerous times for his graffiti drawings in the New York subway system since the police viewed his art as 11._____. Yet, most of his subway drawings were not recorded, as they were either cleaned or covered by new 12._____. It was the ephemeral nature that acted as an impetus for him to reinvent themes with easily 13._____, such as babies, dogs, and angels, all illustrated with outlines. His themes involve 14._____, war, birth, and death, often mocking the mainstream society in 15._____.

As Haring's reputation grew, he took on larger projects. His most notable work is the public mural titled, "Crack is Wack", inspired by his studio assistant who was addicted to 16._____ and addressing the deteriorating 17._____ in New York. The 18._____ is representative of Haring's broad concerns for the American society in the 1980s. He was a social activist as well, heavily involved in socio-political movements, in which he participated in charitable support for children and fought against 19._____. Before his death at age 31, he established the Keith Haring Foundation and the Pop Shop; both have continued his 20._____ till today. Keith Haring has become a worldwide 21._____ of the 20th century Pop Art. His 22._____ is multifaceted, from changing our idea of street art to incorporating social and political

23._____ in Pop Art.

Nowadays, his works are collected by art 24._____ around the world, but he once commented that his drawings on subway panels and those collected in museums mean the same to him, which reflects his ideology that art is inseparable from the mundane.

▶▶ 參考答案

1. cavemen	2. personal emotion
3. historical events	4. political messages
5. sprays	6. stencils
7. fashion designers	8. subway drawings
9. bold lines	10. vibrant atmosphere
11. vandalism	12. advertisements
13. identifiable images	14. sexuality
15. caricatures	16. crack
17. drug issue	18. mural
19. racial discrimination	20. legacy
21. icon	22. contribution
23. messages	24. museums

魯蛇或溫拿

▶▶ 影子跟讀「實戰練習」 🎧 MP3 096

　　此篇為**「影子跟讀實戰練習」**，此章節規劃了由聽**「實際考試長度的英文內容」**的 shadowing 練習，經由先前的兩個部份的練習，已經能逐步掌握跟聽一定句數的英文內容，現在經由實際考試長度的聽力內容來練習，讓耳朵適應聽這樣長度的英文內容，提升在考場時的答題穩定度和適應性，進而獲取理想成績，現在就一起動身，開始由聽**「實戰練習」**！（如果聽這部份且跟讀練習的難度還是太高請重複前兩個部份的練習數次後再來做這部分的練習喔!）

　　"Losers" is a term that used to refer to someone who has failed at doing certain things, but nowadays it incorporates multiple contemporary phenomena. This has led to some intriguing discussions in daily life, whether those are carried out on some websites, Facebook updates, or several key forums or in day-to-day conversations in the office. It is testing our limit to whether or not life will turn out to be smooth sailing, but the fact is life is always pushing us around. For losers, life is like a bigger battle. Some are earning a meager salary. Others can barely pay the rent. By contrast, winners seem to have it all. Some are borne with a silver spoon. Others have a gilded career ahead of them. In life, there are many options along the way, constantly forcing us to make a decision. We all dream of living our lives in a certain way. Of course, no one wants to be a loser. No one wants to even be labeled as losers, but here we are.

魯蛇在過去是用來指有些人未能達成某些事的詞，但現今卻融入了著許多現代社會現象。這也導致一些有趣的討論，不論那些討論是在網頁上、臉書更新或是幾個重要論壇上進行，或在公司裡每天的聊天內容。這也考驗著我們的極限，不論是我們的一生是否會是一帆風順，但事實是生命總是逼著我們走。對魯蛇來說生命就像是個較大的挑戰。有些人賺取著微薄的薪水。另一些人卻勉強能付租金。相對之下，溫拿似乎擁有著一切。有些出生就是銀湯匙。另一些人卻有著鍍金的職涯在他們前方。在生命行進中總是充滿著許多選擇，不斷地促使我們做出決定。我們總夢想著以特定的方式生活著。當然，沒有人想當魯蛇。甚至沒有人想要被貼上魯蛇這個標籤，但我們卻走到這地步。

The loser phenomena have aroused a debate among generations, but it somehow reflects the problems that our generation is currently facing. The problem of not being able to find a wife is simply because you have "loser" values. The ridicule from a friend that you are earning a 22 k salary is also one of them. The issue extends to a bigger one: buying a house. Being able to buy a house means you are heading to the next phase of your life whether it is because you are getting married and having kids so that there are enough

影子跟讀：「短對話」

影子跟讀：「短段落」

影子跟讀：「實戰練習」

雅思聽力必考字彙

261

rooms for them. It is also a commitment to your spouse that you have the ability to start a family. People of the previous generation used to encounter that phase, and they somehow survived. They are now ridiculing how people with a 22 k salary are able to start a family of their own if the salary is ridiculously low.

　　魯蛇的現象已經在幾個世代中引起了辯論，但卻某種程度上反映出我們的世代正面對的問題。無法找到妻子的問題卻因為你有著魯蛇的價值觀。朋友嘲諷你賺取 22k 的薪水也是其中一部分。這個議題延伸到更大的問題上：買房子。具備買房子的能力意味著你朝著人生的下個階段邁進，不論是你將結婚或是有小孩，有著足夠的房間準備給他們。這也是你給予另一半的承諾，你有能力成家。前個世代的人過去經歷了那個階段而他們卻某種程度地存活了下來。他們正嘲諷著賺取 22k 薪資的人要如何能夠成家，如果他們的薪資是如此低呢？

It's a huge burden for today's generation when it comes to buying a house. Losers are thus having a remark of their own that "do you think it is way too early to buy a house" or "not ready to settle down is actually not a bad thing". They don't want to spend money on costlier things. They have come up with more explanations as to why they can't or don't want to do that. But even if these sound reasonable, is it good for them in the long run? In contrast, winners seem to have a different opinion. They think buying a house means you do not just own it. They think it is an investment, an investment that is worthwhile for later life. For them, it is about the long term. No matter what your explanations are or what you have come up with, something like whether you own a house has a total say in whether or not you will get a wife. It's the traditional metrics when it comes to selecting a mate.

對於現今世代這是個很大的負擔,當提到買房子這個話題時。魯蛇卻有著他們的一套說法,難道你們不覺得太早買了嗎?或是不那麼早定下來也不是什麼壞事。他們不想要將錢花費在昂貴的東西上。他們想出了更多的解釋來解釋為什麼他們不會或不想這麼做。但儘管這些都看似合理,這最終對他們來說會是最好的嗎?相對之下,溫拿卻似乎有著不同的看法。他們認為買房子意謂著不只是擁有房子。他們認為這是個投資,對之後的生活來說是很值得的。對他們而言,這是長期的。不論你的解釋為何或你想出的理由是什麼,有些像是不論你是否擁有房子對你能不能交到老婆都有絕對的影響。當提到選擇伴侶時,這是傳統的衡量標準。

Another thing people use to value whether you are losers or not is the way you look. Handsome guys or beautiful ladies are those people desire. People want beautiful things. In addition, it's a hereditary trait. People want to have a beautiful baby, and sometimes people are selfish. Even if they don't look that good, they want their spouse to be that good, perhaps somewhat balancing what they are lacking on the outside.

另一個人們評價你是否是魯蛇的標準是你的長相也就是你的外表。英俊的男生或漂亮的女士是大家所追求的。人們都想要美麗的東西。此外，這是遺傳特徵。人們想要一個漂亮的小孩，而有時候人們是自私的。即使他們長得不怎樣，他們卻想要他們的另一半是那麼好看的，或許某種程度上平衡他們外在所欠缺的。

But all these winner and loser values people place on you have turned people into lunatics. Sometimes it's too extreme. It's quite common for you to see girls who have a small plastic surgery. It's a downside for them. It's distorting some values that we had in the past. Nowadays, men are doing the plastic surgery. The news headline even shocked most of us that a handsome guy wants to have a plastic surgery so that he can be better-looking. People are commenting that "it is just not right", "he is already good-looking" or "I just don't get what he thinks". Eventually, the surgery cost his life. It's the extreme example of the modern phenomenon.

但所有這些溫拿或魯蛇標準人們將它加諸在你身上使人們成了瘋子。有時候太極端了。看到女孩們有微整形手術相當普遍。這是他們的不好的部分。這扭曲了一些我們過去所擁有的價值觀。現在男人也做了整型手術。新聞標題甚至嚇到了我們大多數的人，一個英俊的男人想要作整型手術，他才能看起來更好看。人們評論著這不太對，他已經很好看了，或是我不懂他在想什麼。最後，這手術使他丟了生命。這是個極端的現代化現象。

Regardless of factors that determine how we look or where we are borne, we all need to look at what we can do, not what has been decided. The contrast between losers and winners is how their mind operates. Winners possess positive and optimistic attitudes. They are the ones who say "a handsome face doesn't provide daily bread and butter", "you will have more chances if you have a deep pocket", or "train yourself to stand out of the crowd, and you will be a shining star".

不論是什麼因素決定我們看起來如何或我們的出生為何，我們都需要將重點放在我們能做什麼而非已經無法改變的既定事實上。魯蛇和溫拿的差異在於他們心智是如何運作的。溫拿擁有著正向和樂觀的態度。他們有著「英俊的臉龐並不能提供生活所需」、「如果你口袋夠深的話你會有更多機會」或是「訓練你自己如何鶴立雞群你將成為閃耀之星」。

They are the ones who put themselves out there and commit 100%. Sometimes it's the arduous hard work that's hidden behind. Pure luck, good-looking, being borne into a wealthy family won't last long, if you don't know how to harness it. A one-time lottery winner can eventually be seen living under a bridge in the freezing winter night. We all need to redefine success and values of "losers and winners". We need to know what works best for ourselves and stay true to who we want to be, encountering life risks along the way.

他們將自己置身於該環境中且付出 **100%**的承諾。有時候是隱藏在背後所看不到的艱苦的努力。單純地運氣、長相好看和出生於富有家庭都經不起考驗，如果你不懂得如何駕馭它。曾是樂透贏家的人最終可能被發現在寒冷冬天裡在橋下度過。我們都必須重新定義成功和「魯蛇與溫拿」的價值觀。我們需要知道對我們來說什麼是最適合的，真實地面對我們的內心，迎接一路的人生風險。

▶▶ 影子跟讀「實戰練習」　🎧 MP3 096

　　此部分為**「影子跟讀實戰練習❷」**，請重新播放音檔並完成試題，除了能提升並修正拼寫能力外，也可以藉由音檔注意自己專注力和定位聽力訊息部份，走神或定位錯都會影響在實際考場中的表現，尤其在 section3 和 4 影響的得分會更明顯，現在就一起動身，開始完成**「實戰練習❷」**吧！

　　"Losers" is a term that used to refer to someone who has failed at doing certain things, but nowadays it incorporates multiple 1._____. This has led to some 2._____ in daily life, whether those are carried out on some websites, Facebook updates, or several key forums or in day-to-day conversations in the office. It is testing our limit to whether or not life will turn out to be 3._____, but the fact is life is always pushing us around. Some are earning a 4._____. Some are borne with a 5._____. Others have a gilded career ahead of them.

　　The 6._____ from a friend that you are earning a 22 k salary is also one of them. Being able to buy a house means you are heading to the 7._____ of your life whether it is because you are getting married and having kids so that there are enough 8._____ for them. It is also a 9._____ to your spouse that you have the ability to start a family.

It's a huge 10._____ for today's generation when it comes to buying a house. They don't want to spend money on 11._____. They have come up with more 12._____ as to why they can't or don't want to do that. It's the 13._____ when it comes to selecting a mate.

Another thing people use to value whether you are losers or not is the way you look. 14._____ or beautiful ladies are those people desire. People want beautiful things. In addition, it's a 15._____. People want to have a beautiful baby, and sometimes people are 16._____. Even if they don't look that good, they want their spouse to be that good, perhaps somewhat balancing what they are lacking on the 17._____.

But all these winner and loser values people place on you have turned people into 18._____. The news headline even shocked most of us that a handsome guy wants to have 19._____ so that he can be better-looking.

The contrast between losers and winners is how their mind operates. Winners possess positive and 20._____. They are the ones who say "a handsome face doesn't provide daily 21._____", "you will have more chances if you have a 22._____", or "train yourself to stand out of the crowd, and you will be a shining star".

They are the ones who put themselves out there and commit 100%. Sometimes it's the 23._____ that's hidden behind. Pure luck, good-looking, being borne into a wealthy family won't last long, if you don't know how to harness it. A one-time 24._____ can eventually be seen living under a bridge in the freezing winter night.

▶▶ 參考答案

1. contemporary phenomena	2. intriguing discussions
3. smooth sailing	4. meager salary
5. silver spoon	6. ridicule
7. next phase	8. rooms
9. commitment	10. burden
11. costlier things	12. explanations
13. traditional metrics	14. Handsome guys
15. hereditary trait	16. selfish
17. outside	18. lunatics
19. a plastic surgery	20. optimistic attitudes
21. bread and butter	22. deep pocket
23. arduous hard work	24. lottery winner

虛構世界的未來會是如何

此篇為**「影子跟讀實戰練習」**，此章節規劃了由聽**「實際考試長度的英文內容」**的 shadowing 練習，經由先前的兩個部份的練習，已經能逐步掌握跟聽一定句數的英文內容，現在經由實際考試長度的聽力內容來練習，讓耳朵適應聽這樣長度的英文內容，提升在考場時的答題穩定度和適應性，進而獲取理想成績，現在就一起動身，開始由聽**「實戰練習」**！（如果聽這部份且跟讀練習的難度還是太高請重複前兩個部份的練習數次後再來做這部分的練習喔！）

Ever since Sir Thomas More came up with the term "utopia" in the early 16th century, the unique genre has inspired abundant imagination from novelists and artists. The antonym of utopia, dystopia, also evolved into a literary genre. The origin of dystopia can be traced back to 1605. Both utopia and dystopia refer to the imagined future world. While utopia implies a place that is too good to be true, an ideal human existence that is virtually impossible to achieve, dystopia portrays a world full of darkness in which humans struggle to survive under the oppression of the government or advanced technology.

影子跟讀：「短對話」

影子跟讀：「短段落」

影子跟讀：「實戰練習」

雅思聽力必考字彙

　　自從湯瑪士‧摩爾爵士在十六世紀初期提出「烏托邦」一詞，這個獨特的類型激發了小說家和藝術家的豐富想像力。烏托邦的相反詞，反烏托邦，也演進成一個文學類型。反烏托邦的來源可被追溯到 1605 年。烏托邦和反烏托邦指的都是想像的未來世界。烏托邦暗示一個太好而不可能成真的地方，一個幾乎不可能達到的理想人類生存狀態，而反烏托邦描繪一個充滿黑暗的世界，在政府或高科技的的壓迫下，人類為了生存而掙扎。

　　The word "utopia" derived from Sir Thomas More's novel, *Utopia*, written in Latin in 1516 and translated into English in 1551. More made up this word by combining the Greek words "outopos", meaning "no place" and "eutopos", meaning "good place". Although nowadays the word generally means a perfect world, some experts argue that the connotation arose from misunderstanding More's original intention. More intended to emphasize fictionality, and thus the title simply meant "no place".

　　烏托邦一詞的來源是湯瑪士‧摩爾在 1516 年以拉丁文寫的小說烏托邦，此著作在 1551 年被翻譯成英文。摩爾將希臘文的"outopos"（意為「不存在之地」）和"eutopos"（意為「好地方」）合併，創造出這詞。雖然現在這詞通常指的是完美世界，有些專家主張這涵義是誤解了摩爾的原意。摩爾原本是著重在虛構性，因此書名只是單純表達「不存在之地」。

　　Despite various interpretations, most agree that utopia implies a perfect world which is unattainable, ironically a nowhere place. A much earlier example of utopia is Plato's *The Republic*, in which Plato depicted an ideal society reigned by philosopher-kings. The idea of utopia continued in the 18th and 19th centuries; for example, utopian traits were illustrated in Jonathan Swift's *Gulliver's Travels* and Samuel Butler's *Erewhon*, which is an anagram of the word "nowhere".

儘管有不同的詮釋，大部份的專家同意烏托邦暗喻的是一個不可能達到的完美世界，諷刺地也就是一個「不存在之地」。更早期的烏托邦例子是柏拉圖的《共和國》，柏拉圖描繪了一個由哲學家國王統治的理想社會。烏托邦的概念延續到十八和十九世紀；例如，強納森‧斯威夫特的《格列佛遊記》和山謬‧巴特勒的《烏有之鄉》都描繪了烏托邦特色，《烏有之鄉》這個字是「不存在之地」的顛倒重組字。

What are the characteristics of utopia? In More's book, he described a society with economic prosperity, a peaceful government and egalitarianism for civilians, which are the most obvious traits utopian fictions share. Moreover, technologies are applied to improve human living conditions, and independent thought and free flow of information are encouraged. Although government exists, citizens are united by a set of central ideas, while abiding by moral codes. The term government in a utopia state is very different from our idea of government in the present reality. The government in a utopia is loosely composed of citizenry, without complicated hierarchy. Furthermore, people revere nature and reverse the damage to ecology due to industrialization.

　　烏托邦的特色為何？在摩爾的書裡，他描述一個擁有繁榮經濟，祥和政府和公民平等的社會，這些是烏托邦小説共有的最明顯的特色。此外，科技被應用來改善人類的生活狀態，獨立的思考和資訊自由流通是被鼓勵的。雖然政府存在，公民是被一組中心思想所團結，同時他們遵守道德規範。烏托邦的政府一詞跟我們現在對政府的概念非常不同。烏托邦政府是由公民團體鬆散地組織而成，沒有複雜的階級制度。而且，人們尊敬大自然並反轉了工業化對生態造成的損害。

In today's popular culture, the idea of dystopia is gaining more popularity in young adult fiction and Hollywood movies, as the success of the novels and movies of *The Hunger Games* series has demonstrated. You might know the meaning of dystopia simply from the prefix dys-, implying a negative place with conditions opposite to utopia. In fact, we can trace the origin of dystopian literature way back to 1605, to a satire in Latin called *Mundus Alter et Idem*, meaning "an old world and a new", written by Joseph Hall, Bishop of Norwich, England. *An Old World and a New* satirizes life in London and customs of the Roman Catholic Church. It also served as an inspiration to Jonathan Swift's *Gulliver's Travels*.

　　在今日的流行文化中，反烏托邦的概念在青少年小説和好萊塢

影子跟讀：「短對話」

影子跟讀：「短段落」

影子跟讀：「實戰練習」

雅思聽力必考字彙

電影中越來越受歡迎，如同飢餓遊戲的小說和電影之成功已經證明了。你們可能從字首 dys- 就知道反烏托邦的意思，它暗示的是情況跟烏托邦相反的負面地方。事實上，我們能追溯反烏托邦文學的起源至 1605 年，是一本名為 Mundus Alter et Idem 的拉丁文諷刺小說，書名的意思是「一個舊世界和新世界」，作者是約瑟夫·霍爾，他是英國諾威治的主教。《一個舊世界和新世界》嘲諷倫敦的生活型態及羅馬天主教的習俗。這本書也啟發了強納森·斯威夫特的《格列佛遊記》。

Speaking of Jonathan Swift's *Gulliver's Travels*, some of you might consider it a utopian fiction. It is both utopian and dystopian. *Gulliver's Travels* illustrates utopian and dystopian places. Or a dystopia might be disguised as a utopia, forming an ambiguous genre. One example is Samuel Butler's *Erewhon*, which consists of utopian and dystopian traits. In the 20th century, the most famous dystopian fictions are probably Aldous Huxley's *Brave New World*, written in 1931 and George Orwell's *1984*, written in 1949.

提到強納森·斯威夫特的《格列佛遊記》，你們有些人可能把它視為烏托邦小說。它是烏托邦，也是反烏托邦小說。烏托邦和反烏托邦地區《格列佛遊記》都描述了。或者反烏托邦可能表面上假裝成烏托邦，形成一種模糊的文學類型。一例是在山謬·巴特勒的《烏有之鄉》裡，兩個種類的特色都並存。二十世紀最有名的反烏托邦小說應該是艾爾道斯·赫胥黎 1931 年的著作《美麗新世界》和喬治·歐威爾 1949 年的著作《1984》。

It is not hard to understand that the characteristics of dystopia contribute to its popularity in popular fiction and movies. Those characteristics tend to create tension and anxiety, factors that draw contemporary audience. Those include totalitarian control of citizens, a bureaucratic government, restriction of freedom and information, as well as constant surveillance on civilians with technologies. Civilians' individuality and equality are abolished, while a central head figure or bureaucracy exerts dictatorial control over the society. Other traits are associated with doomsday, such as poverty, hunger, and the destruction of nature.

不難理解，反烏托邦的特色導致了這個概念在流行小說和電影中非常普遍。那些特色會創造緊繃和焦慮感，這些都是吸引當代觀眾的因素。特色包括對公民的獨裁控制，官僚化政府，對自由和資訊的限制，及不斷用科技監視人民。人民的個人特色和平等權被剝奪了，而一位中央領導或官僚體系以獨裁方式控制社會。其他特色跟末日有關聯，例如貧窮，飢餓和對大自然的破壞。

An important reason that dystopia has drawn more attention and has become the recurrent themes in not only novels and movies but also TV series, comic books and computer games is that more and more people realize that it truthfully reflects what has been happening to humanity since the Industrial Revolution. In 2017, the Hollywood adaptation of Margaret Atwood's *The Handmaid's Tale*, published in 1985 and illustrating a dystopian patriarchal society, reminded us again that dystopian scenarios mirror human struggles in reality. Dystopia started off as a fictional genre, yet to our horror, many areas in reality have developed into the near-doomsday scenarios depicted in dystopian novels. It would be too naïve to shy away from the destruction of nature, the totalitarian government, the oppression of women's and minorities' rights, and the censorship of speech, which are all taking place around us.

　　另一個使反烏托邦吸引更多關注，且不斷在小說、電影、電視影集、漫畫和電玩反覆出現的重要原因是因為越來越多人認知反烏托邦真實地反映自從工業革命之後，持續對人類發生的事件。在 2017 年，好萊塢改編瑪格麗特·愛特伍的小說《侍女的故事》，這本小說在 1985 年出版，描述一個反烏托邦的父權社會。好萊塢的改編再次提醒我們反烏托邦的情境呼應了人們在現實的掙扎。反烏托邦最初是虛構類型，但讓人恐懼的是，現實許多方面已發展成反烏托邦小說裡描繪的近乎末日的情境。對大自然的破壞、極權專制政府、對女性及少數族群權力的壓迫和言論的箝制，採取視而不見的態度是太過天真，這些現象在我們周遭都正在發生。

▶▶ 影子跟讀「實戰練習」 🎧 MP3 097

此部分為「**影子跟讀實戰練習❷**」，請重新播放音檔並完成試題，除了能提升並修正拼寫能力外，也可以藉由音檔注意自己專注力和定位聽力訊息部份，走神或定位錯都會影響在實際考場中的表現，尤其在 section3 和 4 影響的得分會更明顯，現在就一起動身，開始完成「**實戰練習❷**」吧！

Ever since Sir Thomas More came up with the term "utopia" in the early 16th century, the unique 1._____ has inspired abundant imagination from novelists and artists. The origin of 2._____ can be traced back to 1605. The word "utopia" derived from Sir Thomas More's novel, *Utopia*, written in 3._____ in 1516. More made up this word by combining the Greek words "outopos", meaning "no place" and "eutopos", meaning "good place". Although nowadays the word generally means a perfect world, some experts argue that the 4._____ arose from misunderstanding More's original intention. More intended to emphasize 5._____, and thus the title simply meant "no place".

Despite various 6._____, most agree that utopia implies a perfect world which is unattainable, ironically a nowhere place. What are the characteristics of utopia? In More's book, he described a society with 7._____, a peaceful government and egal-

影子跟讀：「短對話」

影子跟讀：「短段落」

影子跟讀：「實戰練習」

雅思聽力必考字彙

itarianism for civilians, which are the most obvious traits utopian fictions share. Moreover, 8._____ are applied to improve human living conditions, and independent thought and free flow of information are encouraged.

The government in a utopia is loosely composed of 9._____, without complicated 10._____. You might know the meaning of dystopia simply from the 11._____ dys-, implying a negative place with conditions opposite to utopia. In fact, we can trace the 12._____ of dystopian literature way back to 1605, to a 13._____ in Latin called *Mundus Alter et Idem*, meaning "an old world and a new", written by Joseph Hall, Bishop of Norwich, England. *An Old World and a New* satirizes life in 14._____ and customs of the Roman Catholic Church. One example is Samuel Butler's *Erewhon*, which consists of utopian and dystopian 15._____. It is not hard to understand that the characteristics of dystopia contribute to its 16._____ in popular fiction and movies. Those characteristics tend to create tension and anxiety, factors that draw 17._____. Those include totalitarian control of 18._____, a bureaucratic government, restriction of 19._____ and information, as well as constant 20._____ on civilians with technologies. Civilians' individuality and equality are abolished, while a central head figure or 21._____ exerts dictatorial control over the society. Other traits are associated with doomsday, such as 22._____, hunger, and the destruction of nature. In 2017, the Hollywood adaptation of Margaret Atwood's *The Handmaid's Tale*, published in 1985 and illustrating a dystopian 23._____, reminded us again that dystopian scenarios mirror human struggles in reality. It would be too naïve to shy away from the destruction of nature, the totalitarian government, the oppression of women's and 24._____, and the censorship of speech, which are all taking place around us.

▶▶ 參考答案

1. genre	2. dystopia
3. Latin	4. connotation
5. fictionality	6. interpretations
7. economic prosperity	8. technologies
9. citizenry	10. hierarchy
11. prefix	12. origin
13. satire	14. London
15. traits	16. popularity
17. contemporary audiences	18. citizens
19. freedom	20. surveillance
21. bureaucracy	22. poverty
23. patriarchal society	24. minorities' rights

影子跟讀：「短對話」

影子跟讀：「短段落」

影子跟讀：「實戰練習」

雅思聽力必考字彙

動物和視頻

▶ 影子跟讀「實戰練習」中標 MP3 098

此篇為**「影子跟讀實戰練習」**，此章節規劃了由聽**「實際考試長度的英文內容」**的 shadowing 練習，經由先前的兩個部份的練習，已經能逐步掌握跟聽一定句數的英文內容，現在經由實際考試長度的聽力內容來練習，讓耳朵適應聽這樣長度的英文內容，提升在考場時的答題穩定度和適應性，進而獲取理想成績，現在就一起動身，開始由聽**「實戰練習」**！（如果聽這部份且跟讀練習的難度還是太高請重複前兩個部份的練習數次後再來做這部分的練習喔！）

It has been known that prolonged viewing on the screens of smartphones and computers has caused a widespread concern among educators and parents since it has a detrimental effect on our health. Blue light from these digital devices does cause eye strain, but warnings from the news headlines or health-conscious parents and educators have a very insignificant influence on users of digital devices. What prevents them from doing so has a lot to do with intriguing commercials, appealing footage, and user habits.

眾所皆知，長期觀看智慧型手機和電腦已引起教育者和家長廣泛的關心，因為這對我們的健康會造成有害影響。這些數位裝置的藍

光的確會導致眼睛疲勞，但來自新聞頭條或關注健康的家長及教育者的警告對數位裝置的使用者沒有顯著影響，原因跟有趣的廣告、吸引人的影片及使用者習慣有關。

As competition among companies has become more and more competitive, it is not uncommon for those companies to lure consumers by using innovative technologies or eye-catching videos. A video footage of a blue lobster moving in an aquarium will soon capture the eyes of viewers. The surge of viewers will sooner or later generate more profits for the company. The number of viewers and people who click the like button will be the measurement for ad companies to decide whether this video will bring profits and generate orders.

隨著公司間的競爭越來越激烈，那些公司用創新科技或引人注目的影片吸引消費者是很普遍的。在水族館裡移動的藍色龍蝦影片很快地就能捕捉觀眾的目光。觀眾數量的暴增遲早會替公司帶來更多利潤。觀眾數量和按讚的人數將是廣告公司用來決定這段影片是否能帶來利潤並產生訂單的測量方式。

In addition, novelty also has a say in the viewing population. Among all video footage, animals are by far one of the most interesting to viewers. It is said that animals with a novelty not only add colors to the entire video, but soon generate hit after hit, which is what clients want. They want significant hits within an hour or less. The less time taken, the better.

　　此外，新奇的內容也能決定觀賞者的族群。目前在所有影片中，動物對觀賞者是最有趣的。據說帶有新奇元素的動物不但增加整部影片的趣味，也很快地產生點閱率，而這也是顧客要的。他們想要一小時或更短時間內有大量點閱。花的時間越少越好。

Brown bears have long been known as one of the popular footages among animal videos. Whether it is a warming scene that a mother bear takes her cubs to the river basin, trying to teach them how to fish or several cubs playing along the river bank, the scene is undoubtedly enjoyable. Brown bears inhabit a wide range of habitats. They are omnivorous, and they live in places where foods are abundant. People often associate brown bears with salmon and trout. Footages of brown bears in inland rivers and coastal regions catching salmon are also eye-catching. Torrents won't stop them from going out since salmons offer a rich source of nutrition which enables them to store enough fats, grow to an enormous size, and sustain harsh weather conditions.

　　在動物影片中，棕熊一直是比較受歡迎的影片。不管是母熊帶著幼熊到河床試著教他們捕魚，或幾隻幼熊在河岸玩耍的溫馨影片，這場景絕對是令人愉快的。棕熊棲息在各式各樣的棲息地。他們是雜食性動物，並住在食物豐盛的地區。人們常將棕熊和鮭魚及鱒魚聯想在一起。棕熊在內陸河流和海岸地區捕捉鮭魚的影片也有吸引力。湍流不會阻擋他們，因為鮭魚提供充足的營養來源，讓他們能儲存足夠

脂肪、成長至巨大尺寸並抵抗惡劣的天氣情況。

Despite the cuteness and popularity of brown bears, they can sometimes be very naughty invaders. Invasion into people's houses is not rare. There is footage of them breaking into houses searching for food. Other footage also brings the safety issue to the table. Some brown bears routinely show up in the parks near their habitats, eating dumpster foods perhaps due to habitat destruction and many other factors that result in a scarcity of food.

儘管棕熊可愛又受歡迎，他們有時是非常調皮的侵略者。入侵房屋並不少見，有他們入侵房屋尋找食物的影片。其他影片也引起安全議題。有些棕熊規律地出現在他們的棲息地附近的公園，他們吃垃圾桶裡的食物，可能是因為棲息地被破壞及其他許多導致食物稀少的原因。

In addition, there are other videos that show another side of brown bears that is contrary to popular belief. One of these footages shows that the brown bear invaded a house, playing a piano rather than stealing foods. It also brings numerous hits in less than an hour. People have commented that perhaps brown bears have a talent for music or that's just a playful side of them.

此外，有其他影片顯示與大眾想法相反的，棕熊的另一面。其中一部影片顯示棕熊入侵房子是在彈鋼琴而不是偷食物。這部影片在

一小時內帶來許多點擊。有人評論或許棕熊有音樂的才華或那只是他們好玩的一面。

Another kind of bear also occupies the hearts of millions of people worldwide: raccoons. They live in lowland deciduous forests, related forests along the shore or wetlands so they are able to find abundant foods, such as amphibians and crustaceans. The nimbleness and agility of raccoons is also well-known. The dexterous forelimbs allow them to perform behaviors that are highly unlikely for other creatures.

另一種熊也佔據世界上百萬人的心：浣熊。他們住在低地落葉森林、沿岸邊的森林或濕地，這樣他們能找到充足的食物，例如兩棲動物和甲殼類動物。浣熊也以機靈和敏捷出名。他們敏捷的前肢讓他們能進行其他動物很難進行的行為。

They are also known for their habitual hand washing behavior. Examining and washing an item they receive or catch is one of the reasons why they are favorites among viewers. Footage of raccoons washing cotton candy makes people laugh. People have a sense of sudden euphoria after watching the film perhaps due to the confused look of the raccoon. Repeatedly handing over the cotton candy to the raccoon seems no use. Cotton candy soon dissolves and disappears. Washing a tangible object won't have those hilarious effects, one viewer commented.

浣熊也以習慣性的洗手動作知名。檢視並清洗他們收到或抓到的物品是他們成為觀眾最愛的原因之一。浣熊清洗棉花糖的影片讓人發笑。可能是因為浣熊困惑的表情，人們看完這影片突然有欣喜的感覺。不斷拿棉花糖給浣熊似乎沒用。棉花糖很快融化並消失。一位觀賞者評論，如果浣熊是在清洗實體物品就不會有令人捧腹大笑效果。

Despite their unique charm and cuteness, there are concerns for approaching raccoons or adopting raccoons as pets. Some footage shows raccoons aggressively rob people of their things near the river bank. Some had a less pleasant memory with these creatures. In addition, they carry rabies. Early symptoms of rabies through the bite show little or no sign, which scares parents. Transmission of rabies also raises concerns for related authorities. People really need to give some serious thought when it comes to adopting them as pets.

儘管浣熊可愛，有獨特的魅力，靠近他們或養來當寵物有需要注意的地方。有些影片顯示浣熊在河岸邊有攻擊性地搶奪人們的物品。有些人對這些動物的回憶不是很愉快。而且，他們有狂犬病。被咬之後感染到狂犬病，早期症狀幾乎或完全沒有徵兆，這讓家長感到害怕。狂犬病的散播也引起相關政府官員重視。提到養浣熊當寵物，人們真的需要認真思考。

There are always moments that we feel excited or warm soon after we watch certain animal videos. Whatever messages they convey, it is important for us to have the ability to judge whether or not the decision we made (e.g. adopting a raccoon) is sensible. Another factor that we need to take into account is our safety. Animals all have a wild side in them. Animals' long exposure to human influence does not seem to reduce their wild nature. That animals in captivity killed the person who raised them or was very close to them is not unheard of.

　　我們看完某些動物影片後，總是有感到興奮或溫馨的時光。不管它們傳遞什麼訊息，擁有判斷我們做的決定是否明智的能力是重要的，例如養一隻浣熊。另一個要考慮的因素是安全。動物都有野性。動物長期暴露在人類的影響下似乎不會降低他們的野性。被豢養的動物殺死養大他們的人或跟他們很親近的人，這種事時有所聞。

▶▶ 影子跟讀「實戰練習」　🎧 MP3 098

此部分為**「影子跟讀實戰練習❷」**，請重新播放音檔並完成試題，除了能提升並修正拼寫能力外，也可以藉由音檔注意自己專注力和定位聽力訊息部份，走神或定位錯都會影響在實際考場中的表現，尤其在 section3 和 4 影響的得分會更明顯，現在就一起動身，開始完成**「實戰練習❷」**吧！

It has been known that 1._____ on the screens of smartphones and computers has caused a widespread concern among educators and parents since it has a detrimental effect on our health. 2._____ from these digital devices does cause 3._____.

As competition among companies has become more and more competitive, it is not uncommon for those companies to lure 4._____ by using innovative technologies or eye-catching videos. A video footage of 5._____ moving in an 6._____ will soon capture the eyes of viewers. The 7._____ of viewers will sooner or later generate more profits for the company. The number of viewers and people who click the 8._____ will be the measurement for ad companies to decide whether this video will bring profits and generate orders.

In addition, 9._____ also has a say in the viewing population. 10._____ have long been known as one of the popular footages among animal videos. Whether it is a warming scene that a mother bear takes her cubs to the 11._____, trying to teach them how to fish or several cubs playing along the river bank, the scene is undoubtedly enjoyable. Brown bears inhabit a wide range of 12._____. They are 13._____, and they live in places where foods are abundant. People often associate brown bears with salmon and 14._____. Footages of brown bears in inland rivers and 15._____ catching salmon are also eye-catching. Torrents won't stop them from going there since salmons offer a rich source of 16._____ which enables them to store enough fats, grow to an enormous size, and sustain harsh weather condi-tions.

17._____ into people's houses is not rare. Other footages also bring the 18._____ to the table.

In addition, there are other videos that show another side of brown bears that is contrary to popular belief. One of these footages shows that the brown bear invaded a house, playing 19._____ rather than stealing foods.

They live in 20._____, related for-ests along the shore or wetlands so they are able to find abundant foods, such as 21._____. The 22._____ allow them to perform behaviors that are highly unlikely for other creatures.

Footage of raccoons washing cotton candy makes people laugh. People have a sense of 23.＿＿＿＿＿＿＿＿＿ after watching the film perhaps due to the confused look of the raccoon. Some had a less pleasant memory with these creatures. 24.＿＿＿＿＿＿＿＿＿ also raises concerns for related authorities.

▶▶ 參考答案

1. prolonged viewing	2. Blue light
3. eye strain	4. consumers
5. a blue lobster	6. aquarium
7. surge	8. like button
9. novelty	10. Brown bears
11. river basin	12. habitats
13. omnivorous	14. trout
15. coastal regions	16. nutrition
17. Invasion	18. safety issue
19. piano	20. lowland deciduous forests
21. amphibians and crustaceans	22. dexterous forelimbs
23. sudden euphoria	24. Transmission of rabies

影子跟讀：「短對話」

影子跟讀：「短段落」

影子跟讀：「實戰練習」

雅思聽力必考字彙

電影和環境保護

▶▶ 影子跟讀「實戰練習」　🎧 MP3 099

　　此篇為**「影子跟讀實戰練習」**，此章節規劃了由聽**「實際考試長度的英文內容」**的 shadowing 練習，經由先前的兩個部份的練習，已經能逐步掌握跟聽一定句數的英文內容，現在經由實際考試長度的聽力內容來練習，讓耳朵適應聽這樣長度的英文內容，提升在考場時的答題穩定度和適應性，進而獲取理想成績，現在就一起動身，開始由聽**「實戰練習」**！（如果聽這部份且跟讀練習的難度還是太高請重複前兩個部份的練習數次後再來做這部分的練習喔！）

　　As the awareness of environmental protection has been popularized around the world, protecting endangered species and preserving natural resources have become the mainstream topics in not only school education but also the mass media. Among the various forms of media, commercial films probably are the most powerful medium to convey the message of green awareness to all strata of the society. Viewers can learn about environmental protection while enjoying the entertaining experience. This crucial topic has been covered in virtually all film genres, such as *Avatar*, a 3D sci-fi and global blockbuster in 2009, *Happy Feet*, an animated musical comedy, *Erin Brockovich*, an adaptation of the story about an environmental activist's anti-pollution lawsuit against Pacific Gas & Electric (PG&E), and *An Inconvenient Truth*, a documentary presented by former American vice president, Al Gore, on the threats of global warming.

　　隨著環保意識在全球普及，保護瀕臨絕種動物和維護自然資源在學校教育和大眾媒體上已變成主流議題。在各式各樣的媒體中，商業片可能是傳遞環保意識到社會各階層的最有力媒介。觀眾能一邊享受娛樂經驗，一邊學習關於環保的事物。這個重要議題幾乎所有的電影類型都有著墨，例如《阿凡達》，這部 2009 年的全球賣座 3D 科幻片，動畫音樂喜劇《快樂腳》，改編自環保人士對抗 PG&E 的反污染官司的《艾琳·波洛克維奇》，及《不願面對的真相》，這部由美國前副總統高爾呈現，關於全球暖化威脅的記錄片。

Among the natural resources that are being depleted by human activities, tropical rainforests are in dire need of preservation. We should save tropical rainforests for not only ecological preservation, but also the protection of indigenous peoples whose cultures are inseparable from tropical rainforests.

　　在被人類活動消耗的自然資源中，熱帶雨林需要迫切的保育。我們應該保護熱帶雨林，不只是為了生態保育，也是為了保護原住民族群，原住民族群的生活型態及文化跟熱帶雨林密不可分。

Tropical rainforests are indispensable in stabilizing the

影子跟讀：「短對話」

影子跟讀：「短段落」

影子跟讀：「實戰練習」

雅思聽力必考字彙

water cycle, reducing greenhouse gases, and hosting over 50% of the plant and animal species on the earth, which serves crucial function during the Anthropocene. Since the inception of industrialization in the 19th century, the amount of greenhouse gases has reached an unprecedented height, indicating the urgency in saving rainforests. Yet, the deforestation of tropical rainforests is happening at an alarming rate, which has deprived numerous terrestrial species of their home. Without trees that absorb carbon dioxide and generate oxygen, of which 40% is generated by tropical forests, the greenhouse effect will only deteriorate drastically. With fewer trees to help maintain the equilibrium of the water cycle, humans will face more droughts.

熱帶雨林在穩定水循環，減少溫室氣體，和提供地球上超過50%的植物和動物物種的棲息地等方面是不可或缺的，這在人類世紀元提供關鍵的功能。自從十九世紀工業化起始，溫室氣體總量已經達到前所未有的最高點，顯示了保護雨林的急迫性。然而，熱帶雨林的砍伐以驚人的速度正在進行，也剝奪了許多地棲物種的家。沒有樹群吸收二氧化碳及產生氧氣，且 40%的氧氣是由熱帶雨林產生，溫室效應只會更劇烈惡化。能幫助維持水循環平衡的樹減少了，人類未來將面對更多旱災。

Moreover, the destruction of tropical rainforests is as threatening as the annihilation of species in the movie, *Avatar*. The director of *Avatar*, James Cameron, has publicly acknowledged that the setting of the movie mirrors the Brazilian rainforest and that what happens in the movie is real to numerous indigenous peoples living there. For example, the Brazilian government is building the world's third largest dam, which will flood a vast wildlife habitat in the Amazon and force 40,000 residents to relocate. Worse yet, uprooting the indigenous peoples from their homeland equals destroying their culture.

此外，熱帶雨林的破壞就如同電影《阿凡達》裡的物種滅絕一樣令人感到威脅。《阿凡達》的導演詹姆士‧克麥隆曾公開表示這部電影的場景呼應了巴西的雨林，而且電影裡發生的事對許多住在那裏的原住民族群而言是真實的。例如，巴西政府正在建造世界上第三大的水壩，完成後將會淹沒亞馬遜雨林廣大的野生動物棲息地，並強迫四萬人牽移。更糟糕的是，將原住民族群從他們的家鄉連根拔起等同於摧毀他們的文化。

Tropical rainforests have been described by scientists as the lungs of the earth, and thus it is not difficult to envisage that just as dysfunctional human lungs will induce life-threatening peril, the massive destruction of tropical rainforests will cause a devastating effect on the earth.

熱帶雨林被科學家描述為地球的肺，因此不難想像正如同功能失調的肺會導致威脅生命的危險，對熱帶雨林的大量破壞將導致地球上毀滅性的效應。

Another area of focus is the competition between economic development and the protection of endangered species, which has been going on for decades. Developing an industry should not take precedence over saving the environment for endangered species as destroying natural environment will eventually take its toll on humans in the long run.

　　另一個受到關注的面向是經濟發展及保護瀕臨絕種動物間的競爭，這種競爭已經持續了數十年。我不同意發展產業應該優先於保護瀕臨絕種動物的環境，因為我相信摧毀自然環境最終會讓人類付出代價。

　　First, the infliction on humans due to damaging environment for endangered animals is conspicuous, considering the predicaments of polar bears in the Arctic and emperor penguins in Antarctica. Due to rapid industrialization in the past century, global warming has exacerbated drastically. As a result, polar bears, which spend more time at sea hunting than on land, have suffered from the melting of Arctic ice, forcing them to swim for a longer distance in search of food. What's worse, the shrinkage of the hunting area caused the reduction of seals, polar bears' major prey, which is also affected by commercial overfishing. If industries can take more actions to alleviate global warming, not only human condition will be relieved by the decline of air pollution, but also marine ecology will be better preserved.

　　首先，考慮到北極熊和南極洲帝王企鵝的困境，就能得知破壞瀕臨絕種動物的環境明顯地導致人類磨難。因為過去一世紀的急速工業化，全球暖化的現象已劇烈地惡化。因此，由於北極冰層溶化，花較多時間在海裡狩獵的北極熊備受折磨，牠們被迫覓食時游更長的距離。更糟糕的是，狩獵區域的縮減導致海豹減少，海豹是北極熊主要的獵物，而海豹減少也是受到漁業的影響。如果產業能採取更多行動減緩全球暖化，不只人類生存的狀態會因為空污減少而獲得舒緩，海洋生態也能獲得更佳的保育。

　　Furthermore, emperor penguins in Antarctica have been threatened by the fishing industry. Emperor penguins are not only deprived of their prey, fish and krill, but also jeopardized by climate change, oil spills, and eco-tourism. The decrease of emperor penguins did not draw public attention until the movie, *Happy Feet*, featured an emperor penguin embarking upon a journey to find out why fish was dwindling. The reason is exactly overfishing. The example indicates that the aforementioned industry harms endangered species, altering the food chain, which will eventually harm humans as we are at the top of the food chain.

　　此外，南極洲帝王企鵝一直遭受漁業威脅。不只帝王企鵝的獵物，魚和磷蝦，被剝奪了，帝王企鵝也因氣候變遷，漏油事件和生態觀光而陷入危險。直到《快樂腳》這部電影描繪一隻帝王企鵝展開旅程以找出為何魚量一直減少，帝王企鵝數量的減少才獲得大眾的注意。原因就是過量捕魚。這個例子顯示上述產業傷害瀕臨絕種的動物，改變了食物鏈，而最終將會傷害人類，因為我們處於食物鏈的最

頂端。

Last but not least, since 70% of the earth is covered by ocean, if industries continue damaging marine ecology, it is not difficult to envisage a devastating future for human environment. If we preserve environment for endangered animals, humans might live with them reciprocally.

最後，既然地球的 70%的表面被海洋覆蓋，如果產業繼續損害海洋生態，不難想像出一個對人類環境而言，毀滅性的未來。如果我們保育瀕臨絕種動物的環境，人類可能與動物可以互惠共存。

Movies could be a driving force for the spread of eco-friendly ideas. With 3D animation, enticing plot, and special effects, these ideas are easily comprehensible and highly entertaining to all kinds of viewers despite the differences among their racial, cultural, educational and economic backgrounds. An even more significant message from the movie industry is that protecting mother earth and ensuring human survival are two sides of the same coin. As the bellwether in the movie industry, Hollywood exerts immense influence across borders, and even famous Hollywood movie stars take on the responsibility to promote the importance of environmental protection and preserving natural resources. For example, to equalize water resource access, Matt Damon and Gary White cofounded a charity, Water.org, which educates people on the importance of water resource, and builds water and sanitation facilities in destitute regions, proving that human existence can be elevated by a single act of philanthropy. With constructive solutions, it is not too late to help mother earth recover from industrial damages and the threats of climate changes.

　　電影可能成為推廣環保觀念的動力。伴隨著 3D 動畫，扣人心弦的劇情和特效，這些觀念對所有觀眾都容易理解，而且具備高度的娛樂性，儘管觀眾的種族，文化，教育及經濟背景有所差異。一個來自電影業更重要的訊息是保護地球和確保人類生存是一體兩面。作為電影業的領頭羊，好萊塢能穿越界限施展廣泛的影響力，好萊塢知名影星甚至已負起提倡環保和維護自然資源的責任。例如，麥特‧戴蒙和蓋瑞‧懷特共同成立 Water.org 這個慈善機構，目的是使水資源的取得平等化，這個慈善機構教育人們水資源的重要性，並在赤貧地區建造取水和衛生設施，證明了單一慈善行動能提升人類生存的狀態。若有建設性的解決方案，幫助地球從工業損害及氣候變遷的威脅中恢復還不會太遲。

影子跟讀：「短對話」

影子跟讀：「短段落」

影子跟讀：「實戰練習」

雅思聽力必考字彙

此部分為 **「影子跟讀實戰練習❷」**，請重新播放音檔並完成試題，除了能提升並修正拼寫能力外，也可以藉由音檔注意自己專注力和定位聽力訊息部份，走神或定位錯都會影響在實際考場中的表現，尤其在 section3 和 4 影響的得分會更明顯，現在就一起動身，開始完成 **「實戰練習❷」** 吧！

Among the various forms of media, 1._____ probably are the most 2._____ to convey the message of green awareness to all strata of the society. This crucial topic has been covered in virtually all 3._____, such as *Avatar*, a 3D sci-fi and 4._____ in 2009, *Happy Feet*, an 5._____, *Erin Brockovich*, an adaptation of the story about an environmental activist's 6._____ against Pacific Gas & Electric (PG&E), and *An Inconvenient Truth*, a 7._____ presented by former American vice president, Al Gore, on the threats of global warming.

Among the natural resources that are being depleted by human activities, 8._____ are in dire need of preservation. We should save tropical rainforests for not only ecological preservation, but also the protection of 9._____ whose cultures are inseparable from tropical rainforests.

Tropical rainforests are indispensable in stabilizing the water cycle, reducing 10._____, and hosting over 50% of the plant and animal species on the earth. Since the inception of 11._____ in the 19th century, the amount of greenhouse gases has reached an unprecedented height, indicating the 12._____ to save rainforests. Yet, the 13._____ of tropical rainforests is happening at an alarming rate, which has deprived numerous 14._____ of their home. Without trees that absorb 15._____ and generate oxygen, of which 40% is generated by tropical forests, the greenhouse effect will only deteriorate drastically. With fewer trees to help maintain the 16._____ of the water cycle, humans will face more 17._____.

Moreover, the destruction of tropical rainforests is as threatening as the 18._____ of species in the movie, *Avatar*.

First, the infliction on humans due to damaging environment for endangered animals is conspicuous, considering the predicaments of 19._____ in the Arctic and emperor penguins in Antarctica. What's worse, the shrinkage of the hunting area caused the reduction of 20._____, polar bears' major prey, which is also affected by 21._____.

The example indicates that the aforementioned industry harms endangered species, altering the 22._____, which will eventually harm humans as we are at the top of the food chain.

An even more significant message from the movie industry is that protecting mother earth and ensuring human survival are two sides of the same coin. For example, to equalize 23._____, Matt Damon and Gary White cofounded a charity, Water.org, which educates people on the importance of water resource, and builds water and 24._____ in destitute regions, proving that human existence can be elevated by a single act of philanthropy.

▶▶ 參考答案

1. commercial films	2. powerful medium
3. film genres	4. global blockbuster
5. animated musical comedy	6. anti-pollution lawsuit
7. documentary	8. tropical rainforests
9. indigenous peoples	10. greenhouse gases
11. industrialization	12. urgency
13. deforestation	14. terrestrial species
15. carbon dioxide	16. equilibrium
17. droughts	18. annihilation
19. polar bears	20. seals
21. commercial overfishing	22. food chain
23. water resource access	24. sanitation facilities

無尾熊

▶▶ **影子跟讀「實戰練習」**　🎧 MP3 100

此篇為「**影子跟讀實戰練習**」，此章節規劃了由聽「**實際考試長度的英文內容**」的 shadowing 練習，經由先前的兩個部份的練習，已經能逐步掌握跟聽一定句數的英文內容，現在經由實際考試長度的聽力內容來練習，讓耳朵適應聽這樣長度的英文內容，提升在考場時的答題穩定度和適應性，進而獲取理想成績，現在就一起動身，開始由聽「**實戰練習**」！（如果聽這部份且跟讀練習的難度還是太高請重複前兩個部份的練習數次後再來做這部分的練習喔！）

Koalas are recognised as a symbol of Australia, but the species face many threats in this modernised world. Land exploitation in areas where koalas used to live has posed various risks to this cute creature. Urbanization is depriving and fragmenting koala habitat; human-induced threats such as vehicle strikes or domestic dog attacks are also threatening koala's life. It is also believed the increasing prevalence of koala's diseases are to some extent due to the stress caused by human activities.

無尾熊是澳洲的象徵，但是此物種在現代化世界中面臨許多威

脅。無尾熊過去棲息的地方遭受的土地過度利用，這對這個可愛的生物造成不同的風險威脅。都市化正剝奪和肢解著無尾熊的棲息地。人類引起的威脅像是汽車攻擊或家庭飼養的狗攻擊正威脅著無尾熊的生命。據說，無尾熊疾病的逐漸盛行某些程度上是由於人類活動所引起的壓力。

Some koalas live in the sanctuary where they are cared for by experienced staff. While most koalas live in the wild, they are easily recognized by their appearance and the habitat they are from. Koalas may be given a nickname by local residents if they show up frequently in the neighborhood, so they are more like human's pets rather than wild animals. People enjoy seeing koalas and they make a lot of effort to protect them, such as planting trees and controlling their dogs.

有些無尾熊生活在保護區，在那裡受到具經驗的員工照顧著。雖然大多數的無尾熊生活在野外，能由外表輕易地辨識出它們和它們所處的棲息所在地。如果它們頻繁地出現在社區的話，當地居民可能給予無尾熊暱稱。所以，它們更像是人類的寵物而非野生動物。人們喜愛看到無尾熊而且他們為了保護無尾熊做了許多努力，例如植樹和控制他們的狗狗。

The biggest threat to the koala's existence is habitat destruction, and following this, the most serious threat is death from car hits. I'm going to talk about the koala and the car accident. A koala hit by a vehicle could be killed straight away or suffered from serious injuries. The figure from the Australian Wildlife Hospital and another koala rescue center shows that 3792 koalas were taken to hospitals between 1997 and 2008, and 85% of the injured koalas died after emergency procedures. This number is only the ones that have been calculated, so at least more than 300 koalas are killed each year by motor vehicles.

　　無尾熊生存最大的威脅是棲地破壞,接續這個的原因,最嚴重的威脅是汽車撞擊造成的死亡。我即將會談論到無尾熊和汽車意外。無尾熊被汽車撞到時可能即刻死亡或著遭受到嚴重的傷害。澳洲野生生物醫院和另一個無尾熊拯救中心的數據顯示出在 1997 年到 2008 年間有 3792 隻無尾熊帶往醫院且 85%的受傷無尾熊在緊急程序後死亡。這個僅是已經計算過後的數字,所以至少超過 300 隻無尾熊在每年因汽車意外而死亡。

On June 11 2015, a 6-month-old baby koala clung to his mother during her life-saving surgery after she was hit by a car in Brisbane, Australia. The photo of the baby koala with Lizzy has attracted thousands of views. The mother Lizzy suffered severe injuries including facial trauma and a collapsed lung. The baby koala stayed by his mom's side throughout the entire operation. Luckily Lizzy started recovering after the surgery. How to prevent this kind of situation from happening in the first place has raised public awareness.

　　在 2015 年 6 月 11 日,在牠母親於澳洲的布里斯本受到汽車撞

擊後，六個月大的無尾熊，在母親的急救手術期間緊抓著他母親。無尾熊嬰兒的照片與麗茲以吸引了數千的觀看數。母親麗茲遭受到嚴重的傷害，包含臉部創傷和肺部衰竭。無尾熊嬰兒在整個手術期間都待在自己母親身旁。幸運地是，麗茲在手術後開始康復。首先關於如何使這樣的情況免於發生已經引起大眾的意識。

The Australia government has made a good effort to protect koala from car accidents. When you drive in Queensland, sometimes you can see an overpass built on top of a road. The over-bridge is the koala-crossing infrastructure. The state government has made guidelines for koala safety and required in areas where traffic flow poses risks to koalas, facilities assisting safe koala movement should be built.

澳洲政府已經做了充分的努力來保護無尾熊免於汽車意外。當你行駛在昆士蘭州，有時候你可以目睹在道路上方的高架橋。高架橋是無尾熊跨越的交通建設。州政府對於無尾熊的安全已經制定了指導方針而且要求交通流動會對於無尾熊造成威脅的地區，應該要建造協助無尾熊能安全移動的設施。

At individual level, although it may seem that there is not much we can do since the wild animals cannot be restricted from rushing out onto a road. There are still several things drivers can do to protect koalas, including obeying the speed limit, watching for koala crossing signs, slowing down if seen koalas crossing, especially during the night, and reporting injured or dead koalas if seen one. Wild-life-friendly driving would benefit koalas. The risk of hitting can be reduced by avoiding driving in areas where koalas appear. Driving slowly within the speed limit and scanning the roadside for anything that may move onto the road have a significant preventive effect.

在個人階段，儘管可能看起來沒有甚麼我們所能做的，因為無法限制野生動物不往路上衝去。仍有幾件事是駕駛能做以保護無尾熊的，包括遵守速限、觀看無尾熊跨越標誌、如果看到無尾熊跨越道路時減速，特別是在夜晚的時候，且如果看到時，舉報受傷或死亡的無尾熊。對野生生物友善的駕駛對無尾熊有益。在無尾熊出現的地方，它們被撞到的風險會因此而降低。在速限內緩慢駕駛和掃描道路旁的任何可能出現在道路中的物件對於預防有顯著的成效。

Koalas can sleep up to twenty hours per day and not come to the ground very often. However, nowadays their habitat is fragmented by development. So they have to cross roads to reach some of the food trees. Koala crossing signs are a good indicator to inform drivers that have entered koala's territory. The peak time for them to move across road is most likely to be between July and September usually during the night. If driving through koala habitat during 'koala peak hour', drivers should slow down and check the roadside for koalas and other wild animals.

無尾熊每天能睡長達 20 小時且不常來到地面上。然而，現今它

們的棲息地受到土地開發而支離破碎了。所以它們必須要越過道路抵達一些有食物的樹上。無尾熊跨越的標誌是告知駕駛已抵達無尾熊領域的一項好的指標。對他們來說，越過道路的尖峰時刻最有可能是在七月和九月間，通常發生在夜晚。如果在無尾熊頂峰時刻行駛在無尾熊棲地，駕駛應該要減速且查看道路旁是否有無尾熊和其他野生動物。

During the night, koalas crossing the road have shining eyes. Their eyes reflect the headlights of coming vehicles, which should alert drivers. Driving slowly will give drivers enough time to reflect and avoid the hit. Animals' action can be unpredictable since they might become temporarily blind when confronted by bright light at night, but slowing down can give them time to get off the road.

在夜晚，無尾熊越過道路會有眼睛閃耀的情況。它們的眼睛對通行的車輛的車頭燈會反射出光亮，此能提醒駕駛。緩慢行駛會給予駕駛足夠的時間去反應和避免撞擊。動物的行動會難以預測，因為當在夜晚時遭遇到亮光時，它們可能轉變成短暫性地失明，但減速能給予他們更多的時間離開道路。

What can people do if they see a koala accidentally or encounter an injured koala? It is recommended carrying an old towel or blanket in the car. So the injured koala could be wrapped and moved out off the road. In addition, local wild-life care groups or vet surgeons can be contacted. Most importantly, people should always consider their own safety

影子跟讀：「短對話」

影子跟讀：「短段落」

影子跟讀：「實戰練習」

雅思聽力必考字彙

before intervening, cars need to be parked safely with hazard lights on to alert other drivers. Call the wildlife care groups if you are unsure what actions to take. People who are interested in caring for sick koalas can even attend certain training programs on wildlife rehabilitation to get useful information.

　　如果人們意外地看到無尾熊或遇到受傷的無尾熊，該怎麼辦呢？建議在車子裡攜帶舊毛巾或毯子。如此一來，受傷的無尾熊就能包裹在裏頭或從道路中移開。此外，能連繫當地的野生生物照護團體或外科獸醫。更重要地是，人們應該在干預前，總先考量到自身安全，汽車需要安全地停靠以危急燈警示其他駕駛。致電野生生物照護團體，如果你確定該採取的行動。人們對於照護生病的無尾熊有興趣的話甚至能夠參加特定的野生動物復健的訓練節目以獲取有用的資訊。

▶▶ 影子跟讀「實戰練習」　🎧 MP3 100

　　此部分為「**影子跟讀實戰練習❷**」，請重新播放音檔並完成試題，除了能提升並修正拼寫能力外，也可以藉由音檔注意自己專注力和定位聽力訊息部份，走神或定位錯都會影響在實際考場中的表現，尤其在 section3 和 4 影響的得分會更明顯，現在就一起動身，開始完成「**實戰練習❷**」吧！

　　1.＿＿＿＿＿＿＿＿＿＿＿ in areas where koalas used to live has posed various risks to this cute creature. 2.＿＿＿＿＿＿＿＿＿ is depriving and fragmenting koala habitat; human-induced threats such as vehicle strikes or domestic dog attacks are also threatening koala's life. Some koalas live in the 3.＿＿＿＿＿＿＿＿ where they are cared for by experienced staff. Koalas may be given a 4.＿＿＿＿＿＿＿ by local residents if they show up frequently in the neighborhood. The biggest threat to the koala's existence is 5.＿＿＿＿＿＿＿, and following this, the most serious threat is death from car hits. I'm going to talk about the koala and the car accident. The figure from the Australian Wildlife Hospital and another koala rescue center shows that 6.＿＿＿＿＿＿ koalas were taken to hospitals between 1997 and 2008, and 85% of the injured koalas died after emergency procedures.

　　On June 11 2015, a 6-month-old baby koala clung to his mother during her 7.＿＿＿＿＿＿＿＿＿ after she was hit by a car in Brisbane, Australia. The mother Lizzy suffered severe injuries including 8._____ and a collapsed lung. The Australia government has made a good effort to protect koala from car accidents. When you drive in 9._____, sometimes you can see an 10._____ built on top of a road. The over-bridge is the 11._____. There are still several things drivers can do to protect koalas, including obeying the 12._____, watching for koala crossing signs, slowing down if see koalas crossing, especially during the night, and report injured or dead koala if seen one. 13._____ would benefit koalas. Driving slowly within the speed limit and scanning the roadside for anything that may move onto the road have a significant 14._____.

Koalas can sleep up to 15._____ per day and not come to the ground very often. 16._____ is a good indicator to inform drivers that have entered koala's 17._____. The peak time for them to move across road is most likely to be between 18._____ usually during the night. If driving through koala habitat during 'koala peak hour', drivers should slow down and check the roadside for koalas and other wild animals. During the night, koalas crossing the road have 19._____. Their eyes reflect the 20._____ of coming vehicles, which would alert drivers. It is recommended carrying an old 21._____ in the car. So the injured koala could be wrapped and moved out off the road. In addition, local wildlife care groups or 22._____ can be contacted. Most importantly, people should always consider their own safety before intervening, cars need to be parked safely with 23._____ on to alert other drivers. People who are interested in caring for sick koalas can even attend certain training programs on 24._____ to get useful information.

▶▶ 參考答案

1. Land exploitation	2. Urbanization
3. sanctuary	4. nickname
5. habitat destruction	6. 3792
7. life-saving surgery	8. facial trauma
9. Queensland	10. overpass
11. koala-crossing infrastructure	12. speed limit
13. Wildlife-friendly driving	14. preventive effect
15. twenty hours	16. Koala crossing signs
17. territory	18. July and September
19. shining eyes	20. headlights
21. towel or blanket	22. vet surgeons
23. hazard lights	24. wildlife rehabilitation

影子跟讀：「短對話」　影子跟讀：「短段落」　影子跟讀：「實戰練習」　雅思聽力必考字彙

鯨魚

▶ 影子跟讀「實戰練習」 🎧 MP3 101

此篇為**「影子跟讀實戰練習」**，此章節規劃了由聽**「實際考試長度的英文內容」**的 shadowing 練習，經由先前的兩個部份的練習，已經能逐步掌握跟聽一定句數的英文內容，現在經由實際考試長度的聽力內容來練習，讓耳朵適應聽這樣長度的英文內容，提升在考場時的答題穩定度和適應性，進而獲取理想成績，現在就一起動身，開始由聽**「實戰練習」**！（如果聽這部份且跟讀練習的難度還是太高請重複前兩個部份的練習數次後再來做這部分的練習喔！）

Hi everyone, the topic our group selected for the wild-life case study is the whale. Now I will first present the general features and several species of whales then my group mates will continue with more detailed information.

嗨，各位好，我們這組所選的野生生物研究主題是鯨魚。現在我將首先呈現大致上的特徵和幾種鯨魚種類，然後我的組員夥伴會以更多細節資訊接續講述。

There are more than 90 species of whales, all whale species can be categorised into baleen whales and toothed whales. The baleen whales eat by swimming slowly through fish-rich water and straining food into their mouth. And toothed whales as their names indicate, have teeth. Whales live in marine environment and they are mammals. Just like the continental mammals, whales are also viviparous, which means they reproduce by giving birth to a calf rather than eggs, which leads to fewer offspring and longer-lived individuals. Whales breath with their lungs, and they all have blowholes positioned on top of their head. They breathe in air through the blowholes when they are on the water surface and close it up when they dive. All mammals need to sleep, but whales have to be awake at all times to maintain breath. So whales have a special sleep pattern: half of their brain falls asleep while the other half keeps awake, that makes whales sleep 24 hours per day.

　　有超過 90 種的鯨魚，所有鯨魚物種都能分類成鬚鯨和齒鯨。鬚鯨藉由緩慢游進魚類豐富的水域然後將食物拖進牠們口中的方式進食。而齒鯨則是如牠們名字所示，有著牙齒。鯨魚居住在海洋環境而且牠們是哺乳類動物。如同地面上的補入類動物，鯨魚同樣是胎生動物，這意謂著牠們以產下幼子的方式繁殖，而非生蛋的形式，這也導致生產出較少的後代和較長壽的個體。鯨魚以肺部呼吸，而且他們在頭部頂端裝置著噴水孔。當牠們在水面上或靠近水面而潛入時，鯨魚透過噴水孔吸入空氣。所有的哺乳類動物需要睡覺，但是鯨魚必須總是醒著以維持呼吸。所以鯨魚有著特別的睡眠形式：有一半的腦部睡著而另一半的腦部持續醒著，這使得鯨魚每天能睡眠 24 小時。

Whales have very advanced hearing and they can hear from miles away. They produce low frequency sound, which can be detected over large distances. Now many species of whales are declared as endangered. Apart from human activities such as illegal whaling, these animals collide with ships or get entangled with fishing nets. They are also threatened by pollution and habitat loss from climate change. Now I will briefly talk about four types of baleen whales.

鯨魚有著非常進階的聽覺，而且牠們能聽到數公哩遠的聲音。牠們產生低頻率的聲音，能夠探測著廣大的距離。現在許多鯨魚種類都被宣告是頻臨絕種。除了人類活動，例如違法捕鯨，這些動物可能撞到船或受到漁網纏住。牠們也受到汙染威脅且因氣候改變造成的棲息地損失。現在我將簡短地談論四種類型的鬚鯨。

The first one is the blue whale. The blue whale is the largest animal on the planet. It is also the largest animals ever to have lived, since they are much larger than dinosaurs. Their heart has the same size of a small car, which bumps tons of blood through the circulatory system of the blue whale. The largest blue whale that was ever found was 33.58 meters long and weighed 190 tons. The skin of the blue whale is blue-grey colored. On top of its head, there is a large ridge located from the tip of the nose to the blowhole. The blue whale has a very small dorsal fin and relatively small tail flukes. In terms of feeding and distribution, the blue whale feeds almost exclusively on krill, and you can find the blue whales worldwide. They travel to polar waters to feed during summer time and spend the winter in tropical or subtropical areas. Blue whales like to swim alone or in groups of 2 or 3. In the past century, blue whale has been extensively hunted and the number has deceased to a very low level.

第一種是藍鯨。藍鯨是星球上最大的動物。這也是有史以來現存的最大動物，因為它們比恐龍稍大。它們的心臟與小型車有著相同的大小，透過藍鯨的循環系統充入數噸的血液。目前所發現的最大的藍鯨是 33.58 公噸長且 190 公噸重。藍鯨的皮膚是藍灰色的。在頭部頂端，有著大型的脊狀隆起，位於噴水孔和鼻子頂端。藍鯨有著非常小的背鰭和相當小的尾部倒鉤。關於攝食和分布，藍鯨幾乎專以磷蝦為食而且你可以在世界各地發現藍鯨的蹤跡。牠們在夏季旅行至極地水域進食，而在冬季出現於熱帶或亞熱帶地區。藍鯨喜歡獨自游泳或以兩人或三人一組的方式游泳。過去這個世紀，藍鯨已經廣泛地受到獵捕且數量已降至非常低的等級。

Hence, it is now listed as an endangered species. The second one I will introduce is the fin whale. The fin whale is a fast swimmer. It can swim at the speed of 30 km/hr. Occasionally, the fin whale can jump out of the water. The average length of the fin whale is about 18 to 22 meters and it can weigh up to 70 tons. The fin whale looks long and slender, the head resembles the blue whale but the color is dark grey to brown. The fin whale prefers to stay in deep water

影子跟讀：「短對話」

影子跟讀：「短段落」

影子跟讀：「實戰練習」

雅思聽力必考字彙

and it is also distributed all over the the world's ocean. Unlike the blue whale, the fin whale is more gregarious, which means they live in flocks and are more sociable. Fin whales are generally seen in groups of 10 or more. They mainly feed on small crustaceans such as crabs, lobsters and shrimps. Northern hemisphere fin whales also feed on fish.

因此，現在被列為瀕臨絕種的物種。第二個我要介紹的是鰭鯨。鰭鯨是快速泳者。它可以以每小時 30 公里的速度游泳。偶爾，鰭鯨能跳離水中。鰭鯨的平均長度是大概 18 公尺到 22 公尺長而且重達 70 公噸。鰭鯨看起來長且苗條些，頭部與藍鯨相似但是顏色是暗灰到棕色。鰭鯨偏好待在深水水域且也分布至全世界的海洋中。不像藍鯨，鰭鯨較群居性，這意謂著他們成群生活且較社會性。鰭鯨通常以 10 個或更多數量為一組出現在視線中。他們主要以小型甲殼綱動物，例如螃蟹、龍蝦和蝦子。北半球的鰭鯨也以魚類為食。

The next one is the grey whale, which appears only in the North Pacific Ocean. The grey whale is baleen whale as well. In summer the grey whales move to the Bering Sea to feed and in winter they travel along the US coast down to the Mexican coast. There are lots of whale watching trips organised and sometimes they swim very close to the whale watching boats. The size of the grey whale is relatively smaller compared with the two previous types. They are 15 meters long on average and weigh about 20 tons. The skin of the back of the grey whale has yellow and white coloured patches caused by parasites. Grey whales are also critically endangered and granted protection from commercial hunting; therefore, they are no longer hunted on a large scale.

下個是灰鯨，它們僅出現在北太平洋海洋。灰鯨也是鬚鯨的一種。在夏季，灰鯨移至白令海攝食而到的冬季它們沿著美國海岸旅行至墨西哥海岸。有許多賞鯨旅程的安排而且由時候它們非常靠近賞鯨船。灰鯨的大小與先前兩種類型相比較小。他們平均 15 公尺長且大概 20 公噸重。灰鯨背部的皮膚有著由寄生蟲引起的黃色和白色的補塊。灰鯨也出現嚴重性的瀕臨絕種情況，而且授予商業獵捕的保護，因此，牠們也不再受到大規模的獵捕。

The fourth one on our list is the humpback whale. This is probably the most famous whale species because of its songs that can be heard from a far distance. Only the male sings. So there is a hypothesis that the humpback whale's song has a reproductive reason. Humpback whale is black all over, and it has a unique way of catching fish, it dives down and circles to the surface. On the way up, fishes are encircled in a bubble net and swallowed by the humpback whale. This type of whale also travels long distance; they spend the winter near Hawaii and move to the polar regions in summer. The humpback whale is up to 19 meters long and 48 tons in weight. It feeds on krill, sardines, and small fishes. The humpback whale is considered a vulnerable species and whaling is prohibited as well.

第四種在我們介紹的清單上的是座頭鯨。這可能是最有名的鯨

魚種類因為座頭鯨的鳴叫聲能在遠距離就能聽到。僅有男性座頭鯨鳴叫。所以有個假說是座頭鯨的鳴叫聲有繁殖的目的。座頭鯨全身黑色覆蓋且於捕魚上有獨特的方式。座頭鯨潛入海中並環繞在浮現在水面上。在衝上水面時，魚類環繞在氣泡網中，並且被座頭鯨吞入。這種類型的鯨魚也能夠長距離旅行。牠們冬季會花費時間在夏威夷，而於夏季時移至極地地區。座頭鯨長至 19 公尺長和 48 公噸重。它以磷蝦、沙丁魚和小型魚類為食。座頭鯨被視為是易受攻擊的物種而且捕鯨行為也是禁止的。

▶▶ 影子跟讀「實戰練習」 🎧 MP3 101

此部分為「**影子跟讀實戰練習❷**」，請重新播放音檔並完成試題，除了能提升並修正拼寫能力外，也可以藉由音檔注意自己專注力和定位聽力訊息部份，走神或定位錯都會影響在實際考場中的表現，尤其在 section3 和 4 影響的得分會更明顯，現在就一起動身，開始完成「**實戰練習❷**」吧！

There are more than 90 species of whales, all whale species can be categorised into 1.＿＿＿＿＿＿＿ and toothed whales. The baleen whales eat by swimming slowly through 2.＿＿＿＿＿＿＿ and straining food into their mouth. And toothed whales as their names indicate, have teeth. Whales live in a marine environment and they are mammals. Just like the continental mammals, whales are also 3.＿＿＿＿＿＿＿, which means they reproduce by giving birth to a calf rather than eggs, which leads to fewer offspring and longer-lived individuals. Whales breath with their 4.＿＿＿＿＿＿, and they all have 5.＿＿＿＿＿＿＿ positioned on top of their head. All mammals need to sleep, but whales have to be awake at all times to 6.＿＿＿＿＿＿＿. So whales have a special sleep 7.＿＿＿＿＿＿.

They produce 8.＿＿＿＿＿＿＿, which can be detected over large distances. Apart from human activities such as 9.＿＿＿＿＿＿, these animals can collide with ships or get entangled with 10.＿＿＿＿＿＿. They are also threatened by pollution and 11._____ from climate change. It is also the largest animals ever to have lived, since they are much larger than 12._____. Their heart has the same size as a small car, which bumps tons of blood through the 13._____ of the blue whale. The largest blue whale that was ever found was 33.58 meters long and weighed 14._____ tons. The blue whale has a very small 15._____ and relatively small 16._____. In terms of feeding and distribution, the blue whale feeds almost exclusively on 17._____ and you can find the blue whales worldwide.

Hence, it is now listed as 18._____. The fin whale prefers to stay in deep water and it is also distributed all over the world's ocean. Unlike the blue whale, the fin whale is more 19._____, which means they live in flocks and are more sociable. Fin whales are generally seen in groups of 10 or more. They mainly feed on 20._____, such as crabs, lobsters and shrimps. The next one is the grey whale, which appears only in the North Pacific Ocean. The grey whale is baleen whale as well. In summer the grey whales move to the 21._____ to feed and in winter they travel along the US coast down to the Mexican coast. They are 15 meters long on average and weigh about 20 tons. The skin of the back of the grey whale has yellow and white 22._____ caused by parasites.

Only the male sings. On the way up, fishes are encircled in a 23._____ and swallowed by the humpback whale. This type of whale also travels long distances; they spend the winter near Hawaii and move to the polar regions in summer. The humpback whale is up to 19 meters long and 48 tons in weight. It feeds on krill, sardines, and small fishes. The humpback whale is considered a vulnerable species and 24._____ is prohibited as well.

▶▶ 參考答案

1. baleen whales	2. fish-rich water
3. viviparous	4. lungs
5. blowholes	6. maintain breath
7. pattern	8. low frequency sound
9. illegal whaling	10. fishing nets
11. habitat loss	12. dinosaurs
13. circulatory system	14. 190
15. dorsal fin	16. tail flukes
17. krill	18. an endangered species
19. gregarious	20. small crustaceans
21. Bering Sea	22. coloured patches
23. bubble net	24. whaling

雪梨歌劇院

　　此篇為**「影子跟讀實戰練習」**，此章節規劃了由聽**「實際考試長度的英文內容」**的 shadowing 練習，經由先前的兩個部份的練習，已經能逐步掌握跟聽一定句數的英文內容，現在經由實際考試長度的聽力內容來練習，讓耳朵適應聽這樣長度的英文內容，提升在考場時的答題穩定度和適應性，進而獲取理想成績，現在就一起動身，開始由聽**「實戰練習」**！（如果聽這部份且跟讀練習的難度還是太高請重複前兩個部份的練習數次後再來做這部分的練習喔！）

Hello everyone, I'm delighted to welcome you to the Sydney Opera House, one of the most iconic buildings in the world. Before we step inside this iconic landmark to actually discover this remarkable architecture, I just make a brief introduction of the Opera House.

　　嗨，大家好，我很高興能歡迎你來到雪梨歌劇院，世界上最具指標性的建築物之一。在我們踏入這間指標性的建築物，實際探索這個驚人的建築物前，我會做個簡短的歌劇院介紹。

The Sydney Opera House is a performing arts center and

it is obvious this is a landmark building in the city of Sydney and even a culture symbol of Australia. Every year, there are more than 1600 concerts, operas, dramas and ballets taking place here. You will later be able to put your hands on the world-famous shell tiles and take a seat in the chairs of the concert hall.

雪梨歌劇院是表演戲劇中心和明顯的是這間是地處於雪梨市的地標性建築，而且甚至是澳洲的文化象徵。每年，有超過 1600 場音樂會、歌劇、戲劇和芭蕾再次舉行。你會於稍後感受到世界聞名的由磚瓦堆砌成的歌劇院外殼和入座於音樂會廳的椅子上。

You may feel astonished while walking underneath the vaulted ceilings within the the world's biggest pillarfree chambers. The venues can accommodate several performing arts companies, including Opera Australia, The Australian Ballet, the Sydney Theatre Company and the Sydney Symphony Orchestra. If we are lucky, later we can find a theatre rehearsal in some of the opera halls.

當置身於世界上最大無樑柱的隔間時，走在地窖式天花板下方，你可能感到吃驚。地點能容納幾個表演公司，包括澳洲歌劇院、澳洲人芭蕾、雪梨戲劇公司和雪梨交響樂管弦樂機構。如果我們幸運的話，稍後我們可以看到在一些歌劇院廳的戲劇彩排。

As you can see, the design of Sydney Opera House is quite modern and the Opera House looks different from ev-

影子跟讀：「短對話」

影子跟讀：「短段落」

影子跟讀：「實戰練習」

雅思聽力必考字彙

ery angle. The roof is composed of a couple of precast concrete 'shells'. The opera house is 183 meters long and 120 meters wide, and the whole building is supported by 588 concrete pillars. The two largest spaces are the concert hall in the west and the theatre in the east. Lots of smaller sized performance venues and facilities are also located inside. Surrounding the opera house, is the open public space, where free public performances are always on.

　　如同你所看到的，雪梨歌劇院的設計相當現代化而且歌劇院從每個角度看起來很不同。屋頂由幾個預制的混擬土外殼。歌劇院長 183 公尺且 120 公尺寬，而且整個建築物由 588 個混擬土柱子所支撐。兩個最大的空間式西廂的音樂廳和東側的戲劇院。許多較小型的表演場所和設施也位於內部。環繞在歌劇院周圍的是開放式的大眾空間，免費的大型表演總是在表演中。

　　A noteworthy anecdote is the relationship between Sydney Opera House and its designer. The Opera House was designed by the famous Danish architect Jorn Utzon. He won the competition to design the Sydney Opera House in 1957. Looking from the Sydney Harbor, the Opera House resembles ships' sails or shells. You might wonder what inspired the architect to base this revolutionary design. He acknowledged in an interview that the idea came from the act of peeling an orange. The Opera House has altogether 14 shells, if combined them together, they would form a perfect sphere.

　　值得注意的是雪梨歌劇院和其設計師。歌劇院由著名的建築師約恩‧烏松所設計。他於 1957 年贏得設計雪梨歌劇院的比賽。從雪梨海灘看去，雪梨歌劇院相似於船的帆或外殼。你可能在想是什麼激起設計師的靈感，而以這革命性的設計為基礎。他於面談中承認這個構想是源自於剝柳橙的行為。雪梨歌劇院一共有 14 個外殼，如果結合在一起的話，它們會形成完美的球體。

Although the design was quite innovative, the construction of the Opera House was not smooth. The Opera House was supposed to be opened in 1963 at a cost of 7 million Australian dollars, but it finally opened in 1973 at a cost of around 104 million. This is mainly because the design was too much ahead of its time and available technology; the high cost and extended construction period also raised lots of criticisms from the general public.

　　雖然設計相當地創新，建造雪梨歌劇院不是很順利。歌劇院原先應於 1963 年開放，以 7 百萬澳幣建造成，但是最終於 1973 年才開放，且花費了大約一億零肆百萬元。這主要是因為設計超越當前時空和現有科技所能打造，高額的花費和延伸的建築期間也引起許多大眾的批評。

Sydney Opera House was considered one of the most difficult engineering challenges in the world; since the extraordinary structure of the shells shows out like a puzzle for people who actually build them. The designer team used computer for structure analysis, which was one of the earliest use of computers in architecture.

雪梨歌劇院被視為是世界上最艱困的工程挑戰，既然不尋常的殼狀結構顯示對於實際誰建造它們的人像是個謎團。設計師團隊使用電腦來作結構分析，也是建築最早使用的方式之一。

They calculated the force on each shell and figured out the sequence of assembling arches. They finally came out with a solution and built up the roof. But in 1965, Sydney changed its government and the new government was not as supportive as the previous one towards the construction of the opera house. Utzon was even forced to resign and the construction leadership was handed over to Australian architects team.

他們計算每個外殼內的力量而且試圖了解出組合拱門的順序。他們最終想出解決之道而且建造的屋頂。但是在 1965 年，雪梨政權改變，新政府沒有先前政府那樣支持建造歌劇院。烏松甚至被迫辭職而建築領導權移交制澳洲建築團隊。

Luckily in late 1990s, the Opera House Trust was reconnected with Utzon and they reached reconciliation. You will later visit the "the Utzon Room" which was named after the designer to honor his contribution. In 2007, the Sydney Opera House became the World Heritage of the UNESCO. The official evaluation is "one of the indisputable masterpieces of human creativity". Now lets walk inside to start exploring this world heritage site...

　　幸運地是，在 1990 年晚期，歌劇院信託重新連繫上烏松而且他們達成和解。你將於稍後參觀這個烏松房間，也就是以設計師名字命名以嘉勉他的貢獻。在 2007 年時，歌劇院已成為聯合國國教科文組織的世界遺產。官方評估這是人類創意中無爭議性的傑作。現在讓我們往裡面移動並開始探索這個世界遺址。

▶▶ 影子跟讀「實戰練習」　🎧 MP3 102

　　此部分為「**影子跟讀實戰練習❷**」，請重新播放音檔並完成試題，除了能提升並修正拼寫能力外，也可以藉由音檔注意自己專注力和定位聽力訊息部份，走神或定位錯都會影響在實際考場中的表現，尤其在 section3 和 4 影響的得分會更明顯，現在就一起動身，開始完成「**實戰練習❷**」吧！

　　The Sydney Opera House is a 1.＿＿＿＿＿＿ of Australia. You will later hands on the world-famous 2.＿＿＿＿＿＿ and take a seat in the chairs of the concert hall. You may feel astonished while walking underneath the 3.＿＿＿＿＿ within the the world's biggest 4.＿＿＿＿＿＿. If we are lucky, later we can find a 5.＿＿＿＿＿＿ in some of the opera halls.

　　The opera house is 183 meters long and 120 meters wide, and the whole building is supported by 6.＿＿＿＿＿＿＿. The two largest spaces are the 7.＿＿＿＿＿＿＿ in the west and the theatre in the east. Surrounded the opera house, is the open public space, where free 8.＿＿＿＿＿＿ are always on.

　　A 9.＿＿＿＿＿＿ is the relationship between Sydney Opera House and its designer. The Opera House was designed by the famous Danish architect Jorn Utzon. He won the 10._____ to design the Sydney Opera House in 1957. You might wonder what inspired the architect to base this revolutionary design.

He acknowledged in an 11_____ that the idea came from the act of peeling an 12_____. The Opera House has altogether 14 shells, if combined them together, they would form a perfect 13_____.

Although the design was quite innovative, the 14._____ of the Opera House was not smooth. The Opera House was supposed to be opened in 1963 at a cost of 7 million Australian dollars, but it finally opened in 1973 at a cost of around 15._____ million.

This is mainly because the design was too much ahead of time and 16._____; the high cost and extended construction period also raised lots of 17._____ from the general public.

Sydney Opera House was considered one of the most difficult 18._____ in the world; since the extraordinary structure of the shells shows out like a 19._____ for people who actually build them.

They calculated the force on each shell and figured out the sequence of 20._____. They finally came out a 21._____ and built up the roof.

Luckily in late 1990s, the Opera House Trust was recon-nected with Utzon and they reached 22._____.
You will later visit the "the Utzon Room" which was named after the designer to honor his 23._____. In 2007, the Sydney Opera House has become the World Heritage of the UNESCO. The official evaluation is "one of the 24._____ of human creativity". Now lets walk in-side to start exploring this world heritage...

▶▶ 參考答案

1. culture symbol	2. shell tiles
3. vaulted ceilings	4. pillarfree chambers
5. theatre rehearsal	6. 588 concrete pillars
7. concert hall	8. public performances
9. noteworthy anecdote	10. competition
11. interview	12. orange
13. sphere	14. construction
15. 104	16. available technology
17. criticisms	18. engineering challenge
19. puzzle	20. assembling arches
21. solution	22. reconciliation
23. contribution	24. indisputable masterpieces

租屋概況

　　在租屋時，**房東（landlord）**會與**房客（tenant）**簽訂合約（**contract**）。簽約有時要透過**房屋仲介（real estate agent）**，有時則是房東與房客談妥後自行簽訂。簽約時需要支付**押金（deposit/bond）**，押金金額一般為一到三個月**租金（rent）**。付款則多為採取按月支付的方式（**monthly payment**）。很多學生選擇居住在**寄宿家庭（homestay）**，以得到更好的照料；更多人選擇與人合租（**share house**），這樣生活更為獨立。除了租住一般的房屋，還可以選擇**學生公寓（student apartment）**，短期遊學的同學更可以住在飯店或**青年旅社（youth hostel）**。在租金高的城市，**合租房間（share room）**是一種節約開支的辦法，**室友（share mates）**分擔房間的租金，更加經濟划算。

重要字彙	
landlord	房東
tenant	房客
contract	合約
real estate agent	房仲
deposit	押金
rent	房租
monthly payment	月付

homestay	寄宿家庭
share house	合租房
student apartment	學生公寓
youth hostel	青年旅社
share room	合租屋
share mate	室友
延伸字彙	
single room	單人房
double room	雙人房
suite	套房
services apartment	酒店式公寓
townhouse	連棟屋
studio	設施齊備的單間房
lobby	大廳
courtyard	院子
loft	閣樓
ensuite	帶盥洗室的主臥房
bathroom	浴室
living room/lounge	起居室
garage	車庫
corridor	走廊
central heating	中央供暖
balcony	陽台

影子跟讀：「短對話」

影子跟讀：「短段落」

影子跟讀：「實戰練習」

雅思聽力必考字彙

租屋的外在環境與交通

　　找房子時，房客聯繫房東詢問是否還有**空房（vacancy）**並**預約（make appointment）**、**看房（house inspection）**。房子的**地點（location）**是重要的考量因素，因為關係到就學和打工的方便度。一般來說住在**市中心（downtown）**相對比較貴，而住在**郊區（suburbs）**較為便宜。要考慮住家附近是否有方便的**大眾交通工具（public transport）**，到距離最近的**公車站（bus station）**或**地鐵站（subway／metro station）**要步行幾分鐘。如果自己駕車，則要詢問是否有**停車位（parking lot）**。另外也要確認住家與**醫院（hospital）**、**學校（university）**、**超市（supermarket）**的距離。簽約時要註明**租住時長（duration）**，多久**續租一次（renew the lease）**，何時可以**入住（move in）**，以及開始付房租的時間。

重要字彙	
vacancy	空房
make appointment	預約
house inspection	看房
location	地點
downtown	市中心
suburb	郊區

public transport	大眾交通
bus station	公車站
subway/metro station	地鐵站
parking lot	停車位
hospital	醫院
university	大學
supermarket	超市
duration	時長
renew the lease	續租
move in	入住
延伸字彙	
neighbourhood	附近環境
underground car park	地下停車位
uncovered car park	露天停車位
leasing office	公寓管理處
stairs	樓梯
lift	電梯
basement	地下室
lawn	草坪
fire exit	安全出口
gym	健身房
outdoor swimming pool	室外游泳池
terrace	露台
utility room	儲藏室

影子跟讀：「短對話」

影子跟讀：「短段落」

影子跟讀：「實戰練習」

雅思聽力必考字彙

租屋的傢俱與電器

　　有的房子有附帶傢俱（**furnished**）和電器（**white goods**），可以詢問房東房子有提供（**provide**）什麼傢俱電器。一般情況下，即使是不帶傢俱的房子（**unfurnished**），房間也會提供基本的生活設施如廚房（**kitchen**）裡的煤氣灶（**gas stove**）或電磁灶（**electricity stove**）、嵌入式烤箱（**build-in oven**）、排氣扇（**kitchen ventilator**）、洗碗機（**dishwasher**）等，房間也自帶儲物空間如壁櫥（**cupboard**）和衣櫥（**wardrobe**），盥洗室的沖涼設備（**shower/bath**）也會齊備。一些房間安裝了空調（**air conditioner**），另一些則是吊扇（**ceiling fan**）。搬入不帶傢俱的房子，就需要房客自己採購需要的傢俱和電器，例如床墊（**mattress**）、沙發（**sofa**）、茶几（**tea/coffee table**）、餐桌（**dinning table**）、電視機（**TV set**）、冰箱（**refrigerator**）、洗衣機（**washing machine**）、烘乾機（**dryer**）等。

重要字彙	
furnished	帶傢俱
white goods	電器
provide	提供
unfurnished	不帶傢俱
kitchen	廚房
gas stove	煤氣灶

electricity stove	電磁灶
build-in oven	嵌入式烤箱
kitchen ventilator	排氣扇
dishwasher	洗碗機
cupboard	壁櫥
wardrobe	衣櫥
shower/bath	沖涼設備
air conditioner	空調
ceiling fan	吊扇
mattress	床墊
sofa	沙發
tea/coffee table	茶几
dinning table	餐桌
TV set	電視機
refrigerator	電冰箱
washing machine	洗衣機
dryer	烘乾機
延伸字彙	
stereo system	音響設備
freezer	冷凍庫
kettle	電燒水壺
sink	洗碗池
DVD player	DVD 播放器
book cabinet	書櫃

影子跟讀：「短對話」

影子跟讀：「短段落」

影子跟讀：「實戰練習」

雅思聽力必考字彙

租屋的開銷和注意事項

　　需要和房東確定租金是否包含水電費（**including utilities**），有時房客需要自費各種帳單（**bills**）如電（**electricity**）、水、網路（**internet**）、電話（**telephone**）、有線電視（**cable TV**）等費用。房客一般無須負擔市政管理費（**council rates**）和物業管理費（**body cooperate fee/property management fee**）。房東會負擔房屋裝修（**renovation**）和屋內設施（**facilities**）的維修服務（**maintenance services**），如果由房客墊付，則保留發票（**invoice**）或收據（**receipt**）之後向房東請款。如果入住公寓，也須確認是否禁止吸菸（**no smoking**）或禁養寵物（**no pets**）。一般大樓都有保全系統（**security system**），房客保管好自己的房門鑰匙（**door key**）或門禁卡（**door card**）就可以。洗衣則在自助洗衣房（**laundromat**）使用投幣式洗衣機（**coin operated laundry machine**）。

重要字彙	
including utilities	租金包含其他費用
bills	帳單
electricity	電
internet	網路
telephone	電話

cable TV	有線電視
council rates	市政管理費
body cooperate fee/ property management fee	物業管理費
renovation	裝修
facilities	設施
maintenance services	維修服務
invoice	發票
receipt	收據
no smoking	禁止吸菸
no pets	禁養寵物
security system	保全系統
door key	房門鑰匙
door card	門禁卡
laundromat	自助洗衣房
coin operated laundry machine	投幣式洗衣機
延伸字彙	
radiator	電暖爐
microwave	微波爐
toaster	烤麵包機
table lamp	檯燈
vacuum cleaner	吸塵器
water heater	熱水器
water dispenser	飲水機

影子跟讀:「短對話」

影子跟讀:「短段落」

影子跟讀:「實戰練習」

雅思聽力必考字彙

參觀藝術展

　　來到新的城市，美術館（**art gallery**）和博物館（**museum**）是一定要參觀的目的地（**destination**）。展廳中的雕塑（**sculpture**）和畫作（**painting**）令人想像力（**imagination**）飛馳。博物館的豐富館藏（**collection**）更是學習的最佳素材。徜徉在藝術的海洋中，人文精神和美感意識（**aesthetics**）都會得到滋養（**nourishment**）。展覽（**exhibition**）由主辦方（**host**）策劃多樣的主題（**theme**）。入場（**admission**）後，透過展廳平面圖（**floor plan**）獲得展品的大致位置。每一件展品（**exhibit**）都附有作品説明（**label**），更可以用租來的語音導覽（**audio guide**）獲得展品的詳細訊息。結束藝術館之旅後，可以在紀念品店（**gift shop**）買到展覽的周邊商品（**merchandise**）和明信片（**post card**）。

重要字彙	
art gallery	美術館
museum	博物館
destination	目的地
sculpture	雕塑
painting	畫作
imagination	想像力
collection	館藏

aesthetics	美感意識
nourishment	滋養
exhibition	展覽
host	主辦方
theme	主題
admission	入場
floor plan	平面圖
exhibit	展品
label	作品説明
audio guide	語音導覽
gift shop	紀念品店
merchandise	周邊商品
post card	明信片
延伸字彙	
architecture	建築
treasure	珍寶
display	陳列
visual art	視覺藝術
performance art	表演藝術
decorative art	裝飾藝術
textiles	紡織品
drawings	圖畫
photographs	攝影作品

影子跟讀：「短對話」

影子跟讀：「短段落」

影子跟讀：「實戰練習」

雅思聽力必考字彙

參觀國家公園

　　國家公園（**national park**）是為了保護（**conservation**）生態而劃定的區域，最早和最知名的國家公園是美國的黃石國家公園（**Yellowstone National Park**）。國家公園多為自然生態保護區（**protected areas**），一定要確保遊玩時遵守景區的規定（**regulation**），協助生態保育（**ecological conservation**）。遊客可以自由設計興趣點（**points of interest/POI**），客製化（**customized**）自己的行程。國家公園的景點（**scene spots**）包含各種地貌（**landform**），如山巒（**mountain**）、瀑布（**waterfall**）、峭壁（**cliff**）、火山（**volcano**）、海灘（**beach**）、湖泊（**lake**）等。可以透過書籍和網路得到旅行攻略（**tour suggestion/travelling guide**）。交通（**transportation**）和住宿（**accommodation**）是制定旅行計畫（**travel plan**）的要點，許多人選擇露營（**camping**）以更好的親近自然。由於是戶外旅行，天氣（**weather**）狀況也要列入考慮。

重要字彙	
national park	國家公園
conservation	保護
Yellowstone National Park	黃石國家公園
protected areas	保護區

regulation	規定
ecological conservation	生態保育
points of interest/POI	興趣點
customised	客製化
scene spots	景點
landform	地貌
mountain	山巒
waterfall	瀑布
cliff	峭壁
volcano	火山
beach	海灘
lake	湖泊
tour suggestion/traveling guide	旅行攻略
transportation	交通
accommodation	住宿
travel plan	旅行計畫
camping	露營
weather	天氣

延伸字彙

outdoor recreation	戶外休閒
natural wonders	自然奇蹟
habitat	棲息地
exploration	探索
prohibition	禁令

影子跟讀：「短對話」

影子跟讀：「短段落」

影子跟讀：「實戰練習」

雅思聽力必考字彙

參觀雪梨歌劇院

　　雪梨歌劇院（**Sydney Opera House**）是雪梨市的標誌性建築（**landmark building**）。曾被聯合國教科文組織（**UNESCO/ United Nations Educational Scientific and Cultural Organization**）評為世界文化遺產（**world cultural heritage**）。歌劇院特別的貝殼（**shell**）造型搭配作為背景的港灣大橋（**Sydney Harbor Bridge**），吸引無數遊客來參觀。雪梨歌劇院的兩個主要演出場館（**performance venues**）分別是音樂廳（**concert hall**）和劇場（**drama theatre**），另外還有一些小劇場（**playhouse**）和多功能工作室（**studio**），其中音樂廳內有世界最大的機械管風琴（**organ**）。雪梨歌劇院外主要入口的前庭（**forecourt**）時常舉辦免費的公共演出（**public performance**）。除了用作觀光，歌劇院時常有歌劇（**opera**）、芭蕾舞劇（**ballet**）、音樂會（**concert**）等演出。

重要字彙	
Sydney Opera House	雪梨歌劇院
landmark building	標誌性建築
UNESCO	聯合國教科文組織
world cultural heritage	世界文化遺產
shell	貝殼

Sydney Harbour Bridge	雪梨港灣大橋
performance venues	演出場館
concert hall	音樂廳
drama theatre	劇場
playhouse	小劇場
studio	工作室
organ	管風琴
forecourt	前庭
public performance	公共演出
opera	歌劇
ballet	芭蕾舞劇
concert	音樂會
延伸字彙	
recording studio	錄音室
symphony orchestra	交響樂團
backstage	後台
art centre	藝術中心
structure	結構
audience	觀眾
foyer	門廳
conference	會議
ceremony	儀式
community event	社區活動
entrance	入口

影子跟讀：「短對話」

影子跟讀：「短段落」

影子跟讀：「實戰練習」

雅思聽力必考字彙

遊覽大堡礁

　　大堡礁（**Great Barrier Reef**）位於澳洲昆士蘭（**Queensland**）東北海岸，是全世界最大的珊瑚礁群（**coral reef**）。大堡礁由無數微小的珊瑚蟲（**coral polyps**）建構，整個海域蘊含豐富的海洋生物（**marine life**）。除了令人驚嘆的生物多樣性（**bio-diversity**），大堡礁數百座熱帶島嶼（**tropical island**）的美麗海灘（**beach**）吸引世界各地的遊客感受到自然的靈感（**natural inspiration**）。遊客在大堡礁可以體驗各種娛樂方式如浮潛（**snorkeling**）、潛水（**scuba diving**）、直升機旅行（**helicopter tours**）、郵輪之旅（**cruise ship tours**）、觀賞鯨魚（**whale watching**）、與海豚游泳（**swimming with dolphins**）等。大堡礁的當地文化是澳洲原住民（**indigenous Australians/ Australian aboriginal people**）和托雷斯海峽島民（**Torres Strait islander**）文化，他們已經生活在大堡礁上萬年。

重要字彙	
Great Barrier Reef	大堡礁
Queensland	昆士蘭
coral reef	珊瑚礁
coral polyps	珊瑚蟲
marine life	海洋生物

biodiversity	生物多樣性
tropical island	熱帶島嶼
beach	海灘
natural inspiration	自然的靈感
snorkelling	浮潛
scuba diving	潛水
helicopter tours	直升機旅行
cruise ship tours	郵輪之旅
whale watching	觀賞鯨魚
swimming with dolphins	與海豚游泳
indigenous Australian/ Australian aboriginal people	澳洲原住民
Torres Strait islander	托雷斯海峽島民
延伸字彙	
pastime	休閒
scenic	風景秀美的
rainforest	熱帶雨林
exotic	奇異的
unspoilt	未遭破壞的
ocean view	海景
sailing vessels/yachts	帆船
inshore	近海的
coast	海岸
coastal town	海濱小鎮

影子跟讀：「短對話」

影子跟讀：「短段落」

影子跟讀：「實戰練習」

雅思聽力必考字彙

訂機票

　　訂機票（**book flight**）可以透過旅行社（**travel agency**），也可以直接在航空公司（**airline**）的網頁預訂（**reservation**）。如果是網上直接預訂，第一步先填入基本資訊如出發地（**origin**）、目的地、單程（**one way**）或往返（**return**）票、出發日期（**depart date**）、返回日期、人數等。選擇合適航班後填入乘客信息（**passenger details**），選擇座位（**seats**），最後用信用卡（**credit card**）付款。選擇廉價航空公司（**LCC/Low-cost Carrier**）做短途飛行是節約開支的好辦法，許多廉航有嚴格的行李限制，登機箱（**carry-on luggage**）之外的托運行李（**checked baggage**）要另外購買，也不提供飛機餐。一般的航空公司會不定期推出如機票折扣（**discount**）的優惠（**promotion**），而提前預訂（**book in advance**）通常相對划算。

重要字彙	
book flight	定機票
travel agency	旅行社
airline	航空公司
reservation	預訂
origin	出發地
one way	單程

return	往返
depart date	出發日期
passanger details	乘客信息
seats	座位
credit card	信用卡
LCC/Low-cost Carrier	廉價航空公司
carry-on luggage	登機箱
checked baggage	托運行李
discount	折扣
promotion	優惠
book in advance	提前預訂
延伸字彙	
economy class	經濟艙
business class	商務艙
upgrade	升等
confirm	確認
cancel	取消
window seat	靠窗的位子
aisle seat	靠走道的位子
suitcase	手提箱
fare	票價
check in	辦理登機手續
flight number	航班號
handbag tag	行李牌

影子跟讀：「短對話」

影子跟讀：「短段落」

影子跟讀：「實戰練習」

雅思聽力必考字彙

在機場出境

　　出國旅行應至少在飛機起飛前兩小時到達機場（**airport**）。首先要攜帶機票和護照（**passport**）在航空公司櫃台報到（**check in**），並辦理行李托運。離開報到櫃檯前要確認行李已經通過了機場的 X 光檢查（**X-ray inspection**）。安全稽查（**passenger clearance**）要求乘客走過安全門（**security gate**），以檢查是否攜帶違禁物品（**prohibited items**）。登機行李中的液體（**liquid**）體積不得超過 100ml。海關（**customs**）檢查護照之後可以在機場免稅店（**duty-free shop**）購買免稅商品（**duty-free items**）。大的國際機場有時需要到不同的航廈（**terminal**）登機，所以要確保在登機時間（**boarding time**）之前來到航班的登機門（**boarding gate**）。

重要字彙	
airport	機場
passport	護照
check in	報到
X-ray inspection	X 光檢查
passenger clearance	安全稽查
security gate	安全門

prohibited items	違禁物品
liquid	液體
customs	海關
duty-free shop	免稅店
duty-free items	免稅商品
terminal	航廈
boarding time	登機時間
boarding gate	登機門
延伸字彙	
flight duration	飛行時間
travel mileage	飛行里程
take off	起飛
landing	降落
itinerary	旅行日程表
departure lounge	候機室
delayed	延誤
boarding pass	登機證
transit	過境
domestic departure	國內航班出站
international departure	國際航班出港
goods to declare	報關物品
transfer passengers	中轉旅客
tax return	退稅
currency exchange	貨幣兌換處

影子跟讀：「短對話」

影子跟讀：「短段落」

影子跟讀：「實戰練習」

雅思聽力必考字彙

在機場入境

　　飛機降落前，空服員（**flight attendant**）會請乘客填寫入境申請表（**disembarkation card/immigration form**）以及海關申報表（**customs declaration form**）。入境後先做護照、簽證（**visa**）查驗，去行李提領區（**baggage claim area**）領取行李，海關檢查行李（**baggage inspection**）後即可抵達入境大廳（**arrivals hall**）。入境一個國家前，最好提前對需要申報（**declare**）的檢疫物品（**quarantine items**）做了解。譬如澳洲是入關檢疫非常嚴格的國家，如果沒有申報或丟棄（**dispose**）檢疫物品，則可能被罰款（**fine**）甚至被起訴（**prosecuted**）。機場的訊息中心（**information center**）提供所在城市的各種資訊。遊客可以攜帶國際駕照（**international drivers license**）前往租車處（**car rental**）租車, 也可以乘坐機場巴士（**airport bus**）或接駁巴士（**shuttle bus**）前往目的地。

重要字彙	
flight attendant	空服員
disembarkation card/ immigration form	入境申請表
customs declaration form	海關申報表
visa	簽證

baggage claim area	行李提領區
baggage inspection	檢查行李
arrivals hall	入境大廳
declare	申報
quarantine items	檢疫物品
dispose	丟棄
fine	罰款
prosecuted	被起訴
information centre	訊息中心
international drivers licence	國際駕照
car rental	租車
airport bus	機場巴士
shuttle bus	接駁巴士
延伸字彙	
luggage cart	行李推車
captain	機長
co-pilot	副駕駛
jet lag	時差症候群
meeting point	會面地點
ticket office	購票處
luggage locker	行李寄存處
transfer correspondence	中轉處
scheduled time	預計時間
taxi pick-up point	計程車乘車點

影子跟讀：「短對話」

影子跟讀：「短段落」

影子跟讀：「實戰練習」

雅思聽力必考字彙

藥店買藥

　　在藥店（**pharmacy**）可以直接購得非處方藥物（**OTC drugs ／over-the-counter drugs**）；而購買處方藥物（**prescription drugs**）則必須憑醫生開具的處方（**prescription/Rx**）。處方上記載了病人的姓名、年齡、藥品名稱（**drug name**）、劑量（**dosage**）等，是藥劑師（**pharmacist**）向病人發放（**dispense**）藥品等重要依據。常用藥品如感冒藥（**cold medicine**）、止痛藥（**painkiller**）、非類固醇類消炎藥（**NASID/non-steroidal anti-inflammatory drug**）通常擺放在藥店顯眼位置。除了販賣藥品（**medication/medicine**），藥店也出售保健食品（**healthy food**）、化妝品（**cosmetics**）、皮膚護理品（**skin care**）等商品。如各種維他命（**vitamins**）、嬰兒配方奶粉（**baby formula**）、香水（**fragrance**）、糖果（**confectionary**）、牙齒保健品（**dental care**）。大的藥店會提供全部商品目錄（**catalogue**），以便消費者找到需要的產品。

重要字彙	
pharmacy	藥店
OTC drugs/over-the-counter drugs	非處方藥物
prescription drugs	處方藥
prescription/Rx	處方

drug name	藥品名
dosage	劑量
pharmacist	藥劑師
dispense	發放
cold medicine	感冒藥
painkiller	止痛藥
NASID/non-steroidal anti-inflammatory drug	非類固醇類消炎藥
medication/medicine	藥品
healthy food	保健食品
cosmetics	化妝品
skin care	皮膚護理品
vitamins	維他命
baby formula	嬰兒配方奶粉
fragrance	香水
confectionary	糖果
dental care	牙齒護理
catalogue	目錄
延伸字彙	
hair care	頭髮保養
protein	蛋白質
weight loss	減肥
fish oil	魚油
scar treatment	祛斑
cleansers	潔膚品

露營

　　露營（**camping**）是對環境友善（**environmental friendly**）的旅遊方式。不僅可以親近自然，而且低碳（**LC/low carbon**）節能（**energy saving**）。由於是露天居住，露營前一定要注意天氣的變化。另外也要選擇安全的露營區（**campsite**）。過夜用的裝備有睡袋（**sleeping bag**）、地墊（**floor mat**）和帳篷（**tent**）。露營天數越多，就需要攜帶越多的裝備（**equipment**）。租用露營車（**recreational vehicle/motor caravan**）駐紮在有清潔水源的空間是另一種露營方式。戶外野餐（**picnic**）也很有樂趣，可以用冷飲保藏盒（**chest cooler/esky**）攜帶準備好的食物，或用便攜式瓦斯爐（**camp stove**）烹飪簡單的食物。為了應對戶外過夜，也要準備必要的取暖和照明設備，如露營燈（**camp lantern**）手電筒（**flashlight/torch**）等。

重要字彙	
camping	露營
environmental friendly	環境友善
LC/low carbon	低碳
energy saving	節能
campsite	露營區
sleeping bag	睡袋

floor mat	地墊
tent	帳篷
equipment	裝備
recreational vehicle/motor caravan	露營車
picnic	野餐
chest cooler/esky	冷飲保藏盒
camp stove	便攜式瓦斯爐
camp lantern	露營燈
flashlight/torch	手電筒

延伸字彙

camp fire	營火
compass	指南針
firewood	柴火
lighter	打火機
lime powder	石灰粉
backpack	背包
head torch	頭頂燈
foldable chair	折疊椅
travel pillow	旅行枕頭
first aid kit	急救箱
hike pot	野餐鍋
accessories	附加裝備
umbrella	雨傘

影子跟讀：「短對話」

影子跟讀：「短段落」

影子跟讀：「實戰練習」

雅思聽力必考字彙

遊覽澳洲動物園

　　澳洲動物園（**Australia Zoo**）位在昆士蘭的陽光海岸（**Sunshine Coast**），隔壁的澳洲動物園野生動物醫院（**Australian Zoo Wildlife Hospital**）以救護受傷動物而知名。遊客可以在澳洲動物園觀賞到各種鳥類、哺乳動物（**mammals**）和爬行動物（**reptiles**），體驗親手餵食大象（**hand-feed elephants**），觀賞鱷魚（**crocodile**）表演等。澳洲動物園的特色之一是遊客能夠近距離接觸許多動物（**animal encounters**），除了相對溫馴的袋鼠（**kangaroo**）和無尾熊（**koala**），還可以在工作人員（**staff**）的協助下接近更多野生動物（**wildlife**）如老虎、澳洲野狗（**dingo**）、巨型陸龜（**giant tortoise**）、長頸鹿（**giraffe**）、犀牛（**rhinoceros**）和獵豹（**cheetah**）。

重要字彙	
Australia Zoo	澳洲動物園
Sunshine Coast	陽光海岸
Australian Zoo Wildlife Hospital	澳洲動物園野生動物醫院
mammals	哺乳動物
reptiles	爬行動物
hand-feed elephants	親手餵食大象

crocodile	鱷魚
animal encounters	近距離接觸動物
kangaroo	袋鼠
koala	無尾熊
staff	工作人員
wildlife	野生動物
dingo	澳洲野狗
giant tortoise	巨型陸龜
giraffe	長頸鹿
rhinoceros	犀牛
cheetah	獵豹

延伸字彙

camel	駱駝
possum	袋貂
Tasmania Devils	塔斯馬尼亞惡魔
wombat	毛鼻袋鼠
lizard	蜥蜴
venomous snake	毒蛇
vertebrates	脊椎動物
ectothermic	冷血動物
region	地帶
species	物種
forelimb	前肢

影子跟讀：「短對話」

影子跟讀：「短段落」

影子跟讀：「實戰練習」

雅思聽力必考字彙

申請澳洲的手機門號

　　最方便的辦理手機門號方法是購買預付卡（**pre-paid SIM Card**），這種門號不需要帶護照去特定的電信公司辦理，在便利商店（**convenience store**）或超商（**supermarket**）櫃台就可以購買。用預付卡是打完 SIM 卡中的額度再儲值（**recharge**），不含月租費（**monthly fee**），但卡上金額一般兩個月就會過期（**expire**），如果不繼續儲值門號就會消失。預付卡的通話費率較高，適合短期造訪的人使用。大多數人則是辦理綁約月租卡（**post-paid Card**），需要向電信公司提供身分證明（**proof of identity**），選擇手機型號和通話月租型方案（**monthly plan**），綁約時最好根據自己的需要選擇合適的話費和資料流量方案（**data plan**），因為更改資費方案一般要付一筆違約金（**cancelation fee**）。

重要字彙	
pre-paid SIM Card	預付卡
convenience store	便利商店
supermarket	超商
recharge	儲值
monthly fee	月租費
expire	過期

post-paid Card	月租卡
proof of identity	身分證明
monthly plan	月租型方案
data plan	資料流量方案
cancelation fee	違約金
延伸字彙	
voice message	語音留言
SMS	簡訊
smartphone	智慧型手機
HD camera	高畫素相機
bluetooth	藍牙
touch screen	觸控式螢幕
signal	手機訊號
ringtone	鈴聲
national call	國內通話
international call	國際通話
activate	開通
land line	市內電話
hash key	井字鍵
data usage	資料使用量
add-ons	增加
credit	基本額度
bonus	附贈額度
flag fall	接通費

影子跟讀：「短對話」

影子跟讀：「短段落」

影子跟讀：「實戰練習」

雅思聽力必考字彙

在澳洲申請銀行帳戶

　　澳洲銀行帳戶主要有和銀行卡（**bank card**）綁定的存取帳戶（**access account**）和可以領到利息（**interest**）的儲蓄帳戶（**saving account**）。其中儲蓄帳戶的錢必須轉入存取帳戶裡才能動用。在每間銀行開戶都是這兩個帳戶系統，只是在名稱上有所差異。如聯邦銀行（**Commonwealth Bank**）的這兩個帳戶叫做主帳戶（**complete access**）和網路子帳戶（**net bank saver**）。銀行開戶手續非常簡單，只需攜帶護照去任意分行（**branch**）辦理。一定要將稅號（**tax file number**）提交給銀行，否則利息將被扣去一半。開戶後拿到的提款卡一般是簽帳金融卡（**debit card**），除在ATM 領錢和線上刷卡外，平常可以買東西直接扣款（**EFTPOS/ electronic funds transfer at point of sale**），也可以在買東西的櫃台提款（**cash out**），超市、便利店等收銀機都支持提款功能。

重要字彙	
bank card	銀行卡
access account	存取帳戶
interest	利息
saving account	儲蓄帳戶
Commonwealth Bank	聯邦銀行
complete access	主帳戶

net bank saver	網路子帳戶
branch	分行
tax file number	稅號
debit card	簽帳金融卡
EFTPOS/electronic funds transfer at point of sale	直接扣款
cash out	提款
延伸字彙	
BSB	銀行分行代號
transfer	轉帳
internet banking	網路銀行
account balance	帳戶餘額
cheque	支票
PIN	銀行卡密碼
payment	支付
credit	信用額度
money order	匯款單
security code	客戶服務密碼
account service fee	帳戶管理費
deposit	存款
transaction	交易
foreign exchange rate	匯率
ATM/automatic teller machine	自動提款機
bank statement	銀行帳單

影子跟讀：「短對話」

影子跟讀：「短段落」

影子跟讀：「實戰練習」

雅思聽力必考字彙

診所看病

　　在澳洲，若不是緊急狀況（**emergency**），生病後一般不是去醫院（**hospital**）看病，而是先要去診所（**clinic**）報到。在診所工作的是全科醫師／家醫師（**GP/general practitioner**），GP 會了解病人的身體狀況，如果是不嚴重的常見病如感冒（**cold**）、流感（**flu**）、發燒（**fever**）、外傷（**wound**）等，經驗良好的全科醫師就可以處理。如果需要進一步診斷檢查（**diagnostic examination**）或症狀是診所無法處理的，GP 會寫介紹信（**refer letter**）給專科醫師（**medical specialist**）做進一步診斷。許多 GP 提供診費全額報銷（**bulk billing**），如果是留學生使用海外醫療保險（**overseas health cover**），則需要先自費，再向健康保險公司（**health insurance company**）申請退款（**refund**）。

重要字彙	
emergency	緊急狀況
hospital	醫院
clinic	診所
GP/general practitioner	全科醫師
cold	感冒
flu	流感

fever	發燒
wound	外傷
diagnostic examination	診斷檢查
refer letter	介紹信
medical specialist	專科醫師
bulk billing	全額報銷
overseas health cover	海外醫療保險
health insurance company	健康保險公司
refund	退款
延伸字彙	
physician	內科醫生
allergy	過敏
nurse	護士
patient	病人
injection	打針
appetite	食慾
medical certificate	診斷書
laboratory	實驗室
ambulance	救護車
acupuncture	針灸
blood pressure	血壓
temperature	體溫
pulse rate	心率

影子跟讀：「短對話」

影子跟讀：「短段落」

影子跟讀：「實戰練習」

雅思聽力必考字彙

看牙醫

　　去牙醫診所（**dental clinic**）看診前一般需要先預約（**make an appointment**），若非緊急情況，很少牙醫診所可以隨時入內看病（**walk-in service**）。打電話給牙醫診所後，診所櫃台人員（**medical receptionist**）會詢問姓名、生日（**DOB/date of birth**）和預約的原因，如有症狀（**symptom**）須簡單告知，並在診所提供的可預約時段（**available time**）選擇合適時間前往。如果是常規牙齒保健，牙醫（**dentist**）會檢查（**check-up**）牙齒並做洗牙和拋光（**clean and polish**）；如果是因為牙痛（**tooth-ache**）看牙醫，則需要檢查是否有蛀牙（**dental decay**）、濃腫（**abscess**）、牙齒缺口（**chipped tooth**）等問題。再根據牙齒的狀況做拔牙（**tooth extraction**）、補牙（**fillings**）、根管治療（**root canal therapy**）、做牙冠（**crown**）等醫治（**treatment**）。

重要字彙	
dental clinic	牙醫診所
make an appointment	預約
walk-in service	隨時入內看病
medical receptionist	診所櫃台人員
DOB/date of birth	生日
symptom	症狀

available time	可預約時段
dentist	牙醫
check-up	檢查
clean and polish	洗牙和拋光
toothache	牙痛
dental decay	蛀牙
abscess	濃腫
chipped tooth	牙齒缺口
tooth extraction	拔牙
fillings	補牙
root canal therapy	根管治療
crown	牙冠
treatment	醫治
延伸字彙	
hygienist	衛生保健專家
rinse the mouth	漱口
tongue	舌頭
gum	牙齦
cavity	蛀洞
brush the teeth	刷牙
nerves	神經
drill	鑽頭
anaesthesia	麻醉
floss	牙線

影子跟讀：「短對話」

影子跟讀：「短段落」

影子跟讀：「實戰練習」

雅思聽力必考字彙

配眼鏡

　　視力（**eyesight/vision**）變差就需要去配眼鏡。配眼鏡一般先由驗光師（**optometrist**）檢查視力（**eye check**），許多眼鏡店（**optical store**）都提供免費的視力檢查。近視（**myopia/short-sightedness**）是最常見的眼科問題，驗光師指示念出圖表上的字母（**letters on the chart**）是測試單眼視力的方法。可以透過詳盡的視力檢查來診斷（**diagnose**）和評估（**assessment**）眼睛的（**ocular**）和視力問題。並配戴眼鏡（**glasses**）以功能性修復（**functional repair**）視力障礙（**vision impairment**）。如果驗光師判斷眼睛有更嚴重的問題需要進一步檢查，則會介紹病人去看眼科醫師（**ophthalmologist/oculist**）。驗光後挑選鏡片（**lens/optic**）和鏡架（**frame**）來配眼鏡，有些人則選擇配戴隱形眼鏡（**contact lens**）。

重要字彙	
eyesight/vision	視力
optometrist	驗光師
eye check	檢查視力
optical store	眼鏡店
myopia/short-sightedness	近視
letters on the chart	圖表上的字母

diagnose	診斷
assessment	評估
ocular	眼睛的
glasses	眼鏡
functional repair	功能性修復
vision impairment	視力障礙
ophthalmologist/oculist	眼科醫師
lens/optic	鏡片
frame	鏡架
contact lens	隱形眼鏡
延伸字彙	
corneal	角膜的
retina	視網膜
long-sighted	遠視
astigmia	散光
sunglasses	太陽眼鏡
reading glassed	花鏡
glasses' case	眼鏡盒
wire frames	金屬眼鏡架
contact lens solution	隱形眼鏡護理液
optician	眼鏡商
scratch	(鏡片)刮花
oval frames	橢圓形眼鏡架
rectangular frames	長方形眼鏡架

看足科醫師

　　足踝醫學（**podiatry**）在許多國家是專門的學問，足踝（**ankle**）和腳掌（**feet**）的骨骼（**bone**）、關節（**joint**）和肌腱（**muscle tendon**）承受著身體全部重量，行走和跑步時則承重更多。足科醫師（**podiatrist**）幫助患者解決足踝和下肢（**lower extremity**）的病變，但治療技術和一般的骨科（**orthopedics**）不同。足科診所一般提供基本的足部保健（**foot care**），糖尿病足（**diabetic foot**）照護，兒童（**pediatric**）足科保健，器械矯正（**orthotics**）等。患者在足科診所可以做生物力學（**biomechanics**）和步態分析（**gait analysis**），做趾甲手術（**nail surgery**）；患有血管疾病（**vascular disease**）的高風險病人則可以做下肢感覺神經（**sensory**）的檢查。另外一些足部皮膚病（**dermatitis**）也可以得到治療，譬如香港腳（**athlete foot**）和皮膚真菌感染（**fungal infection**）。

重要字彙	
podiatry	足踝醫學
ankle	足踝
feet	腳掌
bone	骨骼
joint	關節

muscle tendon	肌腱
podiatrist	足科醫師
lower extremity	下肢
orthopaedics	骨科
foot care	足部保健
diabetic foot	糖尿病足
paediatric	兒童的
orthotics	器械矯正
biomechanics	生物力學
gait analysis	步態分析
nail surgery	趾甲手術
vascular disease	血管疾病
sensory	感覺神經
dermatitis	皮膚病
athlete foot	香港腳
fungal infection	真菌感染
延伸字彙	
plantar	足底
knee	膝關節
calf	小腿
thigh	大腿
spasm	痙攣
chiropody	足病治療

影子跟讀：「短對話」

影子跟讀：「短段落」

影子跟讀：「實戰練習」

雅思聽力必考字彙

皇家農業展

　　皇家昆士蘭展覽會（**Royal Queensland Show**）又稱作 EKKA，是澳洲昆士蘭每年最大的節慶活動（**festival**），一般在八月份舉行。EKKA 成立的初衷是做農業（**agricultural**）展覽，由當地農夫（**farmer**）向外界展示新發明（**invention**）的農業機械（**machinery**）裝置（**device**）以及農場動物（**farm animals**）。舉辦超過百年的 EKKA 現在成為了展示本地文化（**local culture**）的視窗，吸引（**attraction**）來到澳洲的外國遊客（**foreign tourist**）。農展會的有趣項目有露天遊樂場（**fairground**）、動物大遊行（**animal parade**）、伐木比賽（**wood chopping competition**）、馬術表演（**equestrian**）、煙火秀（**firework**）等。遊客也可以吃到展會上特別的零食（**snack**）像是棉花糖（**fairy floss**）、漢堡（**burger**）、熱薯條（**hot chips**），和最著名的草莓冰淇淋（**strawberry sundae**）。

重要字彙	
Royal Queensland Show	皇家昆士蘭展覽會
festival	節慶
agricultural	農業的
farmer	農夫
invention	發明

machinery	機械
device	裝置
farm animals	農場動物
local culture	本地文化
attraction	吸引
foreign tourist	外國遊客
fairground	遊樂場
animal parade	動物大遊行
wood chopping competition	伐木比賽
equestrian	馬術表演
firework	煙火秀
snack	零食
fairy floss	棉花糖
burger	漢堡
hot chips	熱薯條
strawberry sundae	草莓冰淇淋
延伸字彙	
sideshow	雜耍
livestock	牲畜
poultry	家禽
paddock	訓馬場
boulevard	林蔭大道
pony	小馬
puppy	小狗

影子跟讀：「短對話」

影子跟讀：「短段落」

影子跟讀：「實戰練習」

雅思聽力必考字彙

澳紐軍團日

　　澳紐軍團日（**ANZAC day/Australian and New Zealand Army Crops day**）是為了紀念（**commemorate**）澳洲和紐西蘭在戰爭（**war**）、衝突（**conflict**）和維和行動（**peacekeeping operation**）中陣亡的軍人而創立的節日。軍團日是每年的 4 月 25 日。這個日子是澳紐軍團參加第一次世界大戰（**the First World War**）時，在土耳其（**Turkey**）的加里玻利（**Gallipoli**）海灘登陸（**landing**）的日子。在這次戰役（**campaign**）中，由於土耳其軍隊（**army**）的頑強抵抗（**defense**），澳紐軍團傷亡（**casualty**）慘重。戰事雖沒有取得勝利（**triumph/victory**），但陣亡的戰士給後人留下偉大的精神遺產（**spiritual heritage**），被稱作 AN-ZAC Legend 精神。現在人們以等待日出（**sunrise**）、軍樂隊（**marching band**）、老兵遊行（**veteran parade**）、紀念儀式（**memorial**）等來渡過這一節日。

重要字彙	
ANZAC day/Australian and New Zealand Army Crops day	澳紐軍團日
commemorate	紀念
war	戰爭
conflict	衝突

peacekeeping operation	維和行動
the First World War	第一次世界大戰
Turkey	土耳其
Gallipoli	加里玻利
landing	登陸
campaign	戰役
army	軍隊
defence	抵抗
casualty	傷亡
triumph/victory	勝利
spiritual heritage	精神遺產
sunrise	日出
marching band	軍樂隊
veteran parade	老兵遊行
memorial	紀念儀式

延伸字彙

revival	復興
national wide	全國
remembrance	紀念
contribution	貢獻
serve	服務
honour	榮譽
anniversary	紀念日
sovereign country	主權國家

影子跟讀：「短對話」

影子跟讀：「短段落」

影子跟讀：「實戰練習」

雅思聽力必考字彙

大洋路

　　大洋路（**Great Ocean Road**）是澳洲維多利亞省（**Victoria**）南部的一條觀光公路（**scenic route**）。大洋路始建於 1919年，以紀念第一次世界大戰中陣亡的士兵，是世界最大的戰爭紀念設施（**war memorial**）。公路沿海岸線（**coastline**）而建，沿途有漂亮的漁村（**fishing village**）、由石灰岩（**limestone**）和砂岩（**sandstone**）構成（**composed**）的懸崖和海灘、遼闊的雨林（**rainforest**）、有時還會遇到鯨魚（**whale**）遷徙（**migrate**）。大洋路上著名的景點十二門徒（**Twelve Apostles**）是岩石受到海潮（**ocean tide**）侵蝕（**erosion**）形成的景觀，人們用耶穌基督（**Jesus Christ**）的十二位弟子命名十二個巨型岩石柱。大洋路步行路線（**Great Ocean walk**）是專門為步行遊客設計的健行步道（**hiking trail**），遊客穿越國家公園，遊覽海洋保護區（**marine reserve**）的美景。

重要字彙	
Great Ocean Road	大洋路
Victoria	維多利亞省
scenic route	觀光公路
war memorial	戰爭紀念設施
coastline	海岸線

fishing village	漁村
limestone	石灰岩
sandstone	砂岩
composed	構成
rainforest	雨林
whale	鯨魚
migrate	遷徙
Twelve Apostles	十二門徒
ocean tide	海潮
erosion	侵蝕
Jesus Christ	耶穌基督
Great Ocean walk	大洋路步行路線
hiking trail	健行步道
marine reserve	海洋保護區
延伸字彙	
invaluable	無價的
rock fall	落石
eco-friendly	生態友好的
landscape	陸上風景
stretch	延伸
hike	遠足
rehabilitation	復原

影子跟讀：「短對話」

影子跟讀：「短段落」

影子跟讀：「實戰練習」

雅思聽力必考字彙

377

考駕照

　　無論是在澳洲學習開車，還是把外國駕照（**driver's licence**）換成澳洲駕照，都必須通過電腦化（**computerized**）交通規則考試（**road rules test**）和路考（**driving test**）。交通規則考試是理論（**theoretical**）考試，檢驗受試者的交通安全（**driving safety**）常識，對交通規則和道路交通號誌（**road traffic signals**）的了解等安全知識。考試通過後獲得學習駕照（**learner licence**），持學習駕照行車必須有正式駕照（**open licence**）持有者監督（**supervision**），並按照要求紀錄行車日誌簿（**logbook**）。拿 L 牌超過一年並積累到 100 小時開車經驗後，就可以向當地交通部（**transport department**）申請參加路考。通過路考後，駕齡超過三年者可以得到正式駕照，不滿三年者則得到臨時駕照（**provisional licence**），需要再經過司機資格考試（**driver qualification test**）換正式駕照。(每個州制度略有差異)

重要字彙	
driver's licence	駕照
computerised	電腦化
road rules test	交通規則考試
driving test	路考
theoretical	理論

driving safety	交通安全
road traffic signals	道路交通號誌
learner licence	學習駕照
open licence	正式駕照
supervision	監督
logbook	日誌簿
transport department	交通部
provisional licence	臨時駕照
driver qualification test	司機資格考試
延伸字彙	
valid	有效
demerit point system	違規扣分制度
upgrade	升級
eligible	有資格的
speeding offence	超速
hazard	危險
perception	感知
alcohol limit	飲酒限量
restriction	限制
suspension	暫停
disqualification	取消資格
speed limit	限速

影子跟讀：「短對話」

影子跟讀：「短段落」

影子跟讀：「實戰練習」

雅思聽力必考字彙

租車

　　澳洲幅員廣闊，租車（**car rental**）可以使旅行更加便利。有網路訂車、電話訂車或親臨訂車等方式，其中網路訂車時常會得到特殊優惠（**concession**）。租車過程（**process**）是選擇租車地點和車型（**vehicle model**）、確認租車價格（**price**）和包含的服務項目（**services**）、填寫個人資料和信用卡資料即可完成。租車一般推薦（**recommend**）購買全險（**fully comprehensive coverage**），需要和租車公司確認理賠費（**excess fee**），這部分是一旦發生意外，承租者先行負擔的部分，之後才由保險公司接手負擔。另外租車者的年齡如果未滿 25 歲，各種費用都會比較高。租車但通例是滿油箱（**full tank**）租車滿油箱歸還，可以根據需要加租導航（**GPS/Global Position System**）、兒童安全座椅（**child safety seat**）等。

重要字彙	
car rental	租車
concession	優惠
process	過程
vehicle model	車型
price	價格
services	服務項目

recommend	推薦
fully comprehensive coverage	全險
excess fee	理賠費
ull tank	滿油箱
GPS/Global Position System	導航
child safety seat	兒童安全座椅

延伸字彙	
unlimited kilometres	不限里程
vehicle registration	車輛註冊
airport tax	機場稅
damage	損毀
automatic	自動檔
manual	手排檔
A/C air-conditioning	空調
reservation	預訂
coupon	兌換點數
discount	折扣
hybrid vehicle	混合動力車
enhance	加強
budget	預算
refund	退款

澳洲高等教育

　　澳洲的高等教育（**tertiary education**）分 技術學院（**TAFE/Technical And Further Education**）和大學（**university**）兩類。技術學院主要提供技術性（**technical**）的課程，一般修習 2 至 3 年；大學則根據科系（**faculty**）不同學習 3 到 7 年不等。TAFE 的專業技術（**professional skills**）訓練偏重實際運用（**practical application**），對職業發展（**career development**）有具體幫助。大學學習比較專精，本科生（**undergraduate**）學習結束後獲得學士學位（**Bachelor Degree**）。有志學術（**academic**）者還可以繼續修讀碩士學位（**Master Degree**）和博士學位（**Doctoral Awards**）。其中碩士學位有研究型（**Master by research**）和修課型（**Master by coursework**）；博士學位則分為一般博士學位（**Doctor of Philosophy**）和針對專業領域的專業博士學位（**Professional Doctorate**）。

重要字彙	
tertiary education	高等教育
TAFE/Technical And Further Education	技術學院
university	大學
technical	技術性
faculty	科系

professional skills	專業技術
practical application	實際運用
career development	職業發展
undergraduate	本科生
Bachelor Degree	學士學位
academic	學術
Master Degree	碩士學位
Doctoral Awards	博士學位
Master by research	研究型碩士學位
Master by coursework	修課型碩士學位
Doctor of Philosophy	一般博士學位
Professional Doctorate	專業博士學位
延伸字彙	
postgraduate	研究生
Honours Degree	榮譽學位
Combined Degrees/Double Degrees	雙學位
LLB/Bachelor of Laws	法學學士學位
MBBS/Bachelor of Medicine, Bachelor of Surgery	內外全科醫學學士
Graduate Certificate	碩士證書
Graduate Diploma	碩士文憑
PhD programme	碩博連讀
PhD candidate	博士候選人

影子跟讀：「短對話」

影子跟讀：「短段落」

影子跟讀：「實戰練習」

雅思聽力必考字彙

申請大學

　　澳洲的大學或研究所（**graduate school**）申請（**application**）可以透過留學代辦（**education agent**）辦理或自己直接申請。在確定好學校和課程（**course**）後，需要準備一些證明文件（**supporting documents**）：最高學歷的成績單（**academic transcript**）以及課程額外（**additional**）要求（**requirements**）的文件，像是設計系（**School of Design**）要求的作品（**production/works**）。或護理系（**Faculty of Nursing**）要求的註冊（**registration**）證照（**licence**）。證明文件必須是經過認證的副本（**certified copies**）。非英文母語國家的申請者需要提供英語水平（**English language proficiency**）證書（**certificate**），如雅思（**IELTS**）和托福（**TOFEL**）成績單。必須在截止日期（**closing date**）之前遞出申請。申請過程（**process**）一般需要一至四週，得到錄取通知書（**offer**）後，即可以安排機票住宿和申請學生簽證（**student visa**）。

重要字彙	
graduate school	研究所
application	申請
education agent	留學代辦
course	課程

supporting documents	證明文件
academic transcript	成績單
additional	額外
requirements	要求
School of Design	設計系
production/works	作品
Faculty of Nursing	護理系
registration	註冊
licence	證照
certified copies	經過認證的副本
English language proficiency	英語水平
certificate	證書
IELTS	雅思
TOFEL	托福
closing date	截止日期
process	過程
offer	錄取通知書
student visa	學生簽證
延伸字彙	
conditional/provisional offer	條件入學許可
preliminary program	大學預科
letter of rejection	拒絕信
scholarship	獎學金

影子跟讀：「短對話」

影子跟讀：「短段落」

影子跟讀：「實戰練習」

雅思聽力必考字彙

正式入學前的英文進修

　　大學常有專門為海外學生（**overseas students**）開設的語言學校（**language school**）。方便英文尚未達到入學要求的學生做英文進修。語言學校開設的主要課程是普通英文（**GE/General English**）和學術英文（**EAP/English for Academic Purposes**）以及專門針對雅思考試的應試培訓等。普通英文課程重在提升交流（**communication**）能力，聽力（**listening**）、閱讀（**reading**）、寫作（**writing**）、字彙（**vocabulary**）都是主要練習的項目。學術英文則依據大學的學習要求培養進階的（**advanced**）英文能力：如報告（**essay**）和論文（**assignment**）寫作、學術引用（**referencing**）、課堂筆記（**note-taking**）和總結（**summarizing**）、專題研究（**research**）技巧、演講（**presentation**）、論文檢索（**article search**）等。這些英文訓練不僅幫助打好英文基礎（**foundation**），也對之後的學業大有裨益。

重要字彙	
Overseas students	海外學生
language school	語言學校
GE/General English	普通英文
EAP/English for Academic Purposes	學術英文

communication	交流
listening	聽力
reading	閱讀
writing	寫作
vocabulary	字彙
advanced	進階的
essay	報告
assignment	論文
referencing	學術引用
note-taking	課堂筆記
summarising	總結
research	專題研究
presentation	演講
article search	論文檢索
foundation	基礎
進階字彙	
competence	能力
proficiency	熟練
word processing	文字處理
database	資料庫
library	圖書館
dictionary skills	辭書檢索能力
method	學習方法

影子跟讀：「短對話」

影子跟讀：「短段落」

影子跟讀：「實戰練習」

雅思聽力必考字彙

大學的學習

　　正式開學前有迎新週（**orientation week**），新生來學校報到（**enroll**）和選課（**select courses**），聽取對專業（**major**）、學習方法（**learning strategies**）、課業任務（**study load**）的介紹（**introduction**）。課程可以自己選擇，除了專業必修課程（**compulsory course**）外還可以修讀選修課程（**elective course**）。普通課程包含講座（**lecture**）和輔導課（**tutorial**），講座一般是兩小時，由教授（**professor**）講解一章知識，輔導課則由導師（**tutor**）解決練習題（**exercise**）和課後學習的問題。一科大學課程通常需要（**require**）每週 10 到 12 小時的學習時間，全職學生（**full-time student**）一般會選擇每學期（**semester**）四或五門（**unit**）課程。大學是完全的自主（**independent**）學習，科目和上課時間都可以自己安排，只得到很少的指導（**supervise**）。

重要字彙	
orientation week	迎新週
enrol	報到
select courses	選課
major	專業
learning strategies	學習方法
study load	課業任務

introduction	介紹
compulsory course	必修課程
elective course	選修課程
lecture	講座
tutorial	輔導課
professor	教授
tutor	導師
exercise	練習題
require	需要
full-time student	全職學生
semester	學期
unit	門／科
independent	自主
supervise	指導
延伸字彙	
part-time student	兼職學生
semester break	假期
guideline	大綱
feedback	反饋
open day	開放日
institute	機構

影子跟讀：「短對話」

影子跟讀：「短段落」

影子跟讀：「實戰練習」

雅思聽力必考字彙

大學的考核

　　撰寫學術報告（**academic essay**）是重要的考核（**assessment**）方式。學術報告一般比較簡短，且需要遵循學術寫作（**academic writing**）的規則，文章結構（**structure**）為緒論（**introduction**）、主要內容（**body**）和結論（**conclusion**）。為了撰寫報告需要大量閱讀，包括老師提供的參考書目（**reading list**）以及從資料庫檢索（**retrieve**）文章。報告的分數（**score**）會按照評分標準（**marking criteria**）給出。學期中會有個人演講（**presentation**）、小組作業（**group work**）、小測驗（**quiz**）等考核，每個項目都佔總成績的一定百分比（**percentage**）。一些科目的期末考試（**final exam**）則以寫論文（**assignment**）方式完成。其中理工科（**science and engineering**）學生需要撰寫實證性（**empirical**）研究論文（**research paper**），論文章節需要介紹研究方法、研究結果（**result**）和討論（**discussion**）。

重要字彙	
academic essay	學術報告
assessment	考核
academic writing	學術寫作
structure	結構
introduction	緒論

body	主要內容
conclusion	結論
reading list	參考書目
retrieve	檢索
score	分數
marking criteria	評分標準
presentation	演講
group work	小組作業
quiz	小測驗
percentage	百分比
final exam	期末考試
assignment	論文
science and engineering	理工科
empirical	實證性
research paper	研究論文
result	研究結果
discussion	討論

延伸字彙

dissertation	學位論文
topic	主題
bibliographies	書目／文獻
proofreading	校對

影子跟讀：「短對話」

影子跟讀：「短段落」

影子跟讀：「實戰練習」

雅思聽力必考字彙

大學的專業

　　澳洲的高等教育在許多學科（**discipline**）都達到國際先進水準，尤其是工程技術（**engineering and technology**）、醫學（**medicine**）、環境科學（**environmental science**）、會計金融（**accounting and finance**）等。有些學科則有高比例的學生修讀雙學位，譬如藝術（**arts**）、管理（**management**）、貿易（**commerce**）、法學（**law**）和健康科學（**health science**）。除了傳統的自然科學（**natural science**）和社會科學（**social science**）專業，澳洲大學的職業（**professions**）與應用科學（**applied science**）也有很高的教學品質，例如農業（**agriculture**）、建築（**architecture**）、教育（**education**）、新聞學（**journalism**）、傳播學（**communication**）、公共衛生（**public health**）、社會工作（**social work**）等。形式科學（**formal science**）方面也建樹頗豐，如計算機科學（**computer science**）、邏輯學（**logic**）、統計學（**statistics**）、數學（**mathematics**）。

重點字彙	
discipline	學科
engineering and technology	工程技術
medicine	醫學
environmental science	環境科學

accounting and finance	會計金融
arts	藝術
management	管理
commerce	貿易
law	法學
health science	健康科學
natural science	自然科學
social science	社會科學
professions	職業
applied science	應用科學
agriculture	農業
architecture	建築
education	教育
journalism	新聞學
communication	傳播學
public health	公共衛生
social work	社會工作
formal science	形式科學
computer science	計算機科學
logic	邏輯學
statistics	統計學
mathematics	數學
physics	物理學
chemistry	化學

影子跟讀：「短對話」

影子跟讀：「短段落」

影子跟讀：「實戰練習」

雅思聽力必考字彙

大學的設施

　　大學的講座通常被安排在座位較多的階梯教室（**lecture theatre**），輔導課則在普通教室（**classroom**）。多媒體（**multimedia**）教室都配有白板（**writing board**）、計算機（**computer**）、投影儀（**projector**）、無線（**wireless**）擴音器（**microphone**）等設備（**equipment**）。圖書館（**library**）有公共電腦房（**computer lab**）、閱覽室（**reference room**）、自習室（**individual study room**），並提供拷貝（**copy**）和列印（**printing**）設施。除實體書外，也提供電子書（**e-books**）借閱服務。大學校園裡有書店（**bookshop**）、餐廳（**canteen**）、健身房（**gym**）、游泳池（**swimming pool**）、學校診所（**school clinics**）、藝術設施（**art facilities**）等。很多大學都設有幼兒中心（**child care center**）和育嬰室（**parenting room**），以幫助有年幼小孩的學生。禱告室（**preyer room**）則為有宗教（**religious**）需要的學生提供空間。

重要字彙	
lecture theatre	階梯教室
classroom	教室
multimedia	多媒體
writing board	白板

computer	計算機
projector	投影儀
wireless	無線
microphone	擴音器
equipment	設備
library	圖書館
computer lab	電腦房
reference room	閱覽室
individual study room	自習室
copy	拷貝
printing	列印
e-books	電子書
bookshop	書店
canteen	餐廳
gym	健身房
swimming pool	游泳池
school clinics	學校診所
art facilities	藝術設施
child care centre	幼兒中心
parenting room	育嬰室
prayer room	禱告室
religious	宗教
campus	校園
security	安全

影子跟讀：「短對話」

影子跟讀：「短段落」

影子跟讀：「實戰練習」

雅思聽力必考字彙

研究方法之量化研究

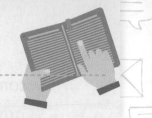

量化研究（**quantitative research**）是一種符合邏輯（**logical**）並以數據（**data**）為基礎的研究方法（**methodology**），被廣泛應用於自然科學和社會科學諸領域。是透過統計（**statistical**）、數學（**mathematical**）及計算（**computational**），對現象（**phenomenon**）進行考察（**investigation**）。研究者（**researcher**）做數據分析（**data analyze**），以期得到（**yield**）可以通用與大範圍人群（**population**）的公正結果（**unbiased result**）。完整的研究進程包括了研究設計（**research design**）、數據分析、及研究的效度（**validity**）與信度（**reliability/credibility**）等問題。取得資料後，要依據各種預測變數（**predictor variable**）和結果變數（**outcome variable**）的數量與性質採取不同的統計方法。如以類別變數（**categorical variables**）測比例（**proportion**）時用卡方檢定（**Chi-square test**）；以兩組連續變量（**continuous variables**）測標準誤差（**standard deviation**）用 T 檢定（**T-test**）；預測（**prediction**）和因果分析（**causal analysis**）則用線性回歸（**linear regression**）。

重要字彙	
quantitative research	量化研究
logical	邏輯
data	數據

methodology	方法
statistical	統計
mathematical	數學
computational	計算
phenomenon	現象
investigation	考察
researcher	研究者
data analyse	數據分析
yield	得到
population	人群
unbiased result	公正結果
research design	研究設計
validity	效度
reliability/credibility	信度
predictor variable	預測變數
outcome variable	結果變數
categorical variables	類別變數
proportion	比例
Chi-square test	卡方檢定
continuous variables	連續變量
standard deviation	標準誤差
prediction	預測
causal analysis	因果分析
linear regression	線性回歸

影子跟讀：「短對話」

影子跟讀：「短段落」

影子跟讀：「實戰練習」

雅思聽力必考字彙

研究方法之質化研究

　　與量化研究相對，質化研究（**qualitative research**）專注在更小更集中（**focused**）的樣本（**samples**），透過個案研究（**case study**）得到的資訊（**information**），深入（**in-depth**）瞭解（**understanding**）人類行為（**behavior**）及其理由（**reason**）。質化研究常被運用於社會科學的眾領域。質化研究最常見的（**popular**）方法個案研究，是以經驗為主（**empirical**）的調查法來研究具體生活（**real-life**）。在個案研究所處理的獨特（**unique**）事件中，研究者可能對事件中的許多變數感興趣，因此需要依賴不同來源（**sources**）的證據（**evidence**）。不限於學術領域，公司（**cooperation**）企業也常利用個案研究法，常見的 SWOT 分析法包含了優勢（**strength**）、劣勢（**weakness**）、機會（**opportunity**）、威脅（**threat**）的分析，從正反兩做綜合（**comprehensive**）分析，為決策制定（**decision making**）提供依據。

重要字彙	
qualitative research	質化研究
focused	集中
samples	樣本
case study	個案研究

information	資訊
in-depth	深入
understanding	瞭解
behaviour	行為
reason	理由
popular	常見的
empirical	以經驗為主
real-life	具體生活
unique	獨特
sources	來源
evidence	證據
cooperation	公司
strength	優勢
weakness	劣勢
opportunity	機會
threat	威脅
comprehensive	綜合
decision making	決策制定
延伸字彙	
sociology	社會學
plausible	貌似合理的
hypothesis	假設
proposition	提議

校園就業服務

　　許多大學都提供就業（**employment**）輔導服務，以及特別針對國際學生（**international student**）的職業（**career**）咨詢（**consultant**）。高年級（**senior grades**）學生可以參加免費的（**free**）為就業做準備（**preparation**）的研討會（**workshop**），得到職業規劃（**career planning**）的建議（**advice**）和就業輔助（**assistance**）。一些大學甚至設有特別為幫助學生求職的導師（**mentor**）計畫（**scheme**），學生可以做面試（**interview**）練習（**practice**），修改簡歷（**resume**），模擬申請（**application**）工作。大學也會組織（**organize**）招聘會（**recruitment fair**），使學生有機會見到潛在（**potential**）雇主（**employer**）。透過學校的就業平台（**platform**），學生也可以得到更多的邁入業界（**industry**）的機會（**opportunity**），譬如應徵到兼職（**part-time**）工作、非正式（**casual**）工作，實習生（**internship**）和培訓生計畫（**graduate program**）。

重要字彙	
employment	就業
international student	國際學生
career	職業
consultant	咨詢

senior grades	高年級
free	免費的
preparation	準備
workshop	研討會
career planning	職業規劃
advice	建議
assistance	輔助
mentor	導師
scheme	計畫
interview	面試
practice	練習
resume	簡歷
application	申請
organize	組織
recruitment fair	招聘會
potential	潛在的
employer	雇主
platform	平台
industry	業界
opportunity	機會
part-time	兼職
casual	非正式
internship	實習生
graduate program	培訓生計畫

影子跟讀：「短對話」

影子跟讀：「短段落」

影子跟讀：「實戰練習」

雅思聽力必考字彙

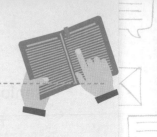

求職

　　求職網站（**job website**）會發布雇主的徵人廣告（**advertisement**），只需鍵入職務名稱（**job title**）、自己的專長（**skills**）、工作地點或郵遞區號（**postcode**），就可以瀏覽（**browse**）符合條件的工作崗位。需要仔細閱讀職位說明（**position description**），尤其是工作任務描述（**duty statement**）和選拔準則（**selection criteria**）。許多崗位要求應徵者（**applicant**）在求職信（**cover letter**）中撰寫自己符合選拔準備的原因。簡歷（**CV/resume**）的書寫原則是簡潔扼要（**concise**），一般不超過兩頁紙，且應當注意拼寫（**spelling**）。人資部門（**HR/human resource**）對簡歷篩選（**screen**）後，會通過電話或電子郵件（**e-mail**）方式通知是否進入面試（**interview**）階段。專業社群網站（**social network**）LinkedIn 搭配應用軟體（**application software**），求職者可以上傳（**upload**）和編輯（**edit**）自己的專業履歷（**professional CV**），也可以獲得最新的行業資訊，也是最常用的求職網站。

重要字彙	
job website	求職網站
advertisement	廣告
job title	職務名稱

skills	專長
postcode	郵遞區號
browse	瀏覽
position description	職位說明
duty statement	任務說明
selection criteria	選拔準則
applicant	應徵者
cover letter	求職信
CV/resume	簡歷
concise	簡潔扼要
spelling	拼寫
HR/human resource	人資
screen	篩選
e-mail	電子郵件
interview	面試
social network	社群網站
application software	應用軟體
upload	上傳
edit	編輯
professional CV	專業履歷
延伸字彙	
recommendation	推薦
background	背景
profile	檔案

影子跟讀：「短對話」

影子跟讀：「短段落」

影子跟讀：「實戰練習」

雅思聽力必考字彙

急救認證

　　安全急救（**First Aid**）認證（**certificate**）課程是被澳洲政府推廣（**promote**）的在全國都被認可的（**accredited**）認證，無論從事何種工作都推薦參加這一訓練（**training**）。許多合法（**legitimate**）註冊的（**registered**）訓練機構（**organization**），如紅十字會（**Red Cross**）、救護車服務站（**Ambulance Service**）等都提供急救認證課程。在課程中學員可以習得職業健康安全（**occupational health and safety**）和危機處理（**crisis management**），了解緊急狀況發生時生命維持（**life support**）的支援方法。學習心肺復甦術（**CPR/cardiopulmonary resuscitation**）的知識和操作，意外受傷（**injury**）如扭傷（**sprain**）、脫臼（**dislocation**）、燒傷（**burns**）、脫水（**dehydration**）、中暑（**heat stroke**）、叮咬（**bites/stings**）、失血（**bleeding**）等狀況發生時，專業醫療介入前的簡單支援也在學習範圍內。

重要字彙	
First Aid	安全急救
certificate	認證
promote	推廣
accredited	被認可的
training	訓練

legitimate	合法
registered	註冊的
organization	機構
Red Cross	紅十字會
Ambulance Service	救護車服務站
occupational health and safety	職業健康安全
crisis management	危機處理
life support	生命維持
CPR/cardiopulmonary resuscitation	心肺復甦術
injury	受傷
sprain	扭傷
dislocation	脫臼
burns	燒傷
dehydration	脫水
heat stroke	中暑
bites/stings	叮咬
bleeding	失血
延伸字彙	
cardiac conditions	心臟病
asthma	氣喘
fracture	骨折
loss of consciousness	失去知覺

影子跟讀：「短對話」

影子跟讀：「短段落」

影子跟讀：「實戰練習」

雅思聽力必考字彙

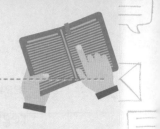

袋鼠

　　袋鼠是彈跳力（**jumping**）最強的哺乳動物（**mammal**），是澳洲地方性的（**endemic**）動物。不同種類（**species**）的袋鼠分佈在不同的自然環境中，其中體型較大的一類被叫做袋鼠（**kangaroo**），體型較小的被稱為沙袋鼠（**wallaby**）。袋鼠有粗壯的後腿（**hind legs**）和大腳以適應跳躍（**leaping**），長尾巴（**tail**）則利於保持平衡（**balance**）。雌性（**female**）袋鼠像其他有袋動物（**marsupials**）一樣，腹部（**abdomen**）前開一個袋子（**pouch**），幼袋鼠（**joey**）就在袋子裡完成出生後（**postnatal**）的發育，直到能夠獨立適應外部生存再脫離母體。袋鼠是澳洲的國家象徵（**symbol**），和鴯鶓（**emu**）一起出現在澳洲國徽（**coat of arms**）上。澳航（**Qantas**）和澳洲皇家空軍（**Royal Australian Air Force**）也都將袋鼠作為標誌。

重要字彙	
jumping	彈跳力
mammal	哺乳動物
endemic	地方性的
species	種類
kangaroo	袋鼠
wallaby	沙袋鼠

hind legs	後腿
leaping	跳躍
tail	尾巴
balance	平衡
female	雌性
marsupials	有袋動物
abdomen	腹部
pouch	袋子
joey	幼袋鼠
postnatal	出生後
symbol	象徵
emu	鴯鶓
coat of arms	國徽
Qantas	澳航
Royal Australian Air Force	澳洲皇家空軍
延伸字彙	
habitat	棲息地
graze	放牧
predator	捕食者
arid	乾旱的
regurgitate	反芻

影子跟讀：「短對話」

影子跟讀：「短段落」

影子跟讀：「實戰練習」

雅思聽力必考字彙

無尾熊

　　無尾熊（**Koala**）也是澳洲特有的有袋動物，Koala 這個名稱來自於原住民方言（**dialect**），意思是「不喝水」。無尾熊的唯一食物是尤加利樹（**eucalyptus**），樹葉（**leaf**）提供的足夠水分使無尾熊無須飲水。由於尤加利樹纖維（**fiber**）堅硬，營養（**nutrition**）和熱量（**calories**）很少，所以無尾熊必須保持靜止不動（**sedentary**）且每天睡眠超過 20 小時的生活模式（**mode**）。無尾熊新陳代謝（**metabolism**）緩慢，又需要耗費大量清醒時光進食，因而個體之間互動（**interaction**）極少，屬於非群居動物（**social animal**）。無尾熊顯著的（**recognizable**）特徵是體態肥胖（**stout**）、身體不長尾巴（**tailless**）、毛茸茸的（**fluffy**）耳朵和黑色的湯匙狀鼻子。它們性情溫順，抱無尾熊拍照是澳洲的動物園受歡迎的項目。

重要字彙	
Koala	無尾熊
dialect	方言
eucalyptus	尤加利樹
leaf	樹葉
fiber	纖維
nutrition	營養

calories	熱量
sedentary	靜止不動
mode	模式
metabolism	新陳代謝
interaction	互動
asocial animal	非群居動物
recognizable	顯著的
stout	肥胖
tailless	不長尾巴
fluffy	毛茸茸的
延伸字彙	
woodlands	樹林
offspring	後代
subspecies	亞種
hairless	無毛的
belly	腹部
insulate	使隔絕
resilient	適應力強的
geographic range	地理分佈
cheek	臉頰
chubby	胖乎乎的

影子跟讀：「短對話」

影子跟讀：「短段落」

影子跟讀：「實戰練習」

雅思聽力必考字彙

全球暖化

　　全球暖化（**global warming**）是由於溫室效應（**Greenhouse effect**）造成的全球平均氣溫（**average temperature**）逐漸（**gradually**）升高（**increase**）。全球暖化被認為會對地球氣候（**climate**）造成永久（**permanent**）改變。近地面（**near-surface**）大氣的（**atmospheric**）溫度升高和海洋（**ocean**）變暖在過去幾十年（**decades**）內呈現出前所未見的（**unprecedented**）趨勢。科學研究（**scientific research**）發現，導致全球暖化的主要原因是人類活動（**human activities**）排放的大量溫室氣體（**greenhouse gases**），如水蒸氣（**vapour**）、二氧化碳（**carbon dioxide**）、甲烷（**methane**）等。全球性的溫度增高使得海平面（**sea level**）上升和降水量（**precipitation**）增多，這進一步導致極端氣候（**extreme weather**）出現更加頻繁（**frequent**），發生更多的洪水（**flood**）、乾旱（**drought**）、熱帶氣旋（**tropical cyclone**），甚至影響農業（**agriculture**）、減少物種和加劇疾病傳播（**spread**）。

重要字彙	
global warming	全球暖化
Greenhouse effect	溫室效應
average temperature	平均氣溫
gradually	逐漸

increase	升高
climate	氣候
permanent	永久的
near-surface	近地面
atmospheric	大氣的
ocean	海洋
decades	幾十年
unprecedented	前所未見的
scientific research	科學研究
human activities	人類活動
greenhouse gases	溫室氣體
vapour	水蒸氣
carbon dioxide	二氧化碳
methane	甲烷
sea level	海平面
precipitation	降水量
extreme weather	極端氣候
frequent	頻繁
flood	洪水
drought	乾旱
tropical cyclone	熱帶氣旋
agriculture	農業
exacerbate	加劇
spread	傳播

影子跟讀：「短對話」

影子跟讀：「短段落」

影子跟讀：「實戰練習」

雅思聽力必考字彙

土壤侵蝕退化

　　土壤（**soil**）是地球的肌膚（**skin**），土壤上充滿活力的（**dynamic**）生態系統（**ecosystem**）為人類和其他生物提供了生存空間（**space**）和資源（**resource**）。人口增多導致對農產品（**agriculture commodities**）需求量增大，許多森林（**forest**）和草場（**grassland**）被改為農地（**farm field**）和牧場（**pasture**）。農作物（**crops**）吸取土壤營養（**nutrition**），不像天然植被（**natural vegetation**）具有水土保持（**conservation**）的作用，土壤更容易被侵蝕（**erosion**）。在過去的 150 年裡，陸地上的表層土（**topsoil**）已經流失過半。除此之外，土壤品質（**quality**）也逐漸退化（**degradation**）。密集種植（**intensive cultivation**）和大量使用殺蟲劑（**pesticide**）加劇了土壤營養物質（**nutrient**）流失，造成土質固化（**compaction**）、鹽鹼化（**salinity**）。唯有土地的可持續（**sustainable**）利用才能阻止（**prevent**）土壤侵蝕退化。

重要字彙	
soil	土壤
skin	肌膚
dynamic	充滿活力的
ecosystem	生態系統

space	空間
resource	資源
agriculture commodities	農產品
forest	森林
grassland	草場
farm field	農地
pasture	牧場
crops	農作物
nutrient	營養物質
natural vegetation	天然植被
conservation	保持
erosion	侵蝕
topsoil	表層土
quality	品質
degradation	退化
intensive cultivation	密集種植
pesticide	殺蟲劑
compaction	固化
salinity	鹽鹼化
sustainable	可持續
prevent	阻止
fertile	肥沃的
pollution	污染
impact	影響

影子跟讀：「短對話」

影子跟讀：「短段落」

影子跟讀：「實戰練習」

雅思聽力必考字彙

沙漠化

　　沙漠化（**desertification**）是土壤退化的一種型態。指土地失去水體（**bodies of water**）、表層植被（**vegetation**）和野生動物，變得乾旱（**arid**）貧瘠（**barren**）。導致沙漠化的直接（**immediate**）原因是植被流失，乾旱、砍伐森林（**deforestation**）、過度放牧（**overgrazing**）等都會導致沙漠化。沙漠化導致沙塵暴（**sandstorm**）增多、人類可利用的生活面積（**area**）減少、生態平衡（**ecological equilibrium**）也受到影響。人們目前掌握的技術可以減輕（**mitigate**）或逆轉（**reverse**）沙漠化帶來的影響，譬如採取（**adopt**）可持續的農耕模式，只是由於成本（**cost**）較高，許多農民難以負擔土地再生利用（**reclamation**）的費用。重新造林（**reforestation**）可以扭轉沙漠化，在雨季（**rainy season**）種下幼苗（**seedling**）有望徹底遏止沙漠化趨勢。

重要字彙	
desertification	沙漠化
bodies of water	水體
vegetation	植被
arid	乾旱
barren	貧瘠

immediate	直接的
deforestation	砍伐森林
overgrazing	過度放牧
sandstorm	沙塵暴
area	面積
ecological equilibrium	生態平衡
mitigate	減輕
reverse	逆轉
adopt	採取
cost	成本
reclamation	再生利用
reforestation	重新造林
rainy season	雨季
seedling	幼苗
延伸字彙	
biodiversity	物種多樣性
threat	威脅
endangered	瀕危的
shelter	遮蓋物
windbreaks	防風林
environmental volunteers	環保志工
rehabilitation	康復

影子跟讀：「短對話」

影子跟讀：「短段落」

影子跟讀：「實戰練習」

雅思聽力必考字彙

國家圖書館出版品預行編目(CIP)資料

一次就考到雅思聽力6.5+ / 倍斯特編輯部
著. -- 初版. -- 臺北市 ： 倍斯特, 2018.8　面
;公分. --（考用英語系列 ;8）
ISBN 978-986-96309-3-1（平裝附光碟）
1.國際英語語文測試系統　2.考試指南

805.189　　　　　　　　　　107011303

考用英語 011

一次就考到雅思聽力6.5+（附英式發音MP3）

初　　版	2018年8月	
定　　價	新台幣450元	

作　　者	倍斯特編輯部
出　　版	倍斯特出版事業有限公司
發 行 人	周瑞德
電　　話	886-2-2351-2007
傳　　真	886-2-2351-0887
地　　址	100 台北市中正區福州街1號10樓之2
E - m a i l	best.books.service@gmail.com
官　　網	www.bestbookstw.com
執行總監	齊心瑪
企劃編輯	陳韋佑
執行編輯	曾品綺
內頁構成	菩薩蠻數位文化有限公司
印　　製	大亞彩色印刷製版股份有限公司

港澳地區總經銷	泛華發行代理有限公司
地　　址	香港新界將軍澳工業邨駿昌街7號2樓
電　　話	852-2798-2323
傳　　真	852-2796-5471